CREATING MEMORIES

Book One of the Scrap Book Trilogy

Jacqueline Gillam Fairchild

Crown and Crumpet Publishing
Creating Memories
Copyright @ 2017 by Jacqueline Gillam Fairchild
Request for information should be addressed to
Crown and Crumpet Publishing, 211 N. Second Street, Dunlap, Ill 61525
ISBN: 154672687X
ISBN: 13-9781546726876
Library of Congress Control Number: 2017908041
CreateSpace Independent Publishing Platform
North Charleston, South CarolinaLibrary Cataloging Data:

Library Cataloging Data:
1.Scrap booking 2. Romance 3. Light fantasy 4. British Shoppe

5. Grand Hotel 6. Murder Mystery 7. Charms 8. Trade Shows

9. Grandmas

For Jerry

ACKNOWLEDGEMENTS

A special thank you to Linda Hartman
Kim Kouski, Paul Maitland, Andy Zach, John Spencer

Nancy Watkins, Colleen Simpson, Doreen Flash
Bonnie Mason, Chad Gillam,
And
Louise Emanuels

ENDORSEMENTS

"Jacqueline is one of the most creative
and interesting persons I have ever met."
J. Peterman, iconic catalog entrepreneur,
TV character and author

ALSO BY JACQUELINE GILLAM FAIRCHILD: ESTATE OF MIND

In praise of Estate of Mind:
"I love your book! I love your book so much that I have to argue with myself about how many chapters I can read in one sitting because I don't want to finish it! What an inspiration. After the first few chapters I I cleaned my entire porch (Some years I haven't used it at all) and have lunch there on weekends while I read. I love the characters, your descriptions are fabulous. I can't say enough good things and just wanted you to know. Thank you for writing this absolutely delightful book. When I finish, I guess I'll just have to read it again!"

Bonnie Mason
Community Business Development Manager
Barnes & Noble, Inc

In praise of Creating Memories:

Take three lonely elderly ladies, add a ditzy young woman from a New York advertising firm, and a Californian race car driver, mix in some magic and put them all in a remote, Midwestern town. POW! Romantic, funny entertainment for everyone.

I categorize this book as romantic, comedic fantasy because it has a little magic from Scotland. There are several laugh-out-loud scenes in here, as well as funny one-liners.

Beach reading? Yes! Fun read on a snowy night? Yes! The novel goes down fast and easy, like a slice of rum cake.

Andy Zach-Author: My Undead Mother in Law and Zombie Turkeys

Dear Readers:

I know you will enjoy Creating Memories, the first in the Scrap Book Trilogy. Meet the very senior Auntie Clara and her chums who take scrap booking to new heights. It seems everything they put in their scrap books happens. Bored with adjusting their living quarters, and hefting their bank books, they want what they think we all want—family.

But manipulating the lives of those young and dear to their hearts might not be a two way wish …

Introducing Lizzie, advertising peon turned scrap book shoppe owner. After all, the aunties need a place to hang out.

And when Lizzie's life is in order (according to Auntie Clara) join me and meet Coco, sweat shop seamstress caught in the middle of a 1940's Murder Mystery week at Grand Hotel, Mackinac Island (Book 2--Grand Memories).

Don't close your scrap book yet, you still have to meet Dee Shannon from the famed Bootles UK jewelry dynasty now designing her own charms (Book 3—Charmed Memories).

The Scrap Book trilogy is just a little bit magical, but who is to say there isn't a little magic all around us, if you just look … or open your scrap book.

Warm regards,

Jacqueline

INTRODUCTION

A very ancient woman sat in her shiny new car outside Fairchild's Ltd, waiting, waiting for them to open so she could burst in with all her news.

Jefferson slipped the key in the lock to Fairchild's Ltd., a tiny shoppe in the middle of the middle of nowhere. A shoppe chocked full with British goodies, from Cadbury chocolates, and Salad Cream, that staple dressing, to Royal Warranted Barbour clothing, and Union Jack sox.

There were hedgerow jams, and Rich Tea Biscuits to go with a never ending assortment of English teas. Silky creams, luxury soaps, and scents from Lavender to Grapefruit spice, all meant to wake up your senses, and pamper you.

Princess dresses for young girls, and girls not so very young--tiaras to match, and shoes--shoes of dreams. Onward to clothing that just didn't fit a category, except maybe charming and romantic.

Jinx, Jefferson's slightly eccentric wife, was right behind him, lugging several huge canvas totes, two miniature Pekinese on leads, and a Chanel hand bag that could double as a carry on. Two of the bags she simply dragged on the sidewalk up to the shoppe's door while trying to convince Maisie and Mrs. Wigglesworth, the Pekes, not to stop and sniff the roses.

Jinx tugged on the door, heaving everything inside, including the dogs, and flipped the hand lettered sign to 'open'. She started going through the routine of waking up the shoppe. Maize and Mrs. Wigglesworth were already asleep in their store beds, having found their own way.

Flipping on the CD player, Jim Hart's newest CD wafted out at her—subtle piano, yet with a pulse of bass to ground it. Jinx smiled as it warmed up. Even though Jim played at Dink's Roadside Diner most nights, this CD was different. Quieter, or maybe more powerful, Jinx couldn't quite decide. She just knew it cleared her head, and somehow made her feel better.

When Jim Hart had dropped off his latest CD offering she'd asked him what it was all about. His music could be bluesy with under tones of classic rock, and hints of country. Good music, good times. He'd just smiled, "See what you think."

And left.

Of course he'd snagged a few Crunchie bars on his way out the door.

Turned out the new music was more poignant that country, gentler than rock, and happier than the blues. It was the kind of music one liked to pop in and let just take over. As the notes started to quietly soar Jinx knew she'd have to call Jim for another stack of CDs. Her customers not only liked it, they seemed to get it, and think it was playing just for them.

And in her own way, Jinx was playing it just for them ...

Jinx straightened a stack of Flake Bars, tucking one in her pocket for her mid morning snack, and headed over to a basket of Popsicle colored cashmere sweaters that needed tidying up, her totes, and bags still heaped by the counter, with bits and pieces spilling out and littering the floor.

"Jinx--what is all that stuff?" Jefferson was turning on the small decorative lights, booting up the computer, getting ready for customers. He looked at her mess and shook his head.

But before Jinx could answer, the first customer toddled in from her car out front—where she'd been waiting.

"Good morning Miss McGillicuddy," Jefferson called out, slipping a dust rag in his pocket. "You're here nice and early." Jefferson looked at the elderly woman who was ninety or maybe one hundred, it was hard to tell. Her white hair formed a halo around her round and dimpled face, but her eyes held a devilish twinkle of mischief.

"Hello Jefferson dear. Please call me Auntie Clara." Then she eyed the Pekinese sleeping happily side by side. "And the pups--I so love it when you bring the sisters to work." Auntie Clara bent and cooed over the Pekes, who in return gave their doggy best, opening an eye and grinning.

Jinx made a little face at Jefferson as she lugged her totes to her messy desk behind the counter.

Jefferson always said he would just as soon leave the dogs at home, though he was known to give them a little pat when he was stressed. And the small dogs were devoted to him. The pups loved to go to work, and after all, how much trouble was it? Water, a snack, walkies--other than that they slept until someone came in to admire them.

Or pose, as Jefferson would say.

Well, Pekinese were born to be ornamental ...

"Takes me back to me girlhood they do. Pekes were much more popular then." Auntie Clara appeared to be feeding them Fig Newtons from her suit case size hand bag.

Jefferson rolled his eyes, thinking whenever that childhood was, possibly Victorian times--possibly earlier.

"They love you too Miss Clara, er Auntie Clara." Jinx turned and accidentally let one of her totes spill. Rubber stamps, stickers, little pots of glitter, bits of ribbon, news paper clippings, and photos started tumbling out, trying to escape.

"Jinx dear ..." Auntie Clara began, "Whatever ..." She stared at Jinx's mess.

"Oh, I'm making a scrap book!" Jinx's face beamed as she scooped back up the minutia, stuffing it all back in her tote. "You know, all the events we've done, and nice articles in the newspaper. Photographs, and little thank you notes from some of my favorite customers, and of course drawings from some of the children that come in. It's all been just collecting in a tote ..."

And Jinx gave that look that said she'd get to it sometime but at least it was all lumped together ...

Auntie Clara clasped her bejeweled hands in glee! "Oh a fellow scrap booker!"

"You too Miss er Auntie Clara?" After all, a fellow scrap booker should be referred to as Aunt.)

"Absolutely! Why I'm addicted! Me chums and me meet several times a week and work on ours. We each have several going!"

"Really?" This fascinated Jinx; she could barely manage the one. Okay, couldn't manage it at all.

"Oh yes me dear--once you really get into it ... now you'll have to promise to show me yours when you've made some progress." And she placed a wrinkled hand, which twinkled with citrines and amethysts, on Jinx's arm.

"I'd like that." Jinx felt a connection to Miss Clara. Age hadn't dulled Miss Clara's mind, or if this was dull, Jinx hated to think what she had been like. (And even though Miss Clara looked ancient, she seemed to have a beat on everything contemporary.)

"You know Jinx dear, there are actually stores that sell nothing but scrap book supplies. I'm working on getting one here in Wind Star." Auntie Clara nodded as she spoke.

"Really, the village could use another shoppe ..." Jinx wondered how serious she was, as the idea had great appeal. Jinx was constantly trying to fill the little village of Wind Star with other merchants. "Now Miss Clara, I mean Auntie Clara, what can I help you find today?"

The Pekes were already asleep, lulled by the conversation, sure the Fig Newton treats were finished.

"Well me great niece Lizzie just moved here from New York City, and I like to keep a few snacks for when she drags in." Auntie Clara gathered up some Dowager Short Break, McVities Digestives biscuits, and a fist full of Crunchie bars. "And I need a little sachet--maybe lavender. (And I rather like this music.")

And Auntie Clara waved her jeweled hands to take in the air around them, implying that was where the music was coming from. She tapped a tapestry toe ever so slightly in appreciation of the sound.

"Oh that's Jim Hart's newest CD: Reaching into Hart." Jinx scooped one off her display, and plopped it on the counter for Auntie Clara.

"Lovely, so powerful, I have a new CD player, and want to just cruise around listening to it. It puts me in the mood."

The mood for what Auntie Clara didn't say.

Jefferson rolled his eyes but kept right on working. Auntie Clara didn't try for dramatic; it just came naturally to her. But Jefferson had to agree, there was something about this new CD ...

"And the little sachet Jinx dear," Auntie Clara brought Jinx back on track.

"Of course."

"On a ribbon if possible. I want to tie it to me rear view mirror. Is that too corny Jinx dear?"

"Well, no not if it's small enough." Jinx tried to look neutral.

"For me new car ..."

"New car? Miss Clara! You got a new car? The Fairlane? Gone?"

"Yes dear, sold it to a collector, and you know it just wasn't me image anymore. I needed a new one. Image that is. And I think I need that CD to go with it too!"

Jinx swallowed a skeptical look. Miss Clara was so old, a new car! Would she last a week? A month?

A year?

Through the warranty?

Till the first car wash?

"Now I know what you're thinking me dear, but me motto has always been live each day to the fullest. And that Fairlane just wasn't cutting it anymore!"

Auntie Clara had known what I was thinking … Jinx felt guilty but patched it quickly, "What'd you get?"

"Well, come to the door and see!" Auntie Clara beamed.

Sure enough right outside the door sat a shiny red Range Rover.

"Miss Clara! A Range Rover! I love Range Rovers!"

"Me too!" Auntie Clara knew a kindred spirit lived in Jinx.

"I didn't think anyone sold them here." And Jinx liked to think she knew everything that went on.

Literally.

Wind Star was a miniscule village next to a small city. "Well the BMW dealer hadn't--that is Mr. Fred."

"You know the owner of the BMW dealership?" Jinx shook her head, trying not to squint. After all Miss Clara was one of her customers, even if she was terribly old. Maybe she was just fabricating … to keep herself more interesting.

Not that that was needed.

"Uh huh, class mate of mine." And Auntie Clara beamed because of course she'd peaked into Jinx's mind, and knew she didn't believe her.

"Class mate?"

"But Jinx dear I should say did know. Mr. Fred passed."

"On?"

"Uh huh," And Auntie Clara paused for affect. "And the new owner, well, he's expanded."

1

"Elizabeth, although your work is very good ... blah blah blah ..."

Elizabeth crunched her emerald green eyes under heavy black lashes. Pay attention. Why does this not sound like a compliment? Well, maybe it was a compliment, a subtle compliment. Or one of those backwards ones ...

"And it has nothing to do with your being young ... blah blah blah ..."

Of course she was young. Well not that young, okay young-ish. Young enough. Focus. This was starting to get her attention.

"And though we value all our employees ..."

Value, why are they talking about value as though I was a sale at Barney's? Maybe this isn't sounding so good. Elizabeth was breathing heavy now. It wasn't to do with being late, or that extra break? Everyone was late. Everyone took breaks--tons of breaks. Focus. Why aren't I focusing?

"And of course we'll be happy to let you use us as a reference ... blah blah blah ..."

Oh my God, I think they're going to fire me! No, of course they're not going to fire me! How silly am I? They love me here. They need me here ... Why, I'm one of their favorites! I'm sure I am.

"And we think a three week pay check is more than adequate under the circumstances ..."

Circumstances? What circumstances? They're handing me a check? A check? Surely I'm mistaken ... They waved it in front of Elizabeth like a dog biscuit, waiting for her to clasp on to it. As if it were poisonous, she took the very edge of it with one of her perfectly manicured red nails. They aren't going to fire me ... they have fired me! The shock was more than she could handle. The check was in her hand.

Elizabeth tottered on her three and a half inch heels. Being five foot seven, she felt the extra height gave her an edge. An edge on what, she wasn't so sure. I guess these heels didn't help my job ... She tugged on her   Burberry skirt, and clutched the check.

I guess I better leave. Oh yeah, say something, and then leave. Should I ask if they're sure? I mean, really sure? These advertising types are a little arty, and that often means, okay, usually means not terribly business like. But this seems business like--very businesslike. I guess they're sure ...

"Uh well okay--then I'll just clean out my desk." But to her utter shock someone handed her a corrugated box with a picture of Fuzzy, her late cat, on top. "Uh well okay then, off I go." There was really nothing else to say.

She put the check on top of Fuzzy's picture, next to her faux Chanel bag, and grasping the box, tottered off. It was ten o'clock.

Too early for lunch. Lunch? I've just been fired, get a grip! There will be no more sweet little lunches in the city. And then it started to sink in: I wonder how long I'll be able to afford living in the city? Not to mention lunch.

Elizabeth quickly calculated, being four months behind on her rent. Rent for what she referred to as half a room. Not even a real room--the most minuscule efficiency apartment on the planet. "A real efficiency--now that would be living." And she laughed crazily fighting off the beginning of desperation as she took the elevator down.

Down and away from her career.

As an illustrator.

For a big, okay, semi big ad agency.

But an ad agency in New York City. Which she loved--the job and the city. "Well, I'll look for another job, at another semi big agency. Maybe I'll even go to a head hunter. After I get to my flat and freak out that is."

And then she remembered that check she almost hadn't taken.

The one for three weeks pay.

Why pay her rent when surely she would find another job soon, and then could pay her rent. This money was severance pay. Didn't that mean cheer up pay? You know for being let go, okay fired. She was pretty sure that's what it meant. And if that was the case maybe she better, for a change, do what she was supposed to do.

Spend that check to get cheered up.

And her mind whirled from something cute to wear to work, but of course she ruled that out as no instant gratification since she had no work, to cosmetics, and eventually right back to shoes, where of course it had started.

Never left.

So she went shoe shopping. And though it was just temporary, the new shoes did give her a buzz and a bounce.

For awhile.

And besides anyone who was anyone who would hire me would look at my shoes ... wouldn't they?

That was three weeks and ten thousand packages of Oreos ago. Elizabeth had actually saved a little cash for Oreos. She opened one bleary, depressed eye. The newspapers had not been much help.

"The real jobs are never in the newspapers." And she rolled back over and fell asleep. The head hunters hadn't returned any of her calls. Her head wasn't big enough to hunt for. Elizabeth wasn't even big enough to get a return phone call rejecting her.

Elizabeth thought about other jobs. Maybe a waitress, not that she thought she could hack it, but she knew she would probably be able to eat on the job, and she was hungry ... Or a clerk at one of her beloved stores. Yet no one seemed to be hiring.

Well at least the restaurants all said the same thing when she told them she had never waited tables. Well they hadn't exactly said anything, they'd just laughed. But they all did it in a similar way, a way that was pretty clearly a no. And it turns out all her favorite stores only loved her as a customer.

She tried not to spend any money each time she went in to inquire at one store, and each time they rejected her, she was tempted to return her purchase.

Tempted.

Just to show them.

Show them that they'd hurt her feelings.

Certainly she hadn't exhausted all the ad agencies in New York City? It was a pretty darn big city … Well; sadly Elizabeth was pretty sure she'd exhausted all the ones that would talk to her on the phone. She thought about lowly jobs but really couldn't come up with anything. Besides weren't all the lowly people already working at them? Well, she was low, pretty darn low …

Mail had piled up, taking up valuable space in her micro mini flat. The thump of more falling through her door slot woke her up. What time was it anyway? She sadly looked at the new pile of mail on her floor. "Maybe it's time I opened my mail."

The eviction letter from her apartment manager was no surprise.

The overdue utilities ditto.

The sale flyer from Bloomies she held hesitantly, then let drop to the floor. Ditto for Barneys.

(The usual junk mail) and one lavender padded envelope. "How odd …" The hand writing was long and flowing, rather old fashioned--maybe Victorian. A font Elizabeth often used at work.

When she worked, that is.

The return address was C. McGillicuddy. Why that is my name--the McGillicuddy part. It was from Wind Star. Elizabeth had no clue where that was. If it wasn't in the City, well, it just wasn't anywhere.

Many years ago, after a bitter divorce, her mother had packed everything including four year old Elizabeth, and moved to New

York City.It seemed ages ago; Elizabeth had no real recollection as to where they'd moved from. The City had just always been home.

By the time Elizabeth finished high school, and was enrolled at F.I.T., her mother had moved to Europe, bouncing around until she'd settled with an entrepreneur.

What her step dad did, Elizabeth had no clue. She'd only met him twice before he, and her mom, moved to Australia to make their fortune. And had they made that fortune? Elizabeth had no clue.

She certainly could use a fortune about now, or at least a few spare dollars. Okay, maybe just a good pastrami sandwich.

Elizabeth never really had known her relatives, certainly not on her father's side. Squeezing her brain, she couldn't go back that far. Her mother had never talked about them even when she asked. And because they were such a non issue in her life, she'd very rarely asked.

She held the lavender envelope by the tips of her now chipped finger nails as though the letter somehow might be dangerous. It was thicker than the average letter. Well, she never got letters, just bills. It was thicker than most bills. And some of her bills were pretty thick ...

Then she sighed wondering what the debate was about. Slowly she slit the padded envelope. It was padded alright--with money. Eight one hundred dollar bills drifted out onto the floor. Someone had sent her cash! In the mail!

Auntie Clara, turns out, was her grandmother's sister, on her father's side, technically her great aunt. Auntie Clara remembered Lizzie as a child in pig tails.

Lizzie?

Auntie Clara, for whatever reason Elizabeth couldn't begin to imagine, was offering her a job.

With an apartment.

In Wind Star.

Where ever that was.

Elizabeth's hands trembled. There was one shrunken apple in her fridge, and one bag of hard butterscotch candy. She'd spent her last twenty dollars on lipstick, foolishly thinking it would cheer her up.

5

It hadn't.

Depression was a black fog creeping along the edges.

Until ...

Elizabeth tried to conjure an image of this Auntie Clara but failed. It just wasn't there. Auntie Clara spoke fondly of her and had somehow tracked her down. "Did she know I was desperate?"

Auntie Clara advised her to buy a used car, pack her belongings, and come to Wind Star.

To family.

Elizabeth looked at the eight hundred dollars and shook her head. "Right ..."

But the note had included the address of a car dealer in Brooklyn, and a name of someone to see. Elizabeth was afraid she'd use her entire eight hundred dollars on public transportation just to get to Brooklyn.

Looking around her dingy flat, she thought why not? She really had no other options ... What else could she possibly be waiting for?

Turned out the BMW dealership was several blocks long and quite smashing! Elizabeth trudged from the bus stop laughing at the foolishness of her being at a Beamer dealer clutching her letter, and her crisp one hundred dollar bills. The lobby looked like an Art Deco movie set--all chrome and red leather.

Music wafted out at her as she took it all in. It was soft piano with just enough of a jazzy tone to match the deco décor. Then she grinned, "Of course, Jim Hart's newest CD."

Funny her favorite music should be as at home here among the priceless imported cars as it had been soothing her cubby hole at her job ... the job she no longer had. Still the sounds made her feel good.

If she did get a car, which of course she was highly doubting would actually happen with her tiny stash of cash, she'd have to remember to take her Jim Hart CDs as company on the road.

Three aggressive salesmen in shiny silk suits pounced on her. Why, Elizabeth couldn't guess. She certainly didn't look like she could afford a new BMW or Range Rover, or anything. She didn't look like she could afford anything here.

Maybe they thought she'd just stumbled in by accident. Her legs in her pink three inch heels glided forward, refusing to be intimidated ... too much. Her   pink Burberry skirt swayed as she headed to the main counter leaving the three sales men in her wake.

Flipping back her waist length chestnut hair, she turned her green eyes to the middle aged receptionist, "I'd like to see a Mr. Basil." Clutching her faux pink Burberry, and wondering what she was even doing there she added, "If he's in and free that is." Well she hoped that counted as manners. Just because she was desperate didn't mean she didn't have manners.

A few manners ...

The receptionist raised a penciled eyebrow, nodded, and picked up a phone. "Young lady to see you," Was all she said.

A studded padded leather door opened and the oldest man Elizabeth had ever seen sauntered out. She was shocked he could move as well as he could. And for such a tiny man, he stood proud. He was ninety if not one hundred.

What was left of his silver hair was combed over a shiny head. He was so small or was he bent over--she couldn't tell ...

But he was dressed in a tweed jacket, dapper bow tie, and she thought she glimpsed red braces on his starched pin striped shirt. His luxurious handle bar mustache twirled up at the ends, and came to life as he smiled! His eyes danced, and his papery wrinkled face lit with humor.

And Elizabeth liked him immediately.

Liked him a lot.

He approached her, gnarled hand out stretched, "I'm Basil Herrington. And you--you must be Lizzie!"

Lizzie? Elizabeth blushed to the tip of her nose but accepted the out stretched hand.

"Clara told me you'd be by--so nice to finally meet you."

"You know my Aunt Clara?" She stammered.

And Basil had a faraway look in his eyes, "Ah yes." But he said no more.

Elizabeth fidgeted on her heels, swaying a bit.

Finally Basil spoke, "You resemble her, my dear."

Look like great Aunt Clara? Preposterous! Elizabeth snuffled up any reaction and just smiled.

But the melancholy look vanished as quickly as it had appeared, and Mr. Herrington got down to business, "A car--Clara said you'd be needing a car--that you'll be leaving our fair New York."

Elizabeth only nodded with a little tilt of her head. Besides it wasn't feeling as fair as it used to.

"Come this way my dear." And he led her out a side door to the used lot. They walked past rows of older Beamers in to a series of used Range Rovers. Elizabeth passed what she was sure were a couple of Rolls, just sitting out in the day light, and a lovely old MG.

There was a basic yet classy car whose name plate read Vauxhall, a row of pristine Austin's, which really were impressive, and one grand lady of them all, a Daimler, the jewel. She only knew the name by reading it off the hood.

Lovely.

Finally at the end of the row sat a Mini Cooper, stripped of all paint, primed silver, almost naked, sadly alone. It was dusty.

"This is what I had in mind," Basil beamed.

Elizabeth looked mortified.

She'd barely stopped when Basil stopped, almost falling forward off her heels.

"Two hundred dollars."

"Two hundred dollars?"

Elizabeth couldn't believe her ears. Surely he was kidding her. No matter how pitiful it looked she knew two hundred dollars barely bought you a decent pair of shoes. Okay, didn't buy you a decent pair of shoes. Shoes she would probably never get to buy again.

"Yes my dear and I will have the boys paint it." Basil grinned and in spite of his years she saw boyish charm.

"Paint it?" Well it was down to primer. At least that's what she thought it was.

"That's right--just talk to Ray in the paint shop. You name it."

She clutched her Burberry bag and sighed. Even she knew this was the deal of a lifetime. "Uh okay," And she was at the brink … And it was a sad little car--sad like her.

Alone.

Certainly out of its league …

It might have personality. It might work … And Elizabeth knew she had no other options. She looked carefully at the tiny car. Maybe it didn't either. Who was going to come into this elegant car dealership for this? No one, that's who, no one at all.

Well she'd save it.

They'd save each other.

Basil smiled. Of course he knew it was okay, and she had no other options. "Fine, I'll have Madge draw up the paper work while you go meet Ray in the paint shop." And he gestured to yet another building. And in spite of himself he smiled.

Elizabeth teetered off on her heels to the paint shop. A stubby, serious man approached her. "The Mini--you're here about the Mini Cooper."

"Uh yes--yes." He was so serious. But, yes, she was here about the Mini. Now wasn't the time to back down. Back down to what?

He said it as though he'd been expecting her. Maybe he had been. Maybe Auntie Clara had called Mr. Basil, and this is what they decided on, and maybe … well, it didn't really matter.

Not at all.

She was here with no other options.

Ray wore paint splotched over hauls, and a base ball hat, also with paint splotches.

"What color can I have?" Elizabeth hesitated to walk any further into the paint shop for fear of ending up like Ray.

"Mr. Herrington told me anything your little heart desires." When Ray smiled Elizabeth saw a fatherly kindness, and possibly a fellow artist. So she relaxed.

"Anything?" What color to paint that odd little car? She was clueless. Looking down at her pink Burberry bag she raised her eyebrows and smiled, "Can you match this?"

"Pink?" Ray grimaced, despite himself.

"That's right!" And her smile was full wattage. The best she'd felt since she lost her job. Suddenly she could see that dingy little car pinked up and happy.

"Yeah, I suppose I can do that." He shook his head as he spoke, looking at her carefully, wondering who she was ...

Then Elizabeth got bolder. Not even sure why, she just did. "And the roof? Can you plaid the roof?" And she grinned at the idea.

"Plaid the roof?"

She pointed to her bag.

Ray started to protest, and then remembered his orders. Whoever this was must be pretty special. He couldn't begin to put a price on the custom paint job--or the time. "I think I can. Let's have Madge Xerox it for me. I could have you ready in a week." If he hustled, and he guessed he would have no choice.

She was so thrilled she impulsively gave him a hug, and then a little wave as she strode back to the office, forgetting about his paint splotches.

As Elizabeth filled out forms Basil re-appeared. "And you and Ray got things settled?" Of course he knew she had.

"Oh yes," And she grinned thinking how cute her car would be.

"Well I thought it would be the perfect car for you, what with the green interior to match your eyes. I assumed they'd be like Clara's."

And suddenly Elizabeth remembered being a very small child and looking into a weathered face with her very same eyes. The strangest sense washed over her, and the feeling of being alone in the world seemed to lift.

Finally she collected herself and sadly spoke, "Mr. Herrington. I am sure there has been some huge mistake. I cannot afford this car ..." Part of her didn't want to say a word. Not a word. But part of her knew it was just too much--too generous.

And she had to. It was who she was ...

"But Clara said she sent you some money ..." Basil looked concerned. He hoped she hadn't spent it all.

Already.

"Yes but ... the price. It's way too low." Elizabeth finally faced the sad reality even though she could already picture the car with its custom paint job ... and driving it around, while wearing her favorite Burberry outfit.

Still, she could not take advantage of this kind old man.

"I can assure you I mean two hundred dollars," Basil studied her closely.

"But surely your boss will fire you!" Elizabeth probably shouldn't have said that but it was out before she could take it back. She scrunched her face embarrassed for both of them.

"I assure you Miss Lizzie, I am the boss. This is my dealership. In fact I own a chain of British car dealerships, and I can price any car anyway I want!" Basil almost smiled.

Almost.

Elizabeth just couldn't close her mouth! She was shocked! Stunned! This ancient, albeit dapper, man she assumed was simply never fired, and kept on as a charity relic, was the proprietor of not only this dealership, but a chain?

No.

"Now the paper work, well, we'll just let Madge finish that up. And I assumed you wouldn't have insurance, Clara took care of your first six months--to get you started."

Again she nodded numbly.

"And I'm assuming you'll be paying cash, if I know Clara."

Tax, title, everything was figured in as a shocked Elizabeth parted with two of her eight hundred dollar bills.

"Now one of my boys will drive you home and bring you back in a week. I've put a nice little atlas in the glove box to help out the Tom Tom. There's a new CD player so you can have company as you drive. And you'll find one of my brother's BMW dealerships outside of Wind Star when you need servicing."

He went to shake her hand, but Elizabeth bent on her extremely tall strappy heels, and kissed his papery cheek, tears in her eyes, hope in her heart.

Basil blushed to the top of his shiny head, through his comb over. "And you'll give Clara my regards," He said it more as a request than a question though his eyes got stuck in middle space for just a second.

Cooper got out of his NASCAR, well what was left of it, and walked away. "I'm too old," he muttered, "To rack my body up in a crash, and I'm too young to die."

And stopped racing.

"I might not be too old for California, but I'm tired of it." Once he said it out loud he knew he was right.

He thought about the letter on his dresser.

The letter suggesting he come to Wind Star.

He flipped out his cell and called movers.

Elizabeth had no clue what career her Aunt Clara had arranged for her. She just knew it included an apartment and was, well, a job. As city life gave way to country, her journey became a series of endless highways. (The back seat of the pink Mini held all her possessions, mostly clothes, and make up.

She'd used some of her very precious remaining six hundred dollars to have her shoes mailed at Pack N Mail. There was no way (sixty three pairs of shoes) could fit in the Mini. Elizabeth said good bye to them tenderly, and then packed what was left and hit the road.

Ray, the car painter, had outdone himself. He was an artist. (The formerly pitiful stripped Mini Cooper was now a piece of art work, her piece of art work) Well, Ray the painter's, but now hers. It was so cute she hugged it when she saw it, tears in her eyes.

Then she ran to the paint shop and hugged Ray. Despite all the time and labor that he put in while grousing about it, he was tickled Elizabeth was so happy. And he would have done it again just to see her face light up. (It matched her beloved pink Burberry hand bag as though it had come from the factory that way.)

(If Elizabeth had all the money in the world, this was exactly what she would have wanted)

As Elizabeth drove, she went over her job, well, lack of job, at the ad agency--went over it in disbelief. Bits of reality would click in as she got further and further from New York. She was fired.

She was so dazed she hadn't even paid attention to their reasons, and just accepted it, and left. At first she'd been angry, indignant. How could they? Who did they think they were?

Now she just felt remorse and self pity. Elizabeth knew who they were. They were the people who controlled the money. The money they no longer planned on giving her. They were the people who controlled her future.

Well, had controlled her future. Now, as she drove through Ohio, having left New York, and even Pennsylvania, far behind she felt the first glimmer of hope that maybe she controlled her future.

And maybe she had been a tad lax. Okay, she did fall asleep once. Well, not counting the time she went out for a pretzel from a street vendor, and fell asleep on a bench. Okay, it wasn't smart, and she supposed not too safe, to fall asleep in the city, on the side walk. Still, she'd been tired, and well, she'd just closed her eyes for a second.

And the other time had been at her desk. But her computer was hard on her eyes, and she was just resting them for a minute. She would have woken up on her own she was quite sure ... eventually.

Elizabeth knew she did good work. Better than good. She had an eye for design and well, she loved it. A knack that she'd developed over a period of time. Granted there were times, okay many times, when the jobs all blurred together.

She wasn't bored, just easily distracted by shiny objects, or day dreams or … But when she had a special account to work on, well, no one made it more special than her.

Okay, she would miss it, darn it.

At least the special part.

Ohio turned into Indiana. She'd taken one break at a Hampton Inn. Whatever made her think she could just drive straight through? She had no conception of time, or distance for that matter.

She just knew that an awful lot of the country looked the same, like a turnpike or highway or … route something or other. And she'd been tired. So she stopped.

Almost didn't have a choice.

This time she knew she really was tired--very tired. Besides she didn't want to take a chance of crashing her beloved pink Mini. And now that her journey was started, well, she didn't want to end it in a car crash.

So she stopped.

The shower was heaven. The over sized bed a dream. The included buffet breakfast was exceptional. She loaded up, and tossed an extra yogurt in her Burberry handbag. Then she went back and made a tiny sandwich out of two bagel toppers, and snagged an apple.

And felt better.

As tired as Elizabeth had been, and as late as it was when she stopped, she couldn't believe she hadn't just slept like a zombie. She dreamt she was still working at the ad agency, and they were firing her again, and again. And still she didn't seem to be getting it.

In her dream she just kept showing up and the whole humiliating experience continued to unfold. Finally she'd woken up, disoriented, and freaked. But the cheerful Hampton Inn brought her back to reality. Yes, she was fired, but only once. And she was on her way, her new adventure was unfolding. And her breakfast was waiting for her ...

Jim Hart continued to sing for her, play the piano for her, and basically keep her company. Well, Jim's music. Basil had installed a CD player that she was sure cost far more than the car itself. Well, pretty sure. It said Bose and it sounded like her own personal concert.

And she mentally thanked him repeatedly for his kindness and generosity--and the Tom Tom GPS. How lovely and very clever that it was John Cleese's voice.

Elizabeth just listened to the directions in his very proper, and yet comical British accent, and did as she was told, the atlas forgotten. She joked that she was traveling to parts unknown with two very interesting men: Jim Hart and John Cleese.

Finally the Tom Tom, and John Cleese, took her off the interstate. She'd left Indiana and finally saw signs that said Illinois. It was flatter, was her first reaction--flatter and fewer cities. Well she didn't see a lot of cities on the freeways.

Or stores.

She hoped they had stores, nice stores in Illinois. She couldn't believe she was on this marathon driving trip and thinking about shopping. She tuned back into her CD and kept driving.

Towns got even smaller, and eventually she wound her way to a tree lined street with some ancient stone four story brown stones. If you called them brown stones in the middle of God help her, she had no clue. Weren't they just apartments?

Yet, the buildings were old; weathered, beautifully appointed--the look of New York City brown stones that she always coveted, surprising herself that something so lovely could exist outside of New York City.

Maybe she was just a tad narrow minded.

Probably not.

Still ...

Elizabeth found her aunt's address, and headed to the ancient glass door, past shabby over grown flower beds, and a weed strewn sidewalk. A reedy voice replied to her ring telling her to come up.

And then her nerves kicked in. This was it, it was time. She was finally here. No more long distance hauling on the highways being tossed about by the big trucks. No more rest stops or gas stations. Her journey was over, and this is where it had taken her. And she couldn't go back.

Back where?

Besides she'd already pressed the world's oldest intercom, and her aunt knew she was down here. So she took a deep breath and started.

Four flights of marble stairs.

To the top floor.

Elizabeth wondered if she'd missed the elevator but was pretty sure she hadn't. She'd scoured the lobby before she gave up, and just started to climb. Her shoes definitely were not meant to climb all those stairs. Nor was she, for that matter.

It wasn't as though she was out of shape; she certainly looked like a model. Okay, so she possibly had no muscle tone. Still, it was an awful lot of steps to climb … She let out a deep breath and fluffed her long hair. Okay, I'm ready …

The door was heavy carved oak, all stained almost black. It was the only door so she figured it was the one.

The one that housed her great aunt.

Elizabeth lifted a knocker shaped like a book, and gently tapped. Nervous, why was she nervous now? She certainly wasn't going to climb back down all those stairs just because she was nervous.

She was also desperate.

Desperate won out.

She could hear someone padding to answer her knock. The door cracked open and they both just stared. Thinking maybe she shouldn't have worn the tiny cut offs and tight red tee shirt, Elizabeth held her pink Burberry purse in front of herself as if it were extra clothing.

Auntie Clara was probably a few inches shorter than her, filled out in a grandmotherly way yet wore a rainbow chenille bath robe. Elizabeth noticed her toe nails were painted electric pink, peeking out of her furry scuffs. Her hair was silver, tied back with wisps about her face almost like a halo; framing her twinkling green eyes.

Elizabeth's eyes.

"Lizzie--you finally made it!" And Auntie Clara held out her arms, and Elizabeth let herself be embraced in the warmth and softness of this very ancient woman who claimed to be her aunt. And with that they started chattering like two old friends.

It just happened.

Relief washed over Elizabeth as Auntie Clara asked about the roads, and when she had left, and what all she'd packed. "Let me put the kettle on." And they both headed to a vintage nineteen thirties kitchen complete with a bubble shaped fridge. In turquoise. And the oldest stove Elizabeth had ever seen, also turquoise.

Elizabeth's eyes darted to plastic canisters with art deco lettering 'tea, flour, and sugar' as Auntie Clara found some tea bags in the one marked sugar.

They sat at a chrome and red table, Elizabeth would have killed for. Auntie Clara tore into a package of McVities Digestives which turned out to be a combination shortbread and graham cracker little cookie. Heaven.

They eyed each other cautiously, but it was really too late.

They knew they liked each other right off the bat.

"And the car?" Auntie Clara began.

Elizabeth beamed, "Oh yes, thank you so much. I love it! I never ever could have bought a car. And, well, I was at a bit of a low point ..." Such an underestimation but she didn't want Auntie Clara to think she'd been nothing short of desperate.

But Auntie Clara nodded, as if she knew.

"And Basil sends his regards," Elizabeth paused to sip, and over lowered lashes watched her great Aunt Clara fuss, brushing back wisps of hair, nervously pleating her napkin.

"And your things--they arrived a couple of days ago. Several huge boxes, so smart to have things sent." Even though they'd come freight collect. And Clara tilted her head toward the dining room where in fact five gigantic corrugated boxes sat, consuming one wall.

"My shoes!" Elizabeth beamed, relieved that they had made it.

"Oh me ..." Auntie Clara just sipped more tea but Elizabeth noticed a faraway look in her eyes. Eventually the pot ran dry, and the cookies finished to a crumb.

"Well now Lizzie, I think it is time to find your apartment." Clara gathered an old skeleton key off a hook. Not bothering to change, headed for the door.

Surprisingly Auntie Clara sailed down the four flights of stairs with ease. Elizabeth looked at her high heeled sandals and wished she were wearing trainers.

Well, she didn't own trainers but still ...

They headed to the back of the building where a single flight of stairs led down one more flight.

"Why it's a basement flat," Elizabeth thought, rather charmed.

Auntie Clara was humming a little ditty that sounded like an old time record.

The flat was a single room with windows on one wall--near the ceiling. It was tiny, yet three times the size of her New York City home.

Maybe bigger.

Oak floors gleamed, an old wardrobe stood on one wall, also oak, with intricate carvings on its doors. There was a bed built like a cupboard with drawers below, almost story book like. It held a patch quilt in reds and pinks, and several fluffy pillows in old embroidered cases.

The kitchen 'corner' held a tiny pink bubble refrigerator, and a matching two burner stove. It must have been the trend to have colored appliances way back when, and yet ... they charmed her.

The bathroom, surprisingly, was almost as big as the entire apartment. Another oak armoire and a claw foot tub huge enough for a family, a Victorian pedestal sink, and a faded chintz chaise. Their eyes both lit on the ruffled hemmed chaise.

"I thought it might be a nice touch, and had it moved in here for you," Auntie Clara began, "Of course it can go ..."

"Oh no! I wouldn't dream of it! I love it!" And Elizabeth did. It was so very Ralph Lauren in a faded turn of the century sort of way. In fact it looked like something she'd seen in his Madison Avenue store. But this was old, surely very old.

Her mind drifted to the miniscule bathroom in her New York flat. To use the toilet, one had to go in, and close the door. The shower, that never had hot water, sprayed the child's sink when used. And the smell, well, she never conquered that semi mold, semi old scent that permeated her towels.

And probably her.

Gratitude shown in Elizabeth's eyes. She bent down and gave Auntie Clara a feather kiss on her papery cheek. "I was at the end ..." She whispered.

"I know Poppet." Auntie Clara patted her as if for all the world she was four years old again--and left her to settle.

⚜

Elizabeth wore her ⸳ cut offs and a pink Burberry Her long hair caught up on top of her head, her hands filthy, her nails split and grimy. She tugged at another forty pound bag of mulch.

"Career ..." She spat out! Auntie Clara said nothing, implied nothing, about manual labor. "Grounds keeper!" Thank God the back yard was all paved parking, and the front of the building was relatively small.

Relatively.

It seems Ferguson, the old grounds keeper, had left—permanently, for the cemetery--and by the looks of the weeds, and ratty beds, had not been up to much for a while.

Quite a while.

Elizabeth was, for all practical purposes, on her own. "But Auntie Clara, I haven't a clue ..." She'd whined like a four year old but Auntie Clara didn't seem to notice.

19

"Nonsense me dear. There's a lawn. There's a lawn mower. You can use your artistic abilities with the flowers."

"What flowers?"

"Oh, management will periodically have delivered whatever you need."

Elizabeth grimaced. Need? She needed a job at a desk. This wasn't a career. Not even a job. It was labor. And where could she possibly put flowers. The yard was full of what she was sure once were weeds. Now they were dead.

Dead weeds.

Where were all those flowers supposed to go? And what was supposed to happen to those dead weeds? Where would they go?

"Lizzie, you saw the shed out back?" Auntie Clara was dressed this time. Retro, rayon, olive green, and burgundy dress that Elizabeth wished were her size.

Auntie Clara's shoes had a bit of a platform, and wedge, but tied sensibly in front. Her hose, if Elizabeth wasn't mistaken, had seams. Seams ... Well, possibly she'd seen them at Nordstrom's. Still ...

Elizabeth nodded weakly, returning from Auntie Clara's retro fashion to the shed.

"Well anything you need is in there. And any job too big, you can call the nursery for help."

"Too big, Auntie Clara? What would be too big?"

Auntie Clara's eyes twinkled, "Oh I don't know. If you want to change the side walk, give it an angle or curve or something."

Change the sidewalk? Elizabeth fought back a tear of pity. Her exquisite tapered pink nails were not only chipped but had little hunks of dirt under them. And and, well, she thought she was sweating! In her good pink Burberry

She got down on her knees with her little trowel, and continued weeding the small yard by the front door. She concluded she had to get rid of all those dead plants.

Why, in heavens name if they died they didn't simply go away? So she started weeding. She had a system--loosen and yank, loosen and yank, while her mind just drifted away.

She'd found a tiny CD player in her new flat and brought Jim Hart's latest CD out to keep her company. It only helped a tiny bit. Still, it was company--the same company that had gotten her all the way here to Wind Star.

For the life of her, she didn't think she'd ever planted a thing, not to mention weed. She didn't know a tulip from a turnip so she just yanked it all.

To say the progress was slow was an understatement, but when she'd crawl into her huge claw foot tub, and sink under the bubbles, or look around her sweet vintage flat, she knew she at least had a home--a home without a monthly bill piling up.

Nagging at her.

And a home that was so charming she actually felt comforted and secure. The fact that Elizabeth was in the middle of the middle of no-where hadn't even sunk in—she was so exhausted from her manual labor she'd forgotten to let it bother her. She was more concerned about running out of that wonderful lavender bubble bath ...

The clearing out of brush and weeds, and the cursing of Ferguson the dead gardener, had a pattern of its own. Elizabeth was mid curse when a nursery truck pulled up.

She stood in awe as flats of bright pink petunias, and fuchsia gera-niums were unloaded. Sunny yellow marigolds, and a few small bushes with top knots she later learned were boxwood. There were trailing ivies, and some variegated ground cover--again she was clueless as to its name.

The driver came up to her with paper work, "You McGillicuddy?"

Elizabeth blushed   . "I guess I am." With a soil streaked slash, she signed the invoice. She stared in amaze-ment as the men started to pull out.

Finally she hollered after the truck, "Hey ... who's going to plant all this?" Leave, how could they possibly leave her with all this ...?

One of the old men winked, "We just deliver--my guess is you are!" And he laughed as the truck disappeared. It didn't look like a delivery. It looked like a sale. Shaking her fist, she looked up to see Auntie Clara come out the front door.

"Ah, I see your plants have arrived," She beamed.

"My plants Auntie Clara?"

"Well my dear, you are the grounds keeper."

"But but ..."

"Just use your artistic talents, you'll figure it out." Then Auntie Clara looked up, shielding her eyes. "Looks like another perfect sunny day. Don't forget to give them a good drink." Auntie Clara wandered to the street with two gigantic canvas totes over stuffed with what looked like scrapbooks. "I'm off to me scrap book club."

And as she said it an ancient car chugged to the curb with an equally ancient woman behind the wheel. "That would be Bertie now. She isn't supposed to drive. Poke your head in like a good girl and say hello ..."

Elizabeth lugged the heavy totes for her aunt, and as she started to shove them in the back seat of what she swore was an old Edsel, a scrawny wiry grandmother stuck a paper thin hand out at her. Already assaulted with faded lavender, Elizabeth reached for it.

"And you must be Lizzie. I'm Bertie. Just call me Auntie Bertie. So glad to hear you're settling in. And I see you're planting flowers today. Lovely!" Her reedy voice was faint but held a twinkle of humor. "Well, we're off to our scrap booking."

In a wink Auntie Clara bundled in the front, and Bertie peeled out leaving Elizabeth in the dust.

Elizabeth stood on the curb, inhaling exhaust. She looked at the sea of riotous flower colors and then at her pile of filthy garden tools. "I need help ..." Self pity had cloaked her but she knew she had to shake it off.

There was no help.

She was the help.

Elizabeth looked down the deserted street. Not even a stray dog--no one. Then she looked back at the flats of flowers and squinted. They virtually were a rainbow riot of all her favorite colors--shades of pink from faded, to brilliant fuchsia. All the yellows on earth from butter, to New York taxi cab gold!

The plants started to look like an art project, and the dirty little front yard of the apartment her canvas.

Then it sank in. Why she could create her own collage of color, and no one to tell her how to do it, probably no one to complain either. She could do ... why she could do whatever she wanted! And she began. A border edging the sidewalk started to emerge in trailing petunias.

She alternated bright yellow with fuchsia. Corny--well, yes, but also bright and eye catching. That took most of the morning, carving out the little holes, and patting in the plants. By eleven thirty it dawned on her to soak the next area with the hose, just a bit to remove the dust.

Her days of stripping weeds, and dead shrubs, and wilted taller plants (beyond recognition, not that she knew what they were anyway) had paid off. Her canvas was clear and ready. She grabbed an apple, hunk of Cheddar, and Diet Pepsi, and sat on the last step to observe her border.

Elizabeth decided the two shrubs, label said boxwood, would flank the steps closest to the building, (their little top knots looking like wooden finials) As she surveyed the size of their pots, she realized this would take the big shovel. And the holes would be a project.

(She set in; spraying dirt all over the tiny section she'd left as lawn. Looking at the clumps it sank in, "I'll need those to pat around my plants ..." Painstakingly she tried to finger comb the soil into a pile, and then emptied the next hole more carefully.)

When both spots were dug, Elizabeth picked up the first plant and started to tip it out. By now it was late afternoon, the sun no longer over head. A gentle breeze tickled her   back. She bent, hips in the air, and finally tugged for all she was worth to remove the lodged shrub.

A green Jag roared down the street, and seeing her ﹐
slid onto the tree lawn. Hearing the commotion, she looked up in horror just in time to see a car driving into her mornings work!

"Hey! You idiot!" Grabbing the empty plastic pot from the boxwood, she flung it at the windshield! Loose top soil scattered on the pristine windows as the pot bounced away.

The man started to laugh. The gardener was even prettier in the upright position! But when he heard her curses, and saw her ready to toss a metal trowel, he backed up and sped away.

Elizabeth started after the car, waving her small shovel, "Come back here you you … plant killer!" Then she looked at the tire tracks through the petunias. She sank in all her filth on the first step and wept.

"My my … design!" Then she wailed even harder. "Design? I'm a gardener, a maintenance man!" When she could cry no more she lugged her tools back to the shed and crawled into her claw foot tub.

"Auntie Clara, what's that heavenly scent?"

"Oh, I made a cake for me scrap booking meeting. It's just cooling."

"Well that doesn't smell like just any old cake," Elizabeth persisted. She'd forced herself to climb those dreaded four flights of stairs, shamed into it by her ancient Aunties ability to bounce up and down them.

And lonely.

Lonely for her Aunt.

"Grab the carrier Lizzie and one of me scrap booking totes. It's not just any old cake. It's me ˙ Pound Cake." Auntie Clara's eyes gleamed.

˙ Pound Cake?" Elizabeth raised an eyebrow as she scooped up the Tupperware cake carrier and looped the scrap book tote over her shoulder.

"That's right." They headed down the stairs as they talked. "The cake has _____ soaked raisins in it and then when it's still warm ..."

As it was right now, Elizabeth thought, as she clutched the toasty heavenly bundle.

"I poke holes with me wooden spoon handle ɩ _____."

" _____ "

Shocked beyond words, not to mention shocked _____ ɩ _____ ıs ... Maybe she didn't have a total license on all things great and wonderful ...

"Well dear, a cakes only as good as the ingredients you put in it, now isn't it?" Auntie Clara's eyes twinkled as she spoke, "Tell you what, you stay and meet Blanchie, and we'll cut you a piece."

"And I'm driving you where?"

"Well Blanchie lives at the retirement center now, and though she still has her license, her son took her car away from her." And Auntie Clara glared in disgust. She ran a hand lovingly on the pink Mini. So creative, she thought. Just like me Lizzie ...

"And your car Auntie Clara? What seems to be the problem?"

Now Auntie Clara raised one penciled eye brow. "Problem? I have no clue! A red light keeps flashing when I go to turn it on and well, nothing happens."

"Nothing?" Elizabeth hadn't even seen Auntie Clara's car. It was probably as old as she was. She rarely drove it anywhere, hopping on the corner bus, or persuading Elizabeth to fetch an errand for her. It was tucked in one of the garages in back, probably rusted to the cement floor.

"So that nice young man from the dealership is going to take a look at it. When he stops by just unlock garage #3 for him."

And she handed Lizzie a little key on a gold ring. The garages were so old the doors opened manually, as in, she guessed you yanked the door up.

Blanchie's retirement center looked more like a country club, albeit an old one--still pristine. Like a page out of one of Auntie Clara's books on the English country side; tudor with rolling lawns, flagstone walk ways, and if Elizabeth wasn't mistaken topiaries.

Why the bushes were actually trimmed out to look like ...

"Chocolate pots me dear," Auntie Clara filled in as they headed up the front walk, reading her mind. "One of the residents is from England and had photographs of Great Dixter, some manor house. So she persuaded the gardeners to re-create some of the Great Dixter topiaries."

Persuaded? Elizabeth's eyes widened. Now how would you convince a gardener to undertake such a huge project? Not to mention one that looked like it took maintenance--loads of maintenance.

But these one sided thoughts were conversations with Auntie Clara. She just read Elizabeth's mind and kept talking, "Cash Lizzie. I believe she had piles and piles of cash and well, the gardener is fond of all things green ..."

Lizzie started to question how Auntie Clara could always seem to peak into her mind but got distracted by the over spilling flower beds. "Oh Auntie Clara! How marvelous! And look those look like our petunias don't they?"

Auntie Clara nodded a gleam in her eye, "I do like the way you've alternated the colors better than theirs though," Clara encouraged. "And I believe management is having the nursery deliver a few more to fill in from that wee accident," She said it with a straight face.

"Wee accident? Auntie Clara! That idiot was a road warrior! He better hope he never, and I mean never, crosses my path--or flower beds--again!" And Elizabeth's green eyes flashed, her hands fisted over Auntie Clara's scrapbook totes.

By now a discreet doorman was holding the front door--a doorman in full uniform. "Miss Clara," He nodded but eyed their bundles.

"Jamieson, I'll be saving you a wee piece of me cake."

And Jamieson blushed.

"Miss Bertie and Miss Blanchie are in the west parlor." And he ever so slightly tilted his head in the proper direction.

The 'west parlor' was like a page out of an English magazine--a very old one. Over stuffed rose covered chintz chairs pulled up to a stone fireplace, their gathered skirts and ruffled pillows adding a cozy old lady touch--rich old lady touch.

A polished oak library table was scattered with scrapbooks, glue pots, scissors, and what appeared to be stacks of old magazines. Bertie waved as they entered.

Blanchie rose and came over, arms outstretched. Her day glow red hair, bordering on orange, was loosely captured in a top knot. She wore what appeared to be a rose covered snap coat but over black leggings. On her feet were bright pink satin mules. Something Elizabeth had only seen in the movies.

The old old movies.

"Lizzie--finally we meet!" Blanchie smelled of Chanel #5, much to Elizabeth's surprise. "You will join us for a bit won't you?"

Auntie Clara and Bertie raised an eyebrow. "Just for cake," Auntie Clara put in.

"Nonsense, I sense a fellow scrap booker. Why I've gotten you an album Lizzie, to get started. You'll surely want to put those creative talents to work."

Clara and Bertie both squinted their eyes at Blanchie, but Blanchie ignored them.

"Well, I could stay a little," It was that or keep planting.

"Now the garden dear ..." Auntie Clara piped in.

"Can wait a bit Clara," Blanchie finished. "I want to properly meet your great niece. From New York City you say?"

But Elizabeth hadn't, still she nodded.

"Ah, I have a granddaughter there, I believe, but maybe not. Maybe you've met her? In the design field--fashion design like I was." And Blanchie patted her rose snap coat. "Coco. Named after ..." But Blanchie didn't finish.

"Chanel?" Elizabeth joked.

But all three ladies bowed their heads in reverence and nodded. Elizabeth thought they did a quick, very quick, sign of the cross. Elizabeth snuck a sideways glance at Auntie Clara. Was she making a little sign of the cross too? No, no way.

"Another day Lizzie--I'll tell you about Coco--another day."

Which one, Elizabeth thought.

"Now Lizzie really can't stay too long, there are more flowers being delivered and she's letting the man in to look at me car."

"An hour Lizzie," Blanchie insisted, "And then we'll send you off."

They sat around the library table with scrap books open, scissors flying, glue pots dripping. Blanchie snipped away from a Chanel ad in a magazine, and added it to a pile.

Odd was all Elizabeth could think.

Auntie Clara had several garden and seed catalogs she was having a go at. (The scrap book page she was working on had intricate flower beds pasted at random.)

"How did you get started, er, scrap booking?" Elizabeth was leafing through one of Blanchie's with pictures of Tudor mansions throughout.

"Well dear ..." Bertie began, "We used to play cards--scads of cards." Then she got somber. "You see we were four." And Bertie looked around tenderly. "And of course we weren't as well, affluent shall I say, as we are now."

The other two ancient women shook their heads seriously in agreement.

"But when Ruthie passed ..."

"Passed?" Elizabeth asked, her experience with senior woman was, well, nonexistent.

"On." And Blanchie and Auntie Clara nodded while bowing their heads and possibly sneaking in a little sign of the cross too quick to really tell.

Elizabeth guessed Ruthie must have been something what with all this head bowing.

"So of course that ended the bridge," Auntie Clara said as if that explained it all.

"Even the Old Maid, our particular favorite," Blanchie added.

"But we needed, well, a hobby, a reason to get together."

The others nodded.

"And we were at a loss until Ruthie suggested scrap booking."

Ruthie? Hadn't she passed?

On?

Now all three were smiling, though just a bit misty, "Our first scrap book was in memory of Ruthie. I'll bring it down next time you come."

It was understood Elizabeth would be back.

Now Auntie Clara picked up the thread, "And well, from there it just snow balled. Why there isn't a subject we haven't ..." Then Auntie Clara looked flustered and clasped her today amethyst ringed fingers. They sparkled in response.

Elizabeth coveted her aunt's jewelry collection. It was endless. At least she continued to see her wear different pieces.

Grand pieces.

"Tackled," Bertie supplied.

This being said, all three women picked up their scissors, and became absorbed in their scrap books. Bertie had her Sharpies out, and was calligraphying something--Elizabeth couldn't see what.

"You know ladies ..." Elizabeth began, looking at their odd supplies. "There are stickers you can buy, and rubber stampers with a huge array of inks, even glittery ones. And stencils. And and ..."

"Please call us Auntie," All three chorused.

"Oh." Suddenly Elizabeth felt like family. "Oh okay." Why Elizabeth didn't feel awkward she couldn't say. She felt ... like family.

"And we shall call you Lizzie. Well, you are Lizzie after all ... to us."

"We even have a Lizzie scrap book," Bertie piped in but Auntie Clara stomped on her foot, and Blanchie gave her a scowl.

"A Lizzie scrap book ...?" Elizabeth asked quietly. Her bottom lip trembled ever so slightly.

Auntie Clara patted her hand, "Oh nothing, nothing really dear. We've just followed your, well, I guess your life."

"My life?"

"Well …" Now Auntie Clara was back pedaling, "What we knew of it dear."

"You are family," Bertie put in.

"And it's time we cut that cake." Blanchie rose to a side board and returned with plates and a wicked looking knife.

"And tea. Jamieson will bring tea."

He will? Elizabeth thought. But the door opened after a muffled knock and sure enough Jamieson, the door greeter, wheeled in a trolley.

"Lovely!" The ladies exclaimed and the aroma of Earl Grey and pound cake filled the room. Their slices were generous, bordering on ridiculously huge and under complaints of "I can't" from Elizabeth, a plate was foisted on her.

"Nonsense my dear, Clara bakes out all the calories! Don't you Clara dear?"

Auntie Clara nodded between mouthfuls, "-zaps them right away!" And they laughed and forced the remainder of the cake on Jamieson. "For the boys downstairs," Auntie Clara said. And Jamieson bowed his way out clutching his prize.

"Now you need to go Lizzie," Auntie Clara began.

"But she hasn't even begun her scrap book," Bertie protested

"She'll be back," And Blanchie rested a hand tenderly on her cheek.

Elizabeth noticed her nails were a luminous pink.

"Won't you dear?"

Elizabeth laughed, "I think I will."

"Wednesday," It was said. It was decided.

And despite herself Elizabeth smiled--smiled at the Aunties.

And she was off, cruising back in her little pink Mini. As Elizabeth pulled up to the brown stone, a truck from the nursery was just finishing unloading more flowers--to replace the damaged ones. As the truck pulled away, and Elizabeth pulled past it, she almost ran into another car.

In the back parking lot.

A shiny green Jag.

With an arrogant jean clad drop dead gorgeous man leaning against it.

"You!"

Elizabeth pulled her ' legs out of her tiny car and started shrieking! "You! You plant killer!" She had nothing to throw but her pink Burberry hand bag, and she sent it sailing!

"You trashed my flower beds you maniac! You shouldn't be allowed on the road!" Then she eyed her shovel, leaning against a tree. She ran for it but the man ducked back into his Jag, laughing, and sped away. Just a bit crazed by seeing the plant killer, Elizabeth jumped in her car and started after him!

By the time she realized he was long gone, she found herself in a little village. Slowing, she slid the Mini in front of a faded brick building.

The Union Jack flag was flying along with the Scottish Cross, and the Irish orange and green. Flowers grew in riotous mounds, roses spilled onto the sidewalk, their heady fragrance meeting her as she stepped out of the car. Hollyhocks in an almost black color flanked the door. A carved sign said 'Fairchild's'.

Elizabeth was pulled in by sheer curiosity. Once on the other side of the door, the flowers were forgotten, and Elizabeth found herself in an over flowing shoppe. The first counter held cake stands with mounds of chocolate bars--but all unfamiliar to her: Flakes, Crunchies, Whole Nut. "Why I think they're British," she mused.

The bleached pine table in front of her held glass domes over gigantic crunchy topped muffins, and over sized chocolate chip cookies. A portly man with wispy silver hair and red braces was filling a wax bag.

"Hello there," He said to her.

(Elizabeth was very unused to speaking to strangers. She was, after all, from New York City where your personal space was taken very seriously and respected.)

"The muffins are carrot today. Want one before I take them all?" His eyes twinkled, and by his size, Elizabeth had no doubt in her mind he would clear off the platter.

"Well maybe I will. I'll have two--one for my Auntie Clara."

"Clara McGillicuddy? You wouldn't be her niece now would you?" And he extended a hand, "Larson Parsons. I'm Wind Star's top lawyer."

Jinx appeared from the stock room with an armful of pastel sweaters, "You mean only lawyer." But she laughed as she said it. "And I'm Jinx. Welcome to my shoppe. I just love your Auntie Clara."

"Uh thank you." Not knowing quiet what to say Elizabeth put her muffins in a wax bag, and then as an afterthought, added a couple of chocolate chip cookies.

"So you're settling in?" Larson asked, eyeing the rest of the cookies.

"Well, yes. Yes, I suppose I am." Self consciously Elizabeth twisted the wax bag. She was settling in. She had a routine. A routine she was actually becoming rather fond of.

"Have you met many people yet?" Larson asked bold as could be.

And Elizabeth thought of Blanchie and Bertie.

"There's a new Patisserie a couple doors down run by a great couple," Jinx started.

Larson paid for his sweets and as Elizabeth followed suit he put in, "It's just down from my office. I'll buy you a coffee and you can meet them--Colette and Charlie. You'll like them. And if you haven't eaten ..." He patted his round stomach, "Well, maybe we can have a small bite."

As they left Fairchild's Elizabeth called out, "I wanted to ask about your flowers."

"Oh come back—anytime," Jinx smiled, "And I'll give you some starts."

2

The Patisserie was pink and black with awning stripes, and little metal ice cream parlor tables. It was so New York, no Parisian; Elizabeth couldn't believe it was right there in the middle of Wind Star. She almost thought 'in the middle of nowhere' but corrected herself. After all, she lived here now.

Colette was a waif under a huge apron behind a pastry counter. Charlie was gregarious and good looking. They greeted Larson, met Elizabeth.

And suddenly Elizabeth was meeting other tables of people, and felt for all intensive purposes, as though she was at a party.

"So you're the commercial artist," Someone named Margaret O' said.

Elizabeth met someone from a fitness club who invited her to try one of her classes, and someone else with a botanical business out at an apple orchard.

"Stop by and meet my sister in law Randi, and we'll give you some apples. She runs a bed and breakfast."

Elizabeth drove home feeling as though she just might make some friends--and belong. She chugged up the stairs to Auntie Clara's flat thinking also a workout class might do her some good! "Auntie Clara! I've brought snacks!" But no one answered. Leaning in the hall against the window jam, she peered out.

Why that obnoxious green Jag was back! And its owner! The garage door was open to #3. "Oh　　, he's the mechanic! I was supposed to let him in!" Slowly she dragged herself back down the stairs, not sure if she should apologize or have another go at him. But by the time she came out the front door he was pulling out. Seeing her standing with her hands on her hips, and her green eyes flashing, he tooted, saluted and pulled away!

"Ah, there you be Lizzie!"

"Auntie Clara. I'm sorry about the mechanic but I'm glad he caught you."

"Actually dear it was more serious than I thought, and he had it towed away." Eyeing the wax sack still in Elizabeth's hand Auntie Clara sighed, "Could you use a cuppa? What have you got there?"

"Oh Auntie Clara, I bought us treats from someone named Jinx, and met the nicest people at a little Patisserie. I might take a work out class. And someone named Josie invited me to her orchard for apples."

Clara just smiled as she dipped her hand in the bag and came out with one of the gigantic cookies.

"Lizzie, the girls are going to meet here around lunch time to scrap book."

"Car still in the shop?" Elizabeth asked idly as she tucked a few geraniums in front of some tall lemon marigolds. She eyed the combination with approval and kept planting.

"As a matter of fact it might be ready around supper if you'd drive me to get it."

Auntie Clara was wearing a sunny yellow and sky blue dress today in a bird pattern. It was so gorgeous, and so from another era, Elizabeth almost forgot it was on a plus size grandmotherly woman. Auntie Clara's shoes were two tone taxi cab yellow and blue bird blue with perky little ties.

And for the life of her, Elizabeth wished she had the same outfit in her size.

Elizabeth nodded and Auntie Clara admired the plantings, "You know dear, you've got such an artistic eye." After all, Auntie Clara was only being honest.

Elizabeth blushed at the praise; she'd been out to the nursery and added a few surprises to the mix, starting to treat the apartment building like her own garden.

"Will you take a break later and say hi to the girls?" Auntie Clara asked.

Elizabeth snuck some Lamb's Ear in next for contrast. "I should be at a stopping point by noon or so." And as she lost herself planting, her mind drifted to a particular green Jag.

Before too long Bertie and Blanchie pulled up and began tugging their gigantic scrapbook totes out of Bertie's old car.

"Hi ladies, I mean Aunties. Can I help?" Elizabeth swiped at her brow, leaving a dirt streak.

They both stood to admire the front garden as Elizabeth hefted their bags. "Beautiful Lizzie--we knew it would be," Bertie began.

"And just like the pictures," Blanchie added.

"Pictures? What pictures Auntie Blanchie?" Elizabeth stopped. Was there a plan? A plan she was supposed to be following? She didn't want to follow a plan. She wanted to make her own).

"Pictures? Did I say pictures? I meant pictures in gardening magazines. You know. You do it just like the pros."

Elizabeth rolled her eyes but picked back up the totes. Bertie had a covered dish that smelled divine.

"Tuna casserole dear," Bertie said in response to Elizabeth's look. "A throw back, for sure, but a staple, we always pot luck our efforts."

"What did you bring Auntie Blanchie?" Elizabeth asked just to be polite. But Blanchie pulled a frosty looking bottle   ' out of her brown sack and grinned.

By noon Elizabeth was thinking about a break and some lunch.

The ladies were spread out on the dining room table, bits of riff raff in piles, scissors askew, and glue bottles dripping. "Clara, let's see that garden scrap book." Blanchie reached for a moss green book off the shelf. A shelf that was top to bottom with scrap books. She started to flip the pages, "Ah yes, the pink and yellow combination. Quite lovely what our Lizzie has done."

Auntie Clara rifled through a stack of cut out pages from some magazines and held up a picture of a fountain.

Blanchie gritted her teeth, "Too much Clara! That's too much! This isn't England! This is a quiet little brown stone in Wind Star! No fountain!"

"But but ..." Auntie Clara waved the picture like a small child.

"No! No fountain! You know I love 'over-done' but that front yard down there is no more than a stoop! The girl has jammed in, though lovely, enough flowers! No!"

Reluctantly Auntie Clara handed the fountain picture over to Blanchie who in turn ripped it in half and let it drift into a waste basket.

"Now we need to get busy here girls. Bertie's knees are starting to bother her again; we need one of those health and fitness magazines. And I sense my Coco is having a hard time; we need to put our thinking caps on."

Bertie was cutting out ads for miracle wrinkle creams and pasting them in her scrap book.

Blanchie glared. "Bertie, are you even listening? We need to find Lizzie a building if we want her to open a scrap book store. She isn't going to be a gardener forever!"

"Grounds keeper!" Auntie Clara interjected.

"Whatever--it doesn't matter? We need to get the ball rolling." Blanchie rolled her eyes at Clara.

"But ... window boxes--I wanted window boxes," Auntie Clara pouted.

"Fine but she's energetic, Lizzie will knock those off in nothing flat. And eventually she'll get bored, and start looking for a real job--on her own," Blanchie added that for emphasis.

"She wouldn't!" Auntie Clara opened her eyes wide.

"I suspect she will! And possibly out of town. So we need to get busy!" And Blanchie just set her mouth in a straight line, meaning business.

They heard Lizzie on the steps coming for lunch and suddenly all quieted down, a unified front.

"Hi ladies, er Aunties," Elizabeth still had on her   cut offs and a   top from gardening, or maybe it was for sun bathing.

Blanchie thought she smelled Coppertone.

"Is that offer for lunch still on?"

They all nodded and started closing up their scrap books.

"I thought I heard shouting on my way up here?"

But no one said a word. Bertie got up to get the casserole out of the oven.

"Let's eat in the kitchen shall we, so we don't have to clear." Auntie Clara suggested, eyeing all the exposed scrap books.

Tuna casserole took on a whole new light   . After her second glass, Elizabeth told the Aunties about meeting Lucy from Fitness Is. "It's a health club, true, but supposedly there are lazy work-out classes like stretching …"

And she eyed Blanchie's slightly spreading middle. "It could be fun--I'd drive."

Bertie raised an eye brow, "We get all the fitness we need just climbing up these steps to see Clara!" And surprisingly they did manage the steps quite well.

Elizabeth rolled her eyes. "Why don't I just check it out ladies and we'll see. It could give you more energy …"

That hit a nerve and ;   agreed to consider it.

Eventually Elizabeth headed back to her gardening   it   . She'd forgotten to even ask about their scrap books. She looked at several flats yet unplanted, sighed, and stretched out on the grass in the sun and promptly drifted off.

"Lizzie! Lizzie! Wake up! I need that ride to pick up me car before they close!" Auntie Clara looked down on Lizzie's angelic slightly freckled face, peaceful in sleep. Her long chestnut hair was spread out in the grass, she still wore her pink Burberry ⁀ top and cut offs. "I'm afraid we'll need to hurry."

"Hurry Auntie Clara?" Elizabeth opened one eye and realized why her mattress was so hard. She'd fallen asleep on the lawn. "Oh, that's right. Let me grab my keys and purse." She pushed herself up but little twigs clung to her long mane. The sun had toasted her to a golden sheen. "And I'll change."

Auntie Clara shook her head, "I'm afraid we won't have time," and then looked at her watch rather frantically.

They raced along in the pink Mini listening to Jim Hart on disk. "You know I rather fancy this music." Auntie Clara mused. Elizabeth just smiled and kept humming. "Turn left--just a bit further." And Clara pointed as she talked.

Suddenly they were at a BMW dealership. Big, glossy, impressive. "Auntie Clara?" But she didn't get an answer as Auntie Clara had bolted and was rushing into the lobby, afraid they'd close.

Someone pointed out back, and Auntie Clara pointed for Lizzie to follow her. By the time Elizabeth parked, Auntie Clara was in a heated argument with ...

"Why it's that arrogant man with the green Jag!"

Auntie Clara and the man seemed to be hollering back and forth! Cooper was refusing to let Auntie Clara pay her bill. Elizabeth rushed out of her car and ran up to them.

"Now listen here you you ... bully! Quit intimidating my Auntie!" And Elizabeth started to swing her pink Burberry purse at his head! Head of dark blonde streaky shaggy hair, angular nose and flashing blue eyes! Flashing with humor.

"Hold on there Missy!"

"Missy! No one calls me Missy!" And Elizabeth started to swing, but was blocked by a muscular arm.

"It's Lizzie," Auntie Clara piped in, amused by the confrontation.

"Okay Lizzie--hold on!"

"Well you just better be nicer to my Auntie Clara!" And Elizabeth seethed the words. Then she turned to Auntie Clara, "This is the idiot who ran over my flowers!"

Cooper started to laugh but thought better of it. "I'm sorry. I was, er, distracted ⌊ ⌋ . "I owe you. Dinner. Can I buy you dinner?"

"You can buy me flowers!" Elizabeth couldn't believe the casual conceit! Then she had an idea she wasn't going to let him get away with trashing her yard and yelling at her Auntie! "And dinner!" She challenged.

"Fine!"

"Great!"

"Tomorrow night!"

"Perfect!"

It all sounded more like a fight than a date! Auntie Clara just watched; a twinkle in her eye.

Suddenly self conscious, Elizabeth turned to Auntie Clara, "Are you all right? Can you drive home? Do you need a ride to your car?"

But Auntie Clara headed over to a red shiny huge Range Rover. An expensive English status car! She called out, "I'm fine dear, "See you at home!"

Elizabeth was flabbergasted! Her great Auntie owned a Range Rover! "That's--that's your car?"

"Well yes dear, I thought you'd seen it." Auntie Clara grinned, "Fits me image."

Cooper just watched, amused.

"What are you grinning at?" Elizabeth turned on Cooper.

He held his hands up, threw back his long streaked hair and laughed, "Hey--don't pick on your Aunt's car!"

Elizabeth started to storm off, back to the Mini.

"Wait a minute," Cooper called out.

Elizabeth turned and looked over her shoulder.

"That's your car? What the devil have you done to that perfectly wonderful Mini?"

Elizabeth squinted her now smoldering green eyes at him. "That is what is known as a custom paint job! It's art! But what would you know!"

"What would I know?" Cooper was starting to get just a little bit annoyed. "Who would ever allow such a thing to be done to a car?"

"Who? Someone who's life is cars! Who knows more about cars than you'll ever hope to know! Mr. Herrington! Mr. Basil Herrington!" And she stormed off. But before she popped into the Mini she hollered out, "You can pick me up at seven and try to clean up!"

Cooper just stared as her pink Mini kicked up a little dust. Hands in his pockets he kicked at a loose piece of gravel and muttered, "Basil? Basil did that?"

Auntie Clara wandered into Fairchild's for her Cadbury chocolate stash. "Miss Clara ..." Jinx began, "Here for Cadbury's?" Auntie, I'm supposed to call her Auntie. Jinx sighed, and went back to smiling.

Auntie Clara started filling a wire shopping basket with Flakes, and Crunchies, and Whole Nuts. Then for good measure she threw in some Curly Wurly's. "Me chums are coming by later for a little scrap booking and we need our fuel." Auntie Clara's eyes danced as she dumped her goodies on the counter, and then they lit on Jinx's

Jinx followed her eyes and blushed, "I read it for the Miss Clara, er Auntie Clara." Then she bit her bottom lip and admitted, "Okay the articles on men are always helpful. Just because I'm married doesn't mean I can't use a little advice."

"That's right dear." But Auntie Clara really had other ideas. The headline 'Hooking an Unsuspecting Man' had grabbed her. "Now, I've well, .   . And at my age, well, I like to keep up you know Jinx."

Keep up? Miss Clara was quite up in Jinx's opinion. Jinx opened her eyes rather wide but played along, wondering where this conversation was headed.

"And if you were done with that well …"

"   ."

"Now haven't I asked you to call me Auntie Clara?"

Jinx shrugged and nodded.

"And yes dear, I would. I mean, if you're done with it and all."

Jinx nodded again.

"Well then just slip it in with me chocolates."

Blanchie and Bertie were out front talking to Elizabeth when Auntie Clara returned. "You know Lizzie, a bench. A bench would be nice about here." And Bertie pointed to a curl under the maple.

"Uh yes, actually it would look nice." Elizabeth was taking gardening advice now from the rest of the Aunties? But she did like the idea. "One of those little curved Victorian ones."

"Exactly!" And Bertie clapped her hands. "I'll tell Clara to er mention it to management." Then she looked up, "Oh Clara, you're back," While eyeing the Fairchild's shopping bag.

"I got us some chocolates girls." And the ladies headed inside. "Wait until you see what I have …"

They started to spread their scrap books, and clippings, out on Auntie Clara's old mahogany dining table. The Cadbury was in a crystal bowl, within easy reach.

"Girls, I need help with me Lizzie scrap book …"

"But I got a new copy of 'Stock Today' for our money making scrap book." Blanchie put in.

"Well it may have to wait a bit. We have plenty of money, don't we? I have some news."

And Bertie and Blanchie put down their scissors.

"Lizzie has a dinner date tonight with Cooper." After the others sighed she proceeded to fill them in about the sparring match at the BMW dealer.

"What will she wear?" Blanchie, always the fashion maven, "Does she even own a ⸱   ⸱ dress? Or any dress? I've only ever seen her in cut offs."

"Does she wear our shoe size girls?" Bertie asked.

Auntie Clara nodded yes to the shoes, and shrugged for the dress, but didn't worry about the shoes, remembering the endless boxes that Lizzie had mailed ahead.

"Well maybe she can drive me home," Blanchie suggested, "And I can give her something vintage to wear."

"Good … good idea."

"What size is she?" Bertie asked cautiously, knowing she was out of touch with young girls.

"She looks like a six," Blanchie considered. She started flipping through a new issue of Vogue. "Black, shouldn't she wear black? Don't men still fall for that ⸱   ⸱ black dress thing?"

⸱⸱⸱⸱⸱."

The other two agreed as Blanchie flipped through her magazine.

"Now make it look older or she'll never believe it was yours," Auntie Clara warned.

Blanchie kept going and found a pencil straight black. "Looks like silk," Blanchie muttered, "With a bit of a flounce at the hem-- should sway nicely." The neckline was rather high with a lace insert

⸱⸱ "Girls … what do you think?"

"Could be old …"

And with that Blanchie snipped it out of the Vogue and handed it to Auntie Clara, who carefully glued the back with the bottle of Elmer's, and put it in her scrap book. Carefully she closed the cover.

As they agreed it would be perfect, Auntie Clara produced Jinx's copy

"Oh, I've seen that at the grocery store ..." Bertie started, "But never had the nerve to buy one."

"Jinx gave it to me," Auntie Clara beamed proudly.

"Ah that Jinx," They agreed

"Well it was this title article that caught me eye." And Auntie Clara pointed to 'Hooking an Unsuspecting Man'. Since they'd already agreed Cooper was 'the man', as they put it, they wanted in the family, they turned to the article. Reading furiously they all went from shocked to occasionally nodding in agreement. The final conclusion was one word: "Glue."

Auntie Clara ripped the article out and Blanchie adhered it in the scrap book next to the dress.

"Do you think it will connect with Cooper though?" Bertie was always just a tad skeptical. They had, after all, had a few mishaps over the years.

Blanchie picked back up Vogue, found a Jaguar car ad and cut it out. "Add this."

Elizabeth wasn't sure why Bertie couldn't drive Blanchie home. She had a million things to do to get ready for her date with that arrogant mechanic what's his name. "Oh   I don't even know his name!" And then she laughed at herself. Arrogant was plenty.

"What's so funny my dear? Whose name don't you know?" Blanchie was strapped into the pink Mini, her scrap book supplies all in the back seat.

"Oh this mechanic I'm having dinner with tonight." Wondering how Blanchie knew what she was thinking, she tried to sound bored but couldn't totally hide the spark.

"Cooper?" Blanchie let slip and then could have killed herself.

"You know him Auntie Blanchie?" Elizabeth caught a glimpse of Blanchie fidgeting as she drove.

"Er well no, no not really. I mean Clara ..."

"I know, he's Auntie Clara's mechanic."

"Er yes that's right dear, I've heard Clara mention him--fine young man."

To this Elizabeth raised her eyebrows, "Fine my foot! You know he's the one who ran over my flower beds?"

Ah yes, Blanchie had heard, "Well I believe he may be—er--a careless driver but he's supposed to be very nice." Blanchie wasn't even sure if nice was the right word. Did they use nice today?

By this point they'd arrived at the country club slash retirement center. "Can you help me carry my things in dear?"

Elizabeth nodded and yet knew she needed to start getting ready. Seven o'clock wasn't that far off and hadn't Blanchie carried it all a million times? But Elizabeth picked up the two totes and dogged behind Blanchie. After all, she was Auntie Clara's friend, and she'd been so nice to her ...

The doorman practically bounced when they got to the foyer, fawning over Blanchie.

"Gee Auntie Blanchie, they treat you ..." She groped but Blanchie called out as she trundled down the hall.

"Like Royalty?" and then laughed.

"Yeah--like royalty is right. Men, regardless of their age, threat me like ..." But she couldn't seem to find the words. It wasn't exactly trash, or badly or or ... well it was never like Royalty.

"Royalty, my dear, is a state of mind. And men treat you the way you ask them. Maybe you need to ask a little more."

Elizabeth raised her eye brows. Auntie Blanchie, possibly ninety or one hundred years old, was giving her man advice.

"I learned that when I lived in Paris. I dated--well, I shouldn't say, Royalty, for a bi t..."

Auntie Blanchie dated Royalty? "Who?" Elizabeth barely got it out.

"Oh my dear, another time, really--you need to get out the history books. I'm a lot older than I look."

Older than she looked? How long did people live? Blanchie looked ninety, maybe one hundred!

"The point is my dear; you need to work on your self esteem." Blanchie was turning the key in her lock. "You're lovely, and of course bright. And you have a sense of humor. Now what are you planning on wearing tonight?" Blanchie was rifling through her closet.

Suddenly she spied an old box on the top shelf and gave it a tug. Silently she cheered. "You know my dear, I have some of my old things I could never part with, and I was just about your size."

Now Elizabeth started to roll her eyes, but Blanchie paid her no heed as she dragged the box to her bed. The lid of the box had a gentle layer of dust on it that scattered into the air.

Carefully, Blanchie opened to <u>lavender tissue</u>, gingerly she dipped her hands inside. A corner of the lace bodice appeared, and Blanchie let out a breath. Pulling the   black dress out, she gave it a shake.

"What do you think my dear?" Blanchie watched Elizabeth's face carefully, hoping she still had the touch ... the fashion touch.

The dress was nothing short of fabulous! Elizabeth couldn't believe it! "It's ... it's, oh Auntie Blanchie! It's gorgeous! Do you think it will fit?"

Blanchie's smile was full of mischief. "Like a glove dear, but why don't you pop into the bathroom and give it a try." I really want to see it on, she thought.

Fit? It was custom made. Elizabeth gave a little twirl in her bare feet; the look on her face was pure excitement.

"Oh Lizzie, you look ... well, you look like a million! Black heels?

"Auntie Blanchie--I have shoes!" But Elizabeth laughed and swung her arms out.

"My dear, in heels, well, you're the one who'll look like Royalty. Now hurry along. I know you have tons to do to get ready. Off you go." And now it seemed Auntie Blanchie was practically pushing her along.

But not before Elizabeth gave Blanchie a hug and a tender kiss on the cheek.

"Have fun my dear."

But Elizabeth was off, grinning, clutching the faded dress box.

Cooper straightened his tie. Why had he worn a suit? His hair was still sun drenched from California and in need of a trim. He clutched the gigantic bouquet he'd let the florist talk him into.

He'd gone in for roses, and come out with garden flowers: delphiniums, hydrangeas, something trailing the florist said was nasturtium. And roses--a few white ones were sprinkled in.

Cooper had to admit when he explained to the florist he had driven over a lady's flower beds; the florist creatively put together a garden to replace it.

Cooper smiled when he thought of Lizzie . It seemed to be her uniform, well, he'd only seen her twice, once when he destroyed her planting, and then yesterday when she drove Clara McGillicuddy to pick up her car. But she wore the same cute get up. Oh, and when he'd been back to assess Clara's car problems.

It wasn't like he hadn't seen plenty of girls when he lived in Southern California; but there was something about her. Maybe it was that long long mane of chestnut bordering on auburn hair?

Or those emerald green eyes that seemed to flash at him even now. How many years of bored and boring, yet beautiful, women had he experienced in Southern California?

Fire. That's what attracted him and he grinned, thinking of her heaving that flower pot at his Jag. And defending her Aunt Clara--as if Clara McGillicuddy needed someone to go to bat for her ... now there was a dynamic woman!

Cooper had come to Illinois just six months ago when his grandfather died. He had no intention of running Grandpa's BMW dealership--just straightening out a few things until he could sell it.

Cooper had grown up on a used car lot--okay, a Beamer lot. Cars were in his blood. He could take 'em apart, rebuild them, race them. Even as a boy, Cooper had a small business washing them. But he never saw himself selling them.

Still ... the smell in the showroom was irresistible; it was his childhood. He'd hung out at his Grandpa's show room until his father pursued his own racing career, and they moved to California. And now, like his father, only he'd walked away from his last crash. His Grandpa had never forgiven his son for moving ... or dying.

Cooper had only intended to just take a look at the old man's business. After all, he had his masters in business. He could race and still have a practical side. "I never intended to stay." This seemed to be his new chant.

Yet, why then had he packed up lock stock and barrel if he hadn't planned on staying? Well that was six months ago, and he was still living in an apartment over the back garages.

As a child, his Grandpa called the apartment his rescue when he worked late and wanted to crash. It seemed it was his rescue now. But if he was going to stay, he needed real digs ...

Grandpa had run the dealership like a smooth machine. And Cooper found he rather enjoyed the order, so unlike his father's life on the car circuit. And Cooper's own too, actually. The thrill of the race somehow lost its shine yet the drain of traveling to races dragged on. And racing seemed to attract clinging adoring fans.

No flashing green eyes. No independence. No spirit. Maybe it wasn't Southern California women in general, just the type, as a race car driver, he attracted. He didn't know. After awhile he didn't care. He'd simply cut back, way back on his dating.

Cooper pulled up to the brown stone, admired the replanted flowers, and raced up the four flights of stairs to Auntie Clara's flat as if it was nothing. He gave her book shaped knocker a tap, and Auntie Clara cautiously peeked out the security hole.

Flinging the door wide, she beamed, "Oh my Cooper!" To her utter surprise he was decked out. And he was clutching, strangling really, a bouquet--a huge bouquet.

"Is she ready?" Now he felt nervous and well, sixteen.

"Oh Lizzie doesn't live with me!" Her eyes twinkled.

"She doesn't?" Had he gotten it wrong--very wrong?

"Oh no me dear. She's in the back flat on the lower level. Through the first floor hall, in the back and then ..." She was rambling; well he seemed to have that affect on women of all ages.

"The basement? Your niece lives in the basement?" He was stunned.

Suddenly Clara became flustered, "Well, well yes. Yes she does. But it's ..." What was it? She forgot. "Oh yes, small--I mean lovely."

But Cooper was heading down the stairs, scowling at Auntie Clara.

"Oh me ... Maybe it's not nice enough. But I never figured she'd stay long ... I mean just long enough ..."

Cooper found the basemen almost afraid to knock. He figured it was the door marked ½--someone's idea of a joke, as opposed to the door marker 'boiler room'.

Elizabeth was pacing. In a last minute effort to be, well civilized, ⸱ ⸱ ⸱ ⸱ ⸱ ⸱ ⸱ ·ʒ. The box of Teddy Grahams probably wouldn't work as hors d'oeuvres, or the apples, ⸱

The tap on her door startled her. It'd been so long since she had a real date. Her last pathetic love interest dumped her when she got fired. Well, he worked at the agency, and Elizabeth just assumed when she left she'd never hear from him again.

No surprises there.

The man before turned out to have a complicated life. Or so he said. Elizabeth guessed a wife was a complication, or at least after she found out. And he had the nerve to be angry when Elizabeth told him to take a hike.

Still it hurt.

New York was a big city, maybe the biggest, and maybe the loneliest. So many people yet so hard to meet ...

She smoothed the dress and opened the door.

To a garden.

Flowers? Now why had he done that? No one ever bought her flowers. Not even on secretary's day at work. Technically she was an artist and not a secretary, so no flowers. Now she was going to go soft, after she really planned to ride him a bit.

"Uh, come in."

He was so handsome but for one split second he didn't look quite so smooth.

Cooper tried to keep his eyes on her face, . Her hair really was the most glorious color he'd ever seen-- chestnut with shades of red. He wanted to just touch it. Well, maybe tangle up in it.

"You brought me flowers ..."

Now the cockiness Cooper had expected was gone, and her green eyes softened like the sea at sunset, all storm gone.

"Uh well, after I trashed yours ..."

But she was turning away.

"I'll get a vase." And she started climbing up an old metal kitchen stool, painted pink no less, rifling through a cupboard over a pink bubble refrigerator. " ," She called down as she found an art glass vase in the back corner.

But she started to teeter, what between her four inch heels, the vase, and the old metal step stool.

Cooper started to reach to help, one hand on the vase, r . "Let me help," He actually blushed, and Elizabeth was so afraid of falling and possibly splitting Auntie Blanchie's dress, not to mention making a fool of herself, she let him.

"Thanks."

They just stood there, the vase between them, staring.

..." Elizabeth tried to clear her mind. Oh yeah.

Cooper turned away, "Your fridge is pink." He tried to sound like he saw a pink fridge every day.

"So's the stove ..." Elizabeth was filling tap water into the vase. Calmer. "It must have been the fashion a million years ago. Auntie Clara's are all turquoise."

The glasses had little maps of the states on them, and as she handed him one she thought she should have bought real   glasses. But these came with the flat and well ...

"I like the glasses. Idaho. Have you ever been there?"

What's he talking about? Oh yeah, the maps on the glasses. "Uh no. Is that where Hemmingway lived? Or is that where the potatoes are from?" Elizabeth turned her own glass before she sipped. California. "Now I know where California is--I've just never been there."

Cooper stopped with his drink midway to his mouth, "Never been to California?"

"Well no--I'm from the city. New York City."

"Oh, you're one of those people who think the world ends outside the city limits!"

"Uh well, yeah. I guess I was. Until ..." Then she looked around her little flat.

He started thinking she could never be happy outside of New York City. Or was he just projecting his own feelings that he thought he could never live anywhere but Southern California?

"Actually I rather like it here. It's cozy." Cozy? Where did that come from? Sounded like a corny word out of the past. But it was. Her little flat embraced her the way the aunts did. "The country side is so pretty. I never gave two thoughts to the great outdoors, mind gardening. It was possibly too slushy to get to Barney's--that sort of thing. But now, with my garden, well ..."

The garden--he felt rather bad. "I'm sorry." He even looked contrite.

"You are?" Elizabeth looked amazed.

"About the garden I mean," He was staring, he just couldn't help it.

"It's my first attempt. God knows what Auntie Clara was thinking. Thinking I could do it I mean."

"It's very artistic."

Elizabeth beamed, "You think? I am, well, was, a commercial artist." Now why was she going on about her old life? Her failed life. She set her California tumbler down. "Maybe we should get going. You did say something about dinner didn't you?"

Elizabeth had no idea where they were headed. She'd really not explored at all since moving and settling into her new career. Her grounds keeping career ... Cooper's Jag was so slick, she almost purred. She sank into the caramel leather seat. "Lovely." It was more sigh than anything.

"Glad you like it."

Surprised, she'd spoken her thoughts she blushed to the tip of her sun kissed nose. I wonder how a mechanic can afford a Jag? But before she could dwell on it, they pulled up to a tiny dark restaurant. The sign read 'French Toast'. *Clever*, she thought.

The Maitre D' was young and hip with slicked back hair, a tuxedo shirt, and jeans. The aromas assaulted her even before she could look around. French street scenes, vintage posters. The hum of intimate couples mingled with the sound of Pink Martini playing somewhere off in the distance. Very New York. She was shocked! And why not?

Cooper laughed, "My reaction exactly when I found it. I haven't lived here long, California transplant."

"Oh ... I see." And she rather did. He had an air about him, and his hair was definitely streaked from a package or the sun. Either way, seemed a bit hip for the middle of the middle of nowhere. "And what brought you to Wind Star?" She really knew nothing about him.

"My grandfather."

But before she could ask more she found herself at an elegant table with a gigantic menu, and a waiter explaining the nightly specials. They started with some warm Brie baked in puff pastry

)

Conversation somehow became superficial as they ate and gazed at each other. The fish was poached ⁞   ⁞, and by the time she was half way through she started to giggle. "You know, I usually don't drink quite this much." Of course he didn't know. Or eat quite this much either, she thought as she dipped her crusty bread into the sauce pooling off her fish.

Yum. It had been awhile since she had really fine restaurant food--or any restaurant food. Since moving to Wind Star she'd been living on yogurt, apples, and Diet Pepsi. And of course Auntie Clara's   Pound Cake.

She pleated her linen napkin with a faraway look in her eyes. The starched cloth, and elegant candles, well she could get used to it, even if she was a grounds keeper. Cooper seemed to be talking cars, and she drifted in and out, fearing she was getting just a little plastered.

When he suggested dessert, and she found herself tucking into a four layer chocolate torte, she knew she must be out of her mind. The calories on the butter and sauce were already more than she ate all week.

"You know I haven't really been cooking since I moved here." Now why was she telling him this? "I mean, I love my little pink stove and fridge but well ..." She waved her fork after devouring the last chocolate crumb.

Cooper smiled. ⁞   ⁞t at least she wasn't combative. "I haven't either actually, though I normally grill a mean salmon." Now why was he telling her this?

"Really?" A man who cooked? And looked like a California surf God. "And if I bring over Auntie Clara's ⁞   ⁞ Pound Cake, will you grill for me?" And she laughed, wondering what was coming over her.

But Cooper laughed back, "Sure that works for me."

By this time they were back in the Jag and Elizabeth was pretty certain she'd had too much   . She said something to that effect just before she rested her head back on the butter soft leather and let her eyes close.

When Cooper didn't get an answer to his last question, a quick glance confirmed Elizabeth was out. He pulled up to the apartment building and gave her a little shake. "Come on Sleeping Beauty."

Elizabeth was dreaming she was driving around the countryside on a balmy night in a great car. "Oh." Still mussy from sleep, she looked up into Coopers sky blue eyes. Then she winced, "*

She fumbled for her purse and tumbled out of the car before he could even help.

He watched in amazement as she scampered in the front door. As it banged shut behind her, probably waking the whole building, he laughed.

3

"Gee Auntie Clara; I didn't think I was drinking too much ..."

Auntie Clara raised one eye brow. She refused to be judgmental. Well, tried.

"Well, I do remember laughing a lot. Or was I giggling? I don't know. I know I kept staring into those blue blue eyes of his. And well, I guess I was a little intimidated--he can be pretty arrogant."

"Arrogant? Cooper? Now my dear, I think you're wrong there." Auntie Clara was sure. Cooper was very sweet.

"Of course he wouldn't be arrogant to you Auntie." Elizabeth started pleating her paper napkin.

"Well arrogant is arrogant--why not me? Oh you mean me age? Ha! That doesn't stop an arrogant man!" And Auntie Clara whacked off a slice of   pound cake while her mind remembered some arrogant man.

"Well maybe not. I   a. I mean I fell asleep on the drive back."

"Oh." Auntie Clara tsked a little and busily stirred her coffee, clinking her spoon on the bone china.

"And when he told me he could cook, I offered to bring over your   Pound Cake ..." Now she felt mortified thinking how bold she'd been. The part about the cake went right over Auntie Clara's head. She was stuck on 'cook'.

"He can cook?"

Elizabeth nodded, "I know. I've never known a man handy in the kitchen."

"Fancy that! He cooks!"

"Well now, I do remember grill was part of it. Salmon. I think. But seems to me he said cook. And grilling is cooking, isn't it?"

"Lizzie …"

"Well anyway Auntie Clara, I made a fool of myself, and he hasn't called so I suspect he isn't planning on it." And she tucked into her Pound Cake, the calories.

"I'm going to Bertie's for scrap booking in a little bit. Wanna come and take your mind off Cooper? You can tell Blanchie how the dress went over." Auntie Clara knew she'd want to hear. They both would, Bertie too.

Elizabeth was in a bit of a sulk, "Okay. What are you bringing for pot luck?" Eyeing the cake they'd already cut into.

"Well I cleaned some nice strawberries--they're in the fridge and I thought we could stop at that Patisserie you told me about for something flakey or maybe Fairchild's for some Cadbury. What do you think?" Auntie Clara started wiping up crumbs from her speckled Formica counter.

"I can be ready in ten." And Elizabeth pushed away from the table. "Should I bring Auntie Blanchie's dress back?" She really hated to part with it.

Auntie Clara's eyebrows scrunched, "I don't think so dear, I mean she won't be wearing it, and well, you may wear it again …"

Auntie Clara parked the Range Rover in front of Fairchild's. "We may as well get some Crunchie bars while we're here," Auntie

Clara started. "Oh look at those Hollyhocks! They're practically black!"

"Jinx said she'd save me some seeds." Elizabeth fingered a velvet blossom.

"Did she now, that Jinx is a nice girl."

Elizabeth nodded as they walked in.

"Oh Auntie Clara and Elizabeth!" Jinx set down an armful of fluffy mohair sweaters. The pekes lifted their little flat faces and gave their best doggy grins and then closed their eyes again.

"Hi dear, we're on our way to our scrap booking and needed some supplies--chocolate supplies!" Auntie Clara started going over her mental list. She piled some Crunchies and Flakes on the counter, and then added some Whole Nuts, and a couple rolls of plain chocolate Digestives for good measure.

"Oh I've been working on mine too! It's on the counter." And Jinx angled her braided head toward an oversized album. She'd made a bit of progress inspired by Auntie Clara.

"You scrap book?" Elizabeth asked as she started to flip through looking at author events Fairchild's had held, small ads in the local newspaper, sale flyers, the shoppe Christmas card, photos of the displays, and an occasional letter or card from a happy child. All decorated with bits of glitter, stickers, and pieces of ribbon. Jinx had written in little notes in the margins that made it even more personal.

"Well, I wanted to keep all these things together, and it's been so much fun. Plus I can keep adding pages." Jinx was rather proud of herself.

"Oh Jinx you got one of those albums that expand." Auntie Clara was peaking over Elizabeth's shoulders, impressed.

"Ms. Clara, er I mean Auntie Clara; there are tons of scrap book items out there. You and the ladies need to investigate. Look at these little stickers I got in Chicago." And Jinx held out a sheet of Pekinese with goofy grins. They were shiny and rather puffy in a raised sort of way.

"Why me dear, they look just like Maisie and Mrs. Wigglesworth." Then turning to Elizabeth Auntie Clara added, "Her shoppe dogs. They're usually here asleep somewhere.")

And sure enough Elizabeth spotted them in their beds.

"We need a scrap book shoppe in Wind Star. And we have room for you in the village—we'd make room." Jinx said it almost on cue, her enthusiasm for her new hobby bubbling. "I'd support it. I mean I know I can get things from the internet but I want to rummage through all the stickers. Plus I never know what I want until I see it. And Auntie Clara, (there are scissors with scallop edges, and templates) and well, there are just tons of things out there."

Then Jinx turned to Elizabeth. "You're very artistic, or so your Auntie says, and there are a couple of empty buildings down the street. You would be a natural! I mean you can't garden forever." Jinx took in a gulp of air, being on a roll.

Auntie Clara just listened, stunned. Stunned she hadn't programmed Jinx.

"No, no, I suppose I can't." Elizabeth hesitated, but just barely.

"Well once you get the garden established ..." And Jinx pointed out the window at her own flower beds. "It practically takes care of itself." And it did look quite chocked full of flowers.

"Besides just sales, you could hold classes. And kids, and the girl scouts would come, and you could have tables where the Aunts could set up and meet. Don't forget brides, and their attendants working on wedding scrap books, and first day of school books, and vacations and ... And they'd all buy. I'm sure of it. These Pekinese stickers were nine dollars."

"Nine dollars! Jinx!" Auntie Clara held her heart.

"I know but look ... they really do look like Maisie and Mrs. Wigglesworth."

And as Auntie Clara peered at them she was surprised how the little dear's personalities had been captured. Captured on stickers.

"It would be fun Elizabeth--we would be shoppe neighbors." Jinx grinned rather foolishly.

By this time Jinx had rung up Auntie Clara's chocolates and was handing her the bag. "You could design a wonderful logo, and come up with a cute name. Something catchy, about saving the good times to look back on."

"Like 'Creating Memories'?" Elizabeth was lost in middle space thinking about a wood sign shaped like an open book.

A scrap book. The idea taking hold.

Auntie Clara pulled a lace edged hankie out of her Queen Elizabeth looking handbag and started to dab at her faded green eyes. "Lizzie, the Aunts would back you." This could be an answer to her prayers.

"Back me?" Elizabeth was shocked and touched. Hadn't Auntie Clara done so much already by just rescuing her? She hadn't even gotten as far as finances. It was just the idea, the idea of running a tiny little business in the village.

Her business.

Her way.

Still, it was something to take in.

"I think we all would. That is, if you'd let us hang out there." Auntie Clara slipped in because she could already picture her, and Blanchie, and Bertie right there …

"Why Auntie Clara, you and the Aunties could have your own table! Besides, you all know far more about scrap booking than I do." And Elizabeth meant it. The idea of scrap booking to her was more art project than anything. Free form art projects that anyone could do.

But Elizabeth had a feeling once she really set her mind to it she'd know there was a whole lot more. And it dawned on her as they picked up their purchases; she wanted to … set her mind to it that is.

And they headed out the door to look into empty shoppe fronts, the Patisserie forgotten.

Bertie's house was an arts and craft cottage near the park; tucked under giant oaks you almost didn't see it.

"Gee Auntie Clara, this looks a little like Hansel and Gretel's house!" The drive time was close but the park like setting made Elizabeth feel as though they were miles from everything. Which seemed odd in a way since the entire community of Wind Star was miles from everything.

Still ... it had a dreamy escape kind of feeling and she hadn't even gone inside yet.

Bertie laughed from the flagstone path, waving to them. "Everyone says that. In fact it was the gardener's cottage. He was grounds keeper at the park." Then Bertie gave Elizabeth one of her impish grins.

"Really? Another grounds keeper? Interesting ..." And Elizabeth grinned.

"Uh huh, and the house just always stayed in the family. I should give it up but I refuse," Bertie stuck her chin out just a little bit.

And Elizabeth actually admired her for it.

Bertie was now up on the porch leading them in, eyeing the Fairchild's sack; sure it was full of goodies.

They headed in to the heady scent of bread baking. Two golden loaves sat on a board in a kitchen almost as tiny as Elizabeth's. Tiny but loaded with charm--caught in a time warp charm. "Auntie Bertie, that smells heavenly!"

"Thank you dear, I'll give you the recipe."

Elizabeth looked alarmed. Bake bread? Surely she was kidding.

"Blanchie brought meat loaf. She convinced the kitchen staff to make it for her." Auntie Clara added her colander of strawberries, and sack of chocolate bars, minus a couple they'd eaten on the way over.

A scarred oak drop leaf was set up in what must have been a little eating nook. Four old captain's chairs were pulled up. "Lizzie, sit so you can look out the bay window," Bertie started. "And tell us all about your date." Bertie hoped she didn't sound too anxious.

"Yes Lizzie. The dress, did he notice the dress?" Blanchie's eyes twinkled. She'd just wandered back in from the bathroom, excited to hear voices, knowing they were finally here.

"Well Aunties, his eyes nearly popped out of his head. I guess I do clean up pretty good." And Elizabeth looked down at her standard uniform, worn ,   ˉ denim cut offs and tiny tee shirt.

"And shoes?" Blanchie pressed. Details, she needed details.

"Very tall and strappy."

The aunties sighed with their mental image of their protégé.

"We went to a very upscale restaurant called French Toast."

"And what did you have to eat?" Bertie was slicing the bread and called out from the kitchen. Though nowhere was very far in such a tiny house.

Elizabeth looked perplexed, "You know, I don't remember."

The aunties exchanged looks as plates with huge meat loaf sandwiches were passed. "And talk about dear, what did you talk about?" After all, it had been a very long time since the aunties had dated. They stared at Elizabeth waiting for answers.

"I'm not sure." Now Elizabeth stared off into middle space, "But it was--well, it was lovely."

The aunties sighed.

"ᵢ   ," Elizabeth hadn't meant to admit to it but well, it just slipped out.

Alarm shot up on the three old ladies faces, no matter how they tried to mask it. Of course Auntie Clara had heard this part but still couldn't hide her concern.

"I mean I didn't get loud or obnoxious or anything." Elizabeth was back pedaling. At least she was pretty sure she hadn't. She really wasn't a very loud girl.

"You did offer to brink.   ˑ Pound Cake if he cooked." Auntie Clara felt she had the inside scoop.

"Grilled," Then Elizabeth smiled, "He cooks. I know that part was bolder than normal for me but he kept describing this salmon he grills on planks."

"Soaked ⁞   ⁞--saw it on the food channel," Bertie interrupted.

"Exactly!" The aunties really did know what was going on.

"Sounds divine," Blanchie put in. "I would have offered Clara's ⁞ Pound Cake too!" Then she looked over to the kitchen counter to see if they'd brought one.

Auntie Clara just shook her head no in response. "I thought we'd bring pastry from the Patisserie ..."

Blanchie craned her neck; Auntie Clara shook her head no again. "Actually we started at Jinx's for chocolates."

"Ah Jinx." Bertie and Blanchie chorused. Fond, very fond they were.

"And she got to talking ..." Auntie Clara couldn't wait to spring it on them, "About scrap booking."

"So lovely that she's one of us," Blanchie said. "Well sort of." Knowing their scrap books were different.

Very different.

"Anyway, Jinx suggested to Lizzie she open a scrap book shoppe in the village."

Elizabeth nodded actually loving the idea.

"So we looked at empty shoppes, and well, I said we'd back her-- you know until she got it up and running and we'd ... well, we'd have a place to scrap book ... I mean as investors and all." Auntie Clara hoped she was getting it all right.

"Like our own table?" Blanchie beamed, picturing it already.

"To hang out, as the young people put it," Bertie chirped.

And suddenly sandwiches were forgotten, scrap books ignored, and they chattered nonstop about Lizzie's shoppe. "Call it 'Lizzie's'," Bertie suggested.

"Or 'Let's Make a Scrap Book'," Blanchie put in.

But Lizzie and Auntie Clara just shared a look.

"Tell em Lizzie," Auntie Clara coaxed.

"Well, I thought, I mean I rather like 'Creating Memories'."

"Creating Memories," Blanchie and Bertie chorused. "Oh yes." And then they sighed.

"Well, can we come with you to look at it?" Bertie wanted to know.

"There were only <u>two empty shoppe fronts</u>, and I should call the realtor listed I suppose. And I need to <u>apply for a tax number</u>, and <u>figure out if there's a trade show</u> for scrap book supplies and and oh, I don't even know what all I need to do." Elizabeth was finally out of her funk, her blood finally moving.

"<u>Call Score, the small business association</u>," Blanchie seemed pretty business oriented. "Score is an organization of retired business people who give advice to beginning businesses. <u>Google scrap book supplies whole sale</u> and ..."

"You know how to Google Auntie Blanchie?" Elizabeth was amazed.

"Well really dearie, computers are not so difficult. It's a, well, passive way we can stay in touch. We all took a class."

"You did?" And as Elizabeth marveled the other aunts nodded. They inhaled their meat loaf sandwiches and sweets anxious to get going while Auntie Clara called up the realtor on her cell.

They all drove to the village in Auntie Clara's red Range Rover. "I feel like an entrepreneur!" Bertie beamed. Rosemary Hills, Wind Stars favorite realtor was meeting them. "Clara, hurry up! What if someone snaps it out from under us?" And the panic came through in her voice as Auntie Clara maneuvered the Range Rover carefully into a spot.

"Bertie, this is Wind Star! It's barely awake. And Jinx can't remember when these buildings ever had a tenant, mind a business." Auntie Clara hated to admit this but facts were facts.

"Does that mean we can get a cappuccino first?" Blanchie really needed some caffeine.

"No!" The other three chimed in. But as if reading their minds, Rosemary stood in front of the first door with a takeout bag from the Patisserie.

Elizabeth stared. How had that realtor known they'd be desperate for coffee? Hadn't Auntie Clara just called her?

"Hi ladies," Rosemary handed the bag to Auntie Clara and started working the keys in the lock.

Blanchie and Bertie stared like two children, watching their future unfold. Finally the door opened.

They never even looked at the second building. This one was perfect. It looked exactly like the thumb nail sketch Clara had made and put in Lizzie's scrap book. The bay front window would be ideal for a huge work table. The main room was L shaped, allowing another section for possible classes. There was a miniscule stock room, and a bathroom. Granted it needed painting, not to mention serious cleaning, but it had potential.

A lot of potential.

"Charming," Bertie let slip as she sipped her coffee. The others agreed trying not to sound over excited.

Rosemary perked up.

Auntie Clara cleared her throat; "Rosemary, the rent is far too high …"

Elizabeth looked alarmed until she caught a wink from Blanchie.

"It would have to come down at least twenty five percent, and we'll need an exterminator to go over it, treat it, and report back. Also the utilities; see if you can get copies of twelve months running so we can look at hot and cold weather. Taxes, don't forget to check on the taxes for us." Auntie Clara took in a gulp of air, hoping she wasn't forgetting anything.

"We'd like an option to buy. See what you can come up with as a rent to own or an outright purchase. And … it goes without saying it needs a cleaning service in here. We can be back in three days. In the mean time call me with the utilities and a buying price, contingent on it passing inspections, being cleaned, and painted." Auntie Clara said it all in a whoosh.

But to Elizabeth's way of thinking her Auntie was one tough negotiator. Elizabeth looked at her aunt in awe.

Auntie Clara produced a business card, gave it to Rosemary, and nodded to the rest of them. "Girls ..." And she tilted her head toward the door.

Just before she left she turned back. "Mr. Parsons will be handling all our legal situations. He's right here in the village." And they trooped out.

And of course Elizabeth remembered the portly lawyer who purchased all the pastries at Fairchild's. The one who kindly took her out for coffee ...

Once in the Patisserie and settled at a table Blanchie let out her breath. "Brilliant Clara--just brilliant!"

"Ruthie would be proud," Bertie gave a quick bow of the head for the late Ruthie. Auntie Clara snuck in a fast sign of the cross.

"Well we really should invest, and Lizzie can rent from us, and we'll put her rent money toward her ultimate purchase." It all made sense.

More brilliants were sung out.

Elizabeth just stared in amazement.

"Lizzie dear ..." Auntie Clara looked concerned, "You did like it didn't you?" She hated to ask ... still ...

Elizabeth nodded.

"Well then dear, you are as good as in business."

Elizabeth started to sputter.

"Now dear, I took the liberty of googling scrap book businesses, just to well, see what was what. Only because I've been well, thinking about all this. You're right, there's a whole world out there we don't know about. There is a trade show at Javits."

"That's in the city." Elizabeth looked alarmed.

"I've booked you a flight and telephoned Basil."

Elizabeth was shocked that her aunt had appeared to just be doodling on her phone while they were eating pastry and it turns out she was booking her a flight and well, whatever else.

Auntie Clara went on and Elizabeth tuned back in. "Basil will pick you up at the airport, and he says he has somewhere you can stay. I registered you on line as a new business."

Elizabeth was in shock.

"So girls don't you think we should see Lizzie off at the airport tomorrow?"

Tomorrow? Haven't I just seen the building? Proposed the idea? How fast did these aunties move?

Of course the aunties nodded, enthusiasm bubbling. "And these trade shows don't just pop up any old time, you need to get into the city while the show is on and not miss it. It might be a year before there is another one." Auntie Clara was nothing if not efficient.

"But the building, Auntie Clara ... What if ..."

"Nonsense me dear, I'm confident it will all be signed, sealed, and delivered, and hopefully even painted by the time you get back. By the way, what color do you want it painted? After all, you are the artist."

Elizabeth wasn't sure why but she blurted out. "Sea foam green. It's just a color that's so easy to be around."

"Ah," The ladies all nodded, nibbling on their pastries.

Elizabeth didn't have time to worry about Cooper, though she wanted to. Granted she hadn't heard from him since their dinner date. His bouquet had finally dwindled down to the last white rose, which she pressed in the phone book--to put in a scrap book.

"Maybe I did drink too much ..." She let this ramble around her head as she pulled out her suit case and started to dump in clothes.

4

"Ah New York, I've missed you." Elizabeth came through the gate sentimental and sappy. How long had she been gone? Seemed like ages. Already the crush of people, and the sound triggered a reaction--one she loved.

She'd packed light, only a carry on, and planned to head straight to the convention center, but when she looked up she saw a tiny old man waving--a tiny old man with a comb over and a bow tie. "Basil!" Elizabeth rushed to him like a long lost friend.

Basil beamed to be recognized. "Lizzie, Clara said you'd be coming in and well I thought you might like a ride."

"A ride? Why Basil, I'm headed to Javits … it's …"

I know where it is my dear. Come on, I've a car."

A car was a limo. With fresh fruit and bottled water and…"Why Basil, is that Jim Hart playing?"

"Yes it is. Clara has gotten rather hooked and so have I. Thought you might like it." They rode along like old friends, Elizabeth filling Basil in on the pending shoppe and of course Auntie Clara.

As conversation dwindled and she looked out the window of the limo Elizabeth was filled with an overwhelming sense of failure--failure in a city she couldn't hack. She was near her old agency and the taste was bitter, almost pitifully so.

She loved the city and yet her dream career had slipped through her fingers--slipped away, casually, easily. She almost hadn't noticed. Certainly hadn't seen it coming. How could that have been?

Elizabeth's mind jumped to the little shoppe front with the bay window. She had never ever considered running a shoppe of any kind mind owning one. Yet that bubble of anticipation was new--exciting. The idea of making books of memories, personal, and creative, was just under her surface of challenging.

Helping someone put together their story seemed so intimate. The ads she'd drawn, at the agency, after awhile became cookie cutter.

Even now it was hard to face. Face the fact that what she'd always thought was her dream bored her, the similarity from assignment to assignment. The impersonal 'never meeting the client', never really having the final say, or the first say for that matter. She was just part of the machine.

The design machine.

Had she failed? Had she subconsciously sought failure? Of course not--the idea appalled her. How would she live? What would she do? She wouldn't seek it ... would she? Or had she carelessly failed? She hated to admit that thought had possibilities. Her careless days seemed to be behind her, forced out by necessity.

And this new venture ... it was an opportunity, it was a dream. It was ... things she'd never heard of or thought of. Sure, as a child, she'd stuck photographs under acetate pages but she had never made collages, little scenes, each page an art project, part of a story.

This dream--this new one, had found her.

And as that idea washed over her Elizabeth said goodbye to what was expected, even if she had expected it of herself. And embraced what lay ahead. And as this all started to sink in they pulled into the Javits lot. Buses, taxis, and people swarmed.

Along with the excitement.

"Now I'll pick you up when the show closes--right here." And Basil indicated where the driver had pulled up. "And we'll grab a little bite." He seemed to have it all under control.

Elizabeth was speechless. She reached for her carry on.

"Leave it--just take your tote. See you later. Work up an appetite." And he was gone.

And Elizabeth was on the sidewalk. Just like that she was actually at the show. The main doors loomed ahead of her. She put one foot in front of the other and found herself mixed in a crush of people, people all on their way to market. People maybe like her.

She joined a queue. Registration was right there, and true to her word Auntie Clara had called with all the necessary information. All she had to do was give her name, and magically a directory was thrust at her along with a cute little tote advertising the show.

The woman behind the counter told her where to find food, restrooms, and other things that quite frankly she paid no attention to. She was here. She had a name badge she was slipping over her head.

She was beginning. Beginning her new business. So after thanking the woman she moved on, following the throngs of people into the main auditorium size room.

And as the hum of activity washed over her, and the stuffed booths of merchandise jumped out at her, Elizabeth found herself smiling. Already crowded with other shoppers, she simply fell in behind a group of women, who possibly owned a business together.

They seemed like old pros and were consulting their directory with a certain vendor in mind. And they were off in another direction. A direction equally as loaded with vendors and excitement.

Elizabeth stayed her course, with no real plan but to see as much as she could, and hopefully figure out what it would take to fill a store ... Not to mention run one.

The show was a whirl of excitement, and Elizabeth was energetically pulled down aisle after aisle of albums, stickers, templates, scissors that crimped, scalloped and zigzagged.

She saw bolts of ribbon and wasn't even sure she thought of ribbon as part of scrap booking. But the displays showed tiny bits tied here and there over a picture or under a caption, and Elizabeth was charmed.

There were kits with small phrases you could glue under pictures, all in different fonts. And rubber stampers with colored ink pads to add little touches here and there. Some of these items came in kits so a customer could just pick up a themed box and get started. Others came what she called 'loose' so a person could customize and purchase just what they wanted.

And it wasn't just wedding scrap books like she'd thought. There were themes for the engagement, the shower, the wedding (of course), the honey moon, scrap book pages and ideas for the bridesmaids, and maid of honor, and the moms, others for the flower girl--a sentimental one for the father of the bride.

Pages and stickers for just the romance part, and others for the first anniversary.

She was stunned how detailed the ideas were.

Stunned and yet hooked.

Then when that first baby was expected the whole process began again. And the category she thought of as children's scrap books was far more detailed. There were scrap books for every age, and grade, your child had, and every activity from soccer to their first ballet class.

Dance was another area she was overwhelmed with. And more for the first tooth and the first day and and and ... Her head buzzed, her mind was on over load.

Of course there were scrap books just for children to put together. Brighter, tougher pages and an endless variety of cheerful stickers on any subject you could imagine. Little boys could scrap book as well as little girls; there was an equally endless assortment of dinosaurs, sports, fire trucks, pirates, and sports cars to pick from. Sports cars ...

Her mind didn't have time to think about one green Jag ...and its owner.

Disney had a booth, and Elizabeth discovered you could scrap book your entire visit to Disney World from park to park, including stickers of the restaurants.

Of course there were all the Disney characters, and the rides, and the park itself laid out in pages, and stampers, and stickers, just waiting for someone to return home and begin capturing their memories.

Suddenly she could see a young mom getting the Disney scrap book before the trip, to help build the anticipation of the fun to come with her child. And then coming home and putting it all together. It was a way to not only save a memory but to maybe make it a little bigger.

Bigger and better.

Elizabeth had hoped she'd see enough, get enough ideas. Now she was hoping she could narrow it down, and still not leave anything out. And create a feeling in her shoppe that didn't seem to jump in too many directions.

She realized she wanted sweet and nostalgic until she saw those themes so she put them high on her priority list. And then she started looking at themes as to exactly how she'd display them and exactly where.

Part of running a small shoppe was, well small. So editing became an issue. But she continued to wander and just take it all in.

And Elizabeth loved it. She had no idea glitter came in so many colors, or cute containers. She saw stickers that were whimsical, others that looked like little works of art. Scrap books, it turns out, came in every shape and size, elegant, casual, juvenile, romantic.

And the prices varied along with the styles. She picked up a satin one with white roses across the top picturing a bride putting in her wedding photos. The cutting of the cake, the first dance, the 'I do' at the church. Suddenly the price didn't seem so high. Not for a memory. A memory a bride would cherish for the rest of her life.

One booth had children's scrapbooks--colorful, with sturdy pages that tiny fingers would not bend or hurt. The subject matters on the covers went from pirates to faerie princesses.

There were ones with hopping frogs and tall giraffes, possibly for a day at the zoo. Other's read 'My Vacation', 'School Days' and 'Time at Grandma's'.

Elizabeth was charmed by the themes and realized she wanted to carry specifics, not just general books. And then her mind raced with all the themes from graduations to vacations and everything in between.

When she saw Girl Scout scrap books she realized Jinx had been right, she could see the Girl Scouts meeting at her new shoppe to work on their projects. There were endless possibilities to choose from.

Vendors were ultra friendly. Was it the trade show atmosphere or the nature of scrap bookers? Elizabeth wasn't sure. She didn't care. She approached each booth with the same line, "I'm starting a scrap book shoppe and I have no experience." By noon she not only had experience, she had merchandise lined up to be shipped.

And ideas.

They whirled in her head like a kaleidoscope. So many of the booths were set up like mini stores that ideas just propelled at her. She took notes, landed up snapping pictures, and suddenly her own shoppe started to take shape, in her mind.

She thought about Auntie Clara, Auntie Blanchie, and Auntie Bertie and how much they would love everything she'd found so far.

Love it and use it.

And she couldn't wait. She ate a sandwich while still walking, not wanting to take a break and miss a thing. The convention center was endless, the size of many football fields in doors.

And it was six o'clock, and the lights were flashed, when she realized she'd only seen a fraction! Leave? How could she possibly leave now? She wanted to spend the night ...

The crowds outside matched the mobs inside; queues for taxis, a row of busses. And still her mind buzzed. Looking left and right through the commotion she saw someone waving frantically.

It was Basil.

And the limo driver.

Elizabeth almost cried. Lugging her now catalog laden tote, she headed toward them like a beacon in a storm, a storm of other exhausted trade show visitors and merchants. The driver took her tote, and Basil handed her a frosty glass of orange juice.

Orange juice!

She sipped gratefully as she sank into the butter soft leather, her shoes already off. And then she started, almost a mile a minute, "Oh Basil! It was wonderful--absolutely wonderful! I met so many people! And ideas! I have a million! And I placed orders and and ..."

"Hold on there Lizzie." Basil smiled; thrilled that he could be there to experience her enthusiasm and wonder. "Do you think you can eat?"

Food? It had been hours since she'd eaten; whatever it was. Suddenly her stomach went into over drive. And she gave a tiny nod. Yes, food would be great. And she let out a breath she didn't even know she'd been holding.

They sat at a tiny café and shared a pizza. Never would she have figured an elegant man like Basil for a pizza fiend! "Now, I have a little flat ..." And he motioned with his head up. "That's yours while you're here. Your carry on is already up there. My limo will be here in the morning to take you back to Javits, and if you can get up early enough, this little café has a killer breakfast."

Basil dangled a key and aimed her to a door she hadn't even seen.

Next thing she knew she was buried in a cloud of down comforters, asleep, dreaming about her shoppe. But just before she closed her eyes she shot up a little prayer and thanked Basil.

The limo magically appeared after she'd had a croissant and coffee in the café. Miraculously her feet and mind were raring to go. She crammed her neck to take in as many sentimental sites as she could as they whisked along.

This time she wasn't nearly as sad as the day before. It was, well, her old city and even though she moved on, it didn't mean she didn't still love New York.

While stopped at a light she thought she saw ... no of course not! But strained ... The sun drenched hair, lanky build, and cocky walk of Cooper! He was leaving a McDonalds and hailing a cab.

By the time she worked the window and hollered he had vanished in traffic.

Impossible! What would a California car mechanic be doing in New York City? Before she could digest this further the limo was dropping her off. "Ms. Lizzie, I'll be taking you from here to the airport after the show closes." She'd left her carry on behind in the limo along with yesterdays stash of catalogs.

"I can't thank you enough—really ...I can't. What can I do to repay you?" Elizabeth was touched. The limo, and Basil, had made a hectic city easy--very easy. Transportation which normally was a hassle had been luxury.

"Mr. Basil wouldn't hear of it!" And the driver gave her a grandfatherly smile. "Just go in there and have a great day!"

And she did! Cooper was forgotten as she seriously plowed through vendors. Elizabeth was so intrigued with the colors of glitter at one booth she had to force herself to keep moving.

A booth of scissors that crimped, and scalloped, and just straight cut caught her attention. The scissors themselves were in pretty colors, girly colors like pink, and peach, and aqua. Scissors that would be fun to pick up and use. She placed an order, and again asked for advice.

She found filler pages that came in patterns, and colors, and textures. Were there just pages? Plain--she guessed not, or at least not any more. Pages were their own little works of art. There were racks to display them, and more scrap books to hold them. She labored and made her selections.

Stickers were so much fun Elizabeth had to force herself to slow down. There was every theme known to man, and then some from out of this world. Faeries and elves were some of her first to be ordered.

With whimsical books with wooded scenes on the covers—places she imaged the faeries and elves would live, of course, had to be included. And cute little animals, puppies, kittens, and bunnies in flocked and fuzzy stickers were hard to resist. Then she found cupcakes, and slices of pie, cakes, and pizzas.

It dawned on Elizabeth that stickers could go on recipes. And recipes could be their own theme of scrap book. Sure enough she found rubber stampers that said 'recipes' and added them to her assortment. Of course she needed scrap books with food themes, kitchen themes, and dining ideas.

Flower stickers were not only very detailed she suspected they were meant for serious gardeners to keep track of their own flower gardens. She ordered all the flowers she'd been planting, and then moved on to ones she had no clue what they were.

Suddenly Elizabeth could see putting a small bouquet of flower sticker on an envelope when she wrote someone a letter--or when the Aunties wrote.

Perfect.

So with the serious gardeners in mind she found scrap books they could use and back ground pages that looked like the great outdoors.

How cute were the stickers of princess's where you could add a tiara, change the jewelry, even change the hair. They were mini build your own princess composites right down to glass slippers and ball gowns. Almost like paper dolls.

No, she thought no almost about them, they were sticker paper dolls where little girls could peel and stick, and not have to deal with scissors. Tickled she ordered them picturing little girls sitting at her tables wanting to get new shoes or crowns for their princesses.

Armed with catalogs, orders, and samples she rounded the last aisle.

"Charms."

She actually had about an hour and half before closing, and felt she'd seriously conquered the world of scrap booking. Conquered it to at least make a great grand opening, and see what other categories she would want to add.

But conquered enough to feel she could have a grand opening and look real--very real.

But charms ... it renewed her spirits with a fascinating whimsical interest. Charms in scrap books? And suddenly she could see them tucked on a page, adding a dimension, being even more of a keepsake. And possibly customers would want them as charms to wear, not just put in their scrap book ...

Elizabeth danced from booth to booth trying to narrow down her purchases of the tiny pieces of jewelry. She couldn't write orders, even small ones, everywhere. To start, she had forced herself to narrow down key manufactures to fit certain niches. She quickly had decided the specialists were, well, maybe a bit more creative.

Unique.

Her competition was the internet but she felt she had an advantage; her customers would be able to pick up an item and look at it. And her displays would do more than an internet page could. And if a customer wanted to bring her scrap book in, and work on it, she knew this was not possible on the internet.

Her competition was also Wal-Mart, and she knew the smaller vendors would never sell the Wal-Marts, couldn't keep up, and deliver. Her dealings with the family businesses were a touch more genuine and sincere. They sold her, true, but also offered suggestions, gave ideas, took her under their wing.

By the end of the first day the small vendors had led her, and created a confidence level in her that maybe was there all along--just misplaced and waiting to come out and play.

So with charms, she thought she wanted someone small. But ...

Then she saw the booth.

'Magical Charms'.

Yes, that's what she wanted; magical charms. She wasn't even sure what that meant, it just somehow felt right.

The booth was red tartan. Celtic symbols were hand drawn and placed in the folds of the fabric along with the sterling charms. They were on tiny red silk ribbons, in clusters, or just one special charm.

The main sign was an open book, similar to how she had imagined her own sign. The facing 'pages' were bordered in plaid. Instead of showing tons of merchandise, a story was hand lettered. Captivated Elizabeth stood and read it.

"In the heather highlands there is a lovely stretch of valley of the river Dee." At this point there was a photograph, purple to blind the eyes, dipping down to a rolling river. A silver sheep charm was placed on the purple heather, next to a photograph of one.

The text went on, "This sweeps down into the rich woodland where Queen Victoria herself wandered." Now a tiny crown charm dangled from a sliver of red ribbon. "The Monarch gave 'Royal Deeside' her seal of approval when she established her summer home there in 1848."

A photograph of Queen Victoria, in faded sepia, and a castle charm broke the lines.

"Beneficiary of Royal patronage, then as now, was the village of Ballater." Now a photograph of the quaint stone shoppes appeared. A charm of a basket of flowers was next to the Royal Florist.

"Prettily situated in a loop of the fast flowing Dee, Ballater became known for the curative powers of its water. In fact magic seemed to surround Ballater as a veil of goodness and luck. It is here I created my charms."

And then a cluster of silver twinkled--a thistle, a Claddagh, a wish bone, and a tiny bell. "Blessed they be with the heart of Ballater as their heart!" A group of three hearts with ruffled edges were attached.

Elizabeth fingered the little bell and it tinkled ever so gently.

"To call the faeries that be."

Elizabeth jumped back; she'd been so entranced she hadn't noticed another thing--or person. But suddenly before her was a diminutive girl about her own age, cloaked in a red tartan cape. Her wild hair was spun gold itself kissed the red of the river fox.

Now why such a description should come to mind Elizabeth wasn't sure. She blushed to her own roots, pulling back her hand-- just before she touched the tips of that hair.

The young woman laughed at her and picked up a handful herself. "It is in my way of being a Scottish curse. We are a faire race indeed with many a strawberry blonde amongst us. I've tried to change it, over the years, but I cannot get the color to stick."

"Change it? Why it is glorious, why would you ever think of changing it?" Elizabeth was shocked by the very idea.

The woman sighed deeply, "Aye. To have what we don't have--it is again me quest or curse." Then she seemed to pull herself back to the here and now of the trade show, and held out her hand. Her wrist twinkled with charms.

"I am Dee Shannon, named after the River Dee in my beloved home." And she angled her head to her sign.

"I'm Elizabeth McGillicuddy. I love your sign. It's not only beautiful but so creative. I, er, was a commercial artist. But now I am a scrap book shoppe keeper." And Elizabeth explained how she was just starting out, hadn't even opened, wasn't even sure she had the building when she left for the show.

"Well now Lizzie, as I am sure that is what they call you."

Elizabeth squinted her eyes.

"You are, and will always be, an artist. It is who you are." And Dee laid a hand on Elizabeth's arm. "You will just bring it to your scrap booking. And to it you will bring a beauty, and an edge, the other shoppe keepers will not have. Being an artist is who you are. Being a shoppe keeper is what you do."

And Elizabeth swore she heard the tiny bell ring again, just ever so slightly.

"You see Lizzie, you think you pick a dream, but in reality your dream picks you. And it would be a shame now not to follow that dream."

Suddenly too serious, Dee turned to her assortment of charms. They covered the span from a tiny tea pot to a miniature stone church. "See anything you like?"

And she handed Elizabeth a small silver tray to gather up the ones that appealed to her. The charms were all in tea cups--tartan tea cups. Elizabeth dipped her fingers in one, and pulled out a tiny cat sleeping in a curled position, and put it on her tray. And then a heart, and the Claddagh.

"Ahhh everlasting love," Dee murmured. And a faerie, and a piece of pie, and on and on until her tray was over loaded. "And each one magical," Dee started to sort them and list them on an order form.

"Now me dream chose jewelry making for me. I am intrigued by the detail I can fit into a tiny charm, and all the magic. Singularly they are special, but together, well they work together and their magic is stronger." And Dee clutched a ribbon of them around her neck. "Now me charms are not only for scrap bookers. They are to be worn too."

After Dee listed them all on her form she handed the tray back to Elizabeth. "Reach in their Lizzie and feel their weight, and their little worlds. Let some drift through your fingers. Hold on to several."

And as she spoke Elizabeth did just that. Her hand seemed to tingle with silver. Most slipped right away but she clung onto three.

Dee held out a small manila envelope a little bigger than a tea bag. "Now let go the ones you've held on to in here."

Elizabeth heard them clink together.

Dee took the string on the envelope, looped it over the button, and twined it shut. "A gift from me," And handed it back to Elizabeth.

"Oh no--no really."

"You must. These are the charms that chose you Lizzie. Leave them sealed and look at them when you get home. Home to?"

"Wind Star," Elizabeth surprised herself with her answer. Still it was home now. It felt like it.

But as softly as she said the words, a look of alarm came into Dee's eyes.

"Wind Star you say?"

And Elizabeth nodded.

"I have people in Wind Star or so I was told as a wee lass. But I never …" Most likely there were Wind Stars in every state … and this was just another Wind Star, not the one she'd always heard of. So Dee gave her head a little shake to clear it out. Her charms rang and rattled as she shook herself.

"Well it is surely a long way from Ballater but not so far now that you are here? Maybe you can come when my shoppe is open, and see your charms, and see Wind Star." Elizabeth made the offer, and though it sounded casual she meant it from the bottom of her heart.

"I have a wee work shoppe behind me home but I had a chance to rent me cottage to a corporation. As a perk, I suppose. So I took me self to the trade shows here in the colonies," Dee explained.

"So you move around then?"

"Aye. I do. I travel the trade show circuit so to speak. Pack up like a gypsy and move to the next show, the next city. What orders I can't fill from me stock, I send back and me cousin pulls for me."

"But you want to go back don't you?" Elizabeth knew this was getting far far too personal.

"The truth is Lizzie; I don't know what I want. I want to make jewelry. And part of that means sell jewelry. I cannot keep making it if I don't complete the circle and sell it."

"But surely, your charms are so special …" Elizabeth looked around her in wonder at the jewelry, and the tiny island of Scotland that had been created at the trade show.

"Aye. To your eye they are. Maybe me dream took me to the colonies …" And Dee let it hang. But the lights flashed indicating the show was closing. "You need to go and I need to dismantle me booth."

Elizabeth was reluctant to walk away.

"Shoo," Dee laughed. "Management will want you to go. We need to close down. Maybe our paths will cross again Lizzie."

"But …"

"Well …" And a smile broke out on her impish face. "I have your address right here on your order."

And Elizabeth was forced to leave. The show was over, and it was time for her to go. She followed the same crowds out that she had followed in, dragging her feet a little, not wanting it to end, not having the energy to keep going.

She'd spent a fortune, a fortune she didn't have. Her tote bulged with orders of things she hoped she loved as much when they got to Wind Star as she did now.

Hoped she'd remember them all. If she'd come earlier she would have invariably spent even more. More money she didn't have. (Did she have enough merchandise? Enough to satisfy her customers, whoever they may be? Enough to make an impact? To look like she was indeed a serious shoppe keeper? She wasn't sure. She wouldn't really know until everything came in and was unpacked. And displayed.

Unpacked where?

Displayed on what? Was she starting her new business in the wrong order? She didn't know.)

Would Elizabeth really have her store? Would Auntie Clara really have it arranged? And how would she make it look? She was grateful for all the vignettes she'd seen. They were mini stores themselves and loaded with good ideas. Ideas she would try and incorporate.

Did she have the right merchandise? She wasn't a scrap booker so she really didn't know.

She was pretty confident that she had tackled every category she came across. Still ... would the diehard scrap bookers look at her assortment and wince or worse yet just raise a critical eyebrow and leave? Or would they see things in her magical setting that would enchant them the same way Dee's charms had enchanted her?

Dee.

Jewelry maker without a home.

Of course Dee had a home, it was Ballater, and she'd told Elizabeth as much. But Dee's voice had been wistful, and homeless, as though she was still looking, or maybe just deciding.

And Elizabeth felt in a way she could relate to her. New York City had been her home. There never had been any question. Until somehow she'd carelessly let it slip away.

But then she'd landed somewhere so unlike the city she was surprised, okay shocked, to find how much she was loving it.

Her home now.

Her new home.

Elizabeth gave one last look over her shoulder, and hoisted up her now packed tote bag, and left the building. It was bright outside. Why wasn't it night time? She felt as if she'd been shopping the market for hours on end. And of course she had been, but she started at the very beginning of the day, and it just felt as though it should be night fall.

Her feet told her it didn't matter what the time of day was, they were done. And her stomach told her it was ready for something to eat. Maybe she was done. Maybe she had absorbed, committed, and seen as much as she could possibly hold. Maybe it was time to go home.

The limo was a God send. Elizabeth went to it like a beacon almost tearful that she didn't have to wait for a cab, or crawl into a bus. She took off her shoes, dumped her tote, and much to her surprise found a glossy bag, and note, from Basil.

A gift? What kind of gift could Basil possibly leave her? She opened the note and read. "Henry will take you to the airport. I've left a snack for you. Take care dear Lizzie and it goes without saying my love to Clara. Warm regards, Basil."

Lizzie dipped into her sack, and to her delight found a corned beef on rye from a land mark deli. She sighed as she sipped her Diet Pepsi, tackling her sandwich and reviewing the trade show. Her tote was stuffed with orders, catalogs, and samples. Glitter ink stampers, faerie stencils, crimping scissors.

She laughed at all the goodies she'd amassed as give-a-ways from her new vendors, hoping there was something for each Auntie. As the limo skimmed the city back to La Guardia, she realized this was the way to travel, and silently thanked Basil.

Elizabeth found the manila envelope from Dee. Well, now was as good a time as any to take a peak. What an odd, but utterly charming, person Dee had been. All her talk about magic and folk lore seemed whimsical bordering on silly.

Still while they talked she was under its spell. She spilled the charms into the palm of her hand, and suddenly felt a tingle of warmth, as though they were alive.

Before she could even question her doubts she uncurled her fingers. There in the palm of her hand was a miniature silver car. She picked it out and held it up to her eyes. On closer inspection it looked like a little Jag. She couldn't even remember seeing a Jag charm?

How could she possibly have picked one?

Elizabeth sighed, wondered where he was, and why she hadn't heard from him. How did she even know how a man viewed these things? Yes, she had gotten a bit tipsy on her date but other than that minor detail, it had gone fine.

More than fine.

Hadn't they talked, lost in each other's eyes, almost finishing each other's sentences? And they'd talked about? Why it dawned on Elizabeth she knew very little about Cooper. Like his last name even. What was his last name? She knew he was a mechanic at the Mini dealer.

Oh yeah, and he thought her Mini was foolish! Well, it was. And she laughed. That was part of the fun of it. And it was uniquely hers and that was probably a bigger part.

Had she seen him in the morning as the limo took her to the show? Or had she just wanted to? He didn't look like a lot of people, certainly not New Yorkers. Maybe he did look like a Californian.

Certainly what she'd always imagined them to look like; lean, tan, streaked hair a tad too long, angular face with a Roman nose that looked just this side of perfect. Maybe it had been broken once, taking his perfect looks to rugged? She didn't know. She just knew that he fascinated her and when he let that arrogant façade drop, she thought she saw serious bordering on tender. She shook her head. "Silly," and slipped the Jag charm back into the envelope.

The next charm she fingered was a small book. "Why it could be a scrap book!" And she delighted when the tiny cover opened.

The last of the three was a bell. The faerie bell. She rang it and wondered if the diminutive sound was going to summon a diminutive faerie. Maybe ... and smiled as she slipped it back in the envelope with the others.

And before she could think anymore about her little cache of charms she was at the airport.

"Now miss, you have your ticket?" Henry the limo driver looked concerned. He helped her unload.

She nodded and flipped the handle of her carry on, swinging her tote of samples and catalogs over her shoulder and her handbag. "Thank you and again thank Basil for me." And she was gone, tackling the crowds at the airport looking for her check in counter.

Elizabeth was grateful she didn't have to check luggage, or reclaim it for that matter. Her carryon was heavy even with the little wheels, yet it still made her trip simpler.

And once she hoisted it up in the over head bin along with her tote, and was strapped in, she knew she could let her breath out. And with the whoosh of breath she closed her eyes.

And was asleep.

Her shoppe was monstrous. The size of a department store. Cavernous. She hadn't bought enough merchandise, and the little amount she had purchased sat in one corner lonely and insignificant. What had she been thinking? Why was the store so big? It seemed to be the size of Javits Convention center only grubby, dark, and depressing. Shoppers were lined up for opening day and still she hadn't painted, much less cleaned.

Something buzzed by her ears, something scampered past her feet. Surely she couldn't have bugs ... or rodents? Could she? Maybe she even had homeless people for all she knew. She couldn't see the back wall, and had no clue how big her dirty building was. The store was a slum. Her slum.

With no merchandise to speak of and angry anxious people queued up and waiting for her to unlock the door. What had she been thinking when she first looked at it? Did it look like this, and she saw something else? Something through rose colored glasses tinted by her enthusiasm?

Impossible.

Yet here she was …

What had happened to her quaint shoppe while she'd been to market? Had Auntie Clara not been able to close the deal and found this football arena instead? Sweat poured down her neck as she looked around. She was starting off panicked, failing. And she knew you should at least start off as you meant to go along.

The Aunties said they would fund things but there was no pile of money big enough to fill this huge store, mind remodel, and bring it up to date. Or even clean it. And could she even begin to manage something this monstrous? Even if it was lovely, which she highly doubted it ever had been, or ever would be …

The customers started rattling the door and finally just pushed it in. They stormed the store like starving insects, and when they realized it was for all basic intentions empty they started tackling her. She tried to shake them off but they persisted.

"Miss. Miss. We have landed. You need to wake up." A sweet stewardess was shaking her. She was back, in the plane, clutching her handbag. The filthy store was a dream.

Just a monstrous dream.

"Uh, sorry, must have dozed. Thank you." And Elizabeth struggled to pull herself together. She took a few deep breaths, dug out her mints and sighed. Hopefully Auntie Clara had been successful.

Hopefully her tiny shoppe in Wind Star, down the street from Fairchild's, would be hers. A lease settled all of Auntie Clara's requests, or should she say demands met, and cleaning begun.

Hopefully she would have a place for all her new wondrous merchandise as it started to arrive. And hopefully her dream business would start to unfold.

She gathered her meager luggage and left the plane, and her nightmare behind.

"So it was fun Lizzie?" Auntie Clara put the kettle on. A roll of McVities Digestives lay open on a plate. Elizabeth paced with excitement, the cookies ignored.

"Oh Auntie Clara! I think I'm really set!" And Elizabeth elaborated on orders and vendors, displays and merchandise.

Auntie Clara grinned and just listened.

"But the shoppe Auntie? Tell me what progress you've made? Do we even have a shoppe?" Elizabeth had forced her airplane night mare away.

"Well why don't we hop into me Rover and I'll take you over." And Auntie Clara already saw a difference in her niece--a glow of excitement and anticipation. Something she'd been hoping for.

Tea forgotten, they pulled up to the formerly dusty building. Elizabeth sat on the edge of her seat. Now conversation had ended, replaced by nerves. The windows were now news papered over. Elizabeth gave it a quizzical look.

"Bertie's idea for some suspense," Auntie Clara slipped an over sized brass key into the front door. Casually, much to Elizabeth's surprise Auntie Clara turned the key as if she'd done it a million times. She called out. "Girls, she's back!"

And Elizabeth held her breath. And very carefully she stepped through the doorway and stared in awe.

Blanchie and Bertie wore white painter's bibs, bandanas over their hair, and what appeared to be combat boots! Goodness! Elizabeth looked them up and down; their faces were splattered with paint, their hands streaked up to their elbows in more.

Why they had rolled up their denim shirt sleeves, Elizabeth couldn't guess. Even Blanchie's peridots were coated in paint! Jim Hart's 'Surrender' blasted at her and seemed to bounce and echo off the empty room!

The empty room! Why it was painted a clear shiny sea foam green (and seemed to envelope Elizabeth in its mood.) She glanced up, and to her delight the ceiling was a shiny light Robin's egg blue! Elizabeth just stared, her mouth hanging open.

Suddenly Blanchie and Bertie started to squirm. Blanchie reached a stray orange curl on her forehead and attempted to push it back under her bandana, leaving Robin's egg blue now on her forehead.

For one frantic moment Elizabeth wondered if Blanchie would be able to get it out of her hair or if she would forever have delicate streaks of aqua blue mixed in with her silver orange.

Auntie Clara turned down the music. There were no joyous greetings from Auntie's Blanchie and Bertie. Nothing like Auntie Clara had been. Bertie finally spoke, "We've gone too far?" There was a plea in her voice of innocence and perhaps youth long forgotten.

Then Blanchie stepped forward and Elizabeth winced, seeing a turquoise footstep under her. "Well you said you loved light green, and I looked at my old Chanel and saw how she'd paired it with aqua. Subtle. We thought it was subtle."

"But lovely!" Bertie piped in, "We didn't want it so subtle it was …"

"Boring!" Blanchie finished, "We abhor boring!"

And as Elizabeth looked at their paint streaked faces and splattered cover-alls she rushed to them, arms out stretched.

"Boring?" She laughed deep, thorough. "My Aunties could never be boring, nor could any of their projects!" And embraced them in her best bear hug.

Auntie Clara watched relieved. "The paint Lizzie--on your suit …"

But Elizabeth's eyes were over flowing with love for these senior ladies who had tackled her filthy empty shoppe space. "Oh, I'm sure it's water base."

Blanchie and Bertie winced but hugged back.

Elizabeth finally broke free and twirled. The room had a warmth and sparkle.

"The high gloss my dear," Blanchie seemed to read her mind, "Will set it all off like a jewel."

And she was right of course, the room glistened. Elizabeth couldn't wait to begin decorating, and filling it with merchandise! "Oh Aunties! I love it. I simply love it! Why I couldn't have imagined anything better. It is elegant, and happy, and warm and ... well I love it."

Blanchie and Bertie let out their pent up breathes. Blanchie wished she still smoked; she would have liked a cigarette. Bertie wished she had a drink. They'd been nervous. Very nervous. Nervous that they had over stepped ... or taken over. Nervous that they didn't know Lizzie as well as they thought they did.

"But the work! So much work! Have you even slept since I've been gone? I can't believe all you have done! Why it would have taken me days just to narrow down the paint colors. You are geniuses! Hard working geniuses! Thank you!" And Elizabeth swiped at a wayward tear.

A happy one.

"And the details! I haven't heard how you finalized the lease, or sale, or whatever. And the inspections and all those other details! Why it's so pretty I can't even think what else to ask you about!" And Elizabeth knew she was rambling but couldn't help it.

Blanchie, Bertie, and Auntie Clara beamed. This was what they had wanted. This was what all their hard work had been about. Not the hard work of cleaning and painting. The hard work of getting Lizzie to move to Wind Star, to start a new life ... a better one.

And one they would all get to be part of. And her wanting it, grasping it. This is what they quietly referred to as the launching of Lizzie.

"But Lizzie we want to hear all about your market trip." Blanchie looked at her tenderly, as though she were her own granddaughter or great niece. And she knew through Auntie Clara she kind of was. Auntie Clara had so kindly shared everything with her and Bertie for years.

And now family. Auntie Clara shared family.

Elizabeth took a deep breath, "I have so much to tell you--it was fabulous! Simply fabulous! I loved every minute of it!" And suddenly she wanted them to hear it all, see it all as she had. And she knew 'fabulous' just didn't tell them a thing.

"And nice, were they nice to you Lizzie dear?" Blanchie was touching up a corner with light green as she spoke.

Elizabeth considered, "You know, I was surprised how helpful all the vendors were when I told them I hadn't even opened yet. Yes, they were." Then she looked alarmed. "Weren't they going to be?"

Now Blanchie stammered, "Oh my dear, in the apparel world, many zillions of years ago, well, the ready to wear people are ..."

"Snobby Blanchie," Bertie piped in, "Just say it."

Blanchie nodded, "I guess they are or were. It's a hard nut to crack so to speak, and so I worried."

But Elizabeth assured her it was not at all that way, and that vendors had gone out of their way to be welcoming. "Even though I'm not even open, they were gracious to me."

"And the city Lizzie?" Bertie had to ask. It was on all their minds. "How was the city?" What Bertie meant, of course, was how it all felt ...

"New York was New York, frantic, exhilarating, and wonderful. A place I was happy to live in and now happy to leave." And as Elizabeth got the words out three very old ladies let their breath out and sighed. Happy.

Chatter moved on to the shoppe itself, and the paint selections, and of course, the soon to be delivered merchandise. "And I brought you all little gifts! They all seemed to give me samples!" Elizabeth reached into her tote bag and pulled out a pair of scallop edged scissors and handed them to Auntie Clara.

Auntie Clara beamed.

Next came a small suede album in pink and black. "Chanel's color scheme ... isn't it?" Elizabeth had a feeling Blanchie would like it.

And Blanchie wiped a tear.

Then Elizabeth dipped in for glue glitter for Bertie but found her small envelope of charms. Unconsciously she slipped a finger in and peeked. Why there were two bells. But there had been only one. Two faerie bells? Maybe she wasn't seeing it right. She spilled the charms into the palm of her hand. There were four. "Auntie Bertie?"

Bertie stood alert, waiting for her treat.

"I well ..." Elizabeth hesitated.

"Whatever it is Lizzie, I'll love it. It just means a lot to all of us you'd think about us while you were so busy ..."

"Working." Auntie Clara added, but she was snipping at a paper napkin she found in her purse, fascinated by the effect of her new scissors.

But Bertie was tired of waiting. She reached out, and Elizabeth uncurled her hand. "Why they're charms, aren't they?" Bertie was fascinated, "I'd heard people put charms in their albums."

Elizabeth nodded. "I got three as samples but well, now there seem to be four. It seems as though there are two bells, and I think one must be meant for you Auntie Bertie."

"A little bell, how sweet." Auntie Clara felt Lizzie really was the generous girl she'd hoped for. "But what does a bell mean?"

Bertie held it by its miniature ring and gave it a shake. The sound was clear, almost magical. "It's a faerie bell. I haven't seen one since I was a wee lass. You--well, you ring it to summon the faeries." And Bertie was gone in middle space for just a split second.

"Really?" Auntie Clara and Blanchie said in unison.

But Elizabeth was nodding surprised Auntie Bertie knew the lore.

"That's what the rep told me. But..." Then she gave a shy smile to Bertie, "Does it work?"

But Bertie saw no teasing in the question, "Well me dear, the faeries are an odd lot, and they do as they like. Oh they'll hear the bell ring all right, yet they may or may not answer it. But legend has it you should not ring for them lightly. It should be saved for something important. Then if your request is sincere, they will consider it."

A veil of seriousness fell over them all as Bertie spoke.

Finally Blanchie broke it, "Girls, we're grateful Lizzie thought of us. Now let's show her what all we got done while she was gone."

And suddenly a party like atmosphere elevated the mood while the aunties explained their quest for the perfect celadon and Robin's egg blue paint samples. And their search for painting uniforms.

"You know I was rather embarrassed for that young man at Lowes, suggesting we were too old to paint," Blanchie grinned.

"Too old my foot!" Bertie agreed.

The space had gone from dreary and dirty to almost ethereal. "The colors rather embrace you, don't you think?" Elizabeth asked. "In art school we learned these are the two most soothing colors in the entire palette. And they do--sooth. They make me feel welcome and really good."

The aunts beamed, relieved that their choices were approved.

"Now we want you to make a list of fixtures you'll need ..." Auntie Clara began. "You know tables, shelves, whatever."

Elizabeth listed as she wandered thinking about some of the displays she'd just seen at market. The colors were beautiful and the sheen added just enough sparkle to well, bring the space to life. And Elizabeth suddenly could see fixtures in place.

Auntie Clara went on, "We, er, well we have lots of odds and ends in storage. Don't we girls?"

Blanchie and Bertie nodded.

"So just figure out what you'll need and we'll see what we can come up with."

"But Auntie Clara, I'll need, well ..." Elizabeth's mind was spinning.

"An old cash register?" Bertie supplied with a twinkle in her eye. "I might have one. You know the nickel plated ones from the twenties."

She'd just gotten the flyer for Texas' Marburger Antique Show and had seen one.

"And some oak shelves?" Blanchie mentally ran through her magazine supply, wondering if she'd have to stop at Barnes and Noble on the way home.

"A desk? Do you think you'll need a desk?" Bertie wondered out loud. Of course Elizabeth would need a desk, for ... business work.

So Elizabeth nodded yes.

"And tables, with chairs, for people to work at," Auntie Clara was picturing oak herself. Maybe a round pedestal table or ... well, she'd have to look around and decide. Auntie Clara did love the look of those English Small Bone Kitchens ...

But Elizabeth was too busy just nodding her head yes. Her mind reeling.

"Oh, we almost forgot ..." And Blanchie headed to the stock room. She dragged out an old iron cart covered with a sheet. Slowly and dramatically she pulled the sheet away revealing a wooden sign shaped like an open book. It was primed white.

"You mentioned a sign like an open scrap book and we had a friend, Old Tomas, cut this for you." Blanchie looked hopefully at Elizabeth.

"But we thought you'd want to paint it," Bertie added nervous again.

"Because you're so artistic," Auntie Clara finished tenderly.

Tears spilled--at first a few; then the flood. She couldn't help it.

"Oh dear," Bertie started to fidget.

"We've gone too far, haven't we dear?" Blanchie's confidence had fizzled.

Only Auntie Clara opened her arms. "Oh Lizzie--come here dear. Come on." And Auntie Clara patted Elizabeth tenderly when she finally fell into her arms. "Oh Lizzie ... has it been so very long since anyone did anything for you? Cared for you? Loved you?"

But Elizabeth just sobbed.

And when the other aunts understood, they gathered around.

Auntie Clara dabbed at her own eyes, "You're home now Lizzie. You don't have to struggle alone anymore. As a matter of fact dear, you don't have to struggle at all. You're embarking on something that will not only use all your talents but you will be able to do it your way, at your own speed. You can be both artist and boss, your own boss Lizzie."

"We want to give you that freedom to no longer look over your shoulder because your methods are your own. And now, they're good enough. And no longer seek approval, approval from bosses. You can do what you think is right, and you can be your own boss. This is our gift to you Lizzie."

And very shakily Elizabeth let the words soak in through layers and years of self doubt.

The next morning Elizabeth sat in front of the book shaped sign. Her tubes of paint scattered in front of her, along with sketches she'd worked on long into the night until she had it all just so. She'd decided on a rather Victorian font for the actual name--probably because it reminded her of the first letter Auntie Clara had sent her.

The letter that had changed her life.

True, it was old fashioned but something about scrap booking was old fashioned. Elizabeth had drawn the charms, and scissors, and stickers bordering the open pages inspired by the sign at Dee Shannon's charm booth.

The first bit of paint went on. Was it too green? Was it green enough? Since she'd matched the background of the sign to the sea foam of her walls, she wasn't sure.

Hefting the sign, she lugged it outside, in natural light, where the sign would be seen. Elizabeth leaned it against the building and stood back, hands on denim clad hips. It really looked good--no, great. Maybe the lettering should be darker, bolder than she originally thought.

Stepping into the tree lawn for a better view, the tree lawn she planned to turn into a flower bed. Maybe she needed to step a bit farther back--to see if the details sketched in were big enough.

A car slammed on its brakes, and horn rang out at the same time! Startling Elizabeth, she toppled on her wedge heeled sandals! Why she'd backed into the street! But as the thought of possibly being hit sank in she saw stars.

Nothing but stars.

Cooper scooped her up in his arms. He'd been headed to Fairchild's for chocolate and seen her in the street, gazing up at an empty building. And almost hit her!

What was she doing? What was she looking at? All forgotten in a split second.

Was she okay?

"Lizzie! Lizzie!" He was half sobbing.

Her lashes fluttered and suddenly sea green eyes met Robin's egg blue. "Cooper?" It was just a whisper, "Cooper, you saved me." And all thoughts she'd been harboring about him not calling evaporated.

Saved her? I almost ran her over! I almost killed her! But before he could say a word she was back out, only this time with a hint of a smile on her face.

Jinx came running out of Fairchild's after hearing the squeal of brakes. Cooper had set Elizabeth on the grass and was rubbing her wrists—afraid, afraid to shake her. Shock her. By the time Colette came out of the Patisserie with water, Elizabeth was embraced by a small crowd.

"I ... I backed into the street." Then Elizabeth became mortified by the attention. "I'm fine--really. Just a tumble--and Cooper. Cooper saved me."

But Cooper's face was ashen. He'd seen a million car accidents. It went with his racing territory. Thank God he had perfect reflexes and could stop on a dime.

Colette went back in the Patisserie for coffee. Strong and black. Colette forced a cup on each of them. "Shows over! Everyone leave," And shoved away the bystanders.

Elizabeth and Cooper sipped the strong brew, clearing both their heads.

"I could have hit you! I could have hit you!" Cooper's mantra droned on.

"But you didn't," Elizabeth laid a hand on his cheek, brushed a sun streaked strand of hair out of his eyes. "Maybe someone else would have, but you came along--able to stop. React."

Her words were soothing, comforting, and he slowly fought back the panic. Why this crazy girl was affecting him he had no clue! Once he'd plowed into her flower beds, this time he almost plowed into her.

"I'm okay, really." Elizabeth took his hand and patted it for reassurance.

But Cooper's mind short circuited, and all he could think about was crushing her to him.

"Come on. I have something to show you." Elizabeth stretched her ⸻ started to tug him to his feet.

"You need to wear more," He muttered, still in shock. But she only laughed. He was standing now and she reached for her sign to drag it back inside.

"I was contemplating my new sign." She took in a gulp of air. It sounded almost foreign to her, but good, very good, "For my new business."

Once she heard it out loud she smiled full wattage, "My new business! Come on. I'll show you around."

He'd taken the cumbersome sign from her and was carrying it in. Carefully he set it down, still keeping an eye on her.

She led him into the glistening painted space, pointing out where shelves would go.

"But aren't you Clara's grounds keeper?" Cooper sounded stupid but was feeling better, his shock subsiding.

"Oh, I can still do that! I have tons of energy!" Tons of energy she never knew she had! And Elizabeth twirled in her new space, grinning foolishly.

"A scrap booking shoppe?" He wasn't even sure what that meant.

"Uh huh--actually the Aunties are huge scrap bookers, and well, encouraged me." And she beamed.

"Aunties? There are more than Clara?" Cooper shook his head.

"Oh my yes--there's Auntie Blanchie and Auntie Bertie, and they're well, they're somewhat like Auntie Clara, and somewhat their own thing too. I can't explain it--for some reason these ancient ladies have become my friends--my family." Elizabeth said this softly, quietly. "And I was ready for something. I'm a commercial artist by trade but well; let's just say I'm taking a new road."

Cooper thought about his racing, a storage bin full of trophies, and how now he was selling cars, albeit very expensive ones, and with a staff, but still a far cry from racing. "I understand."

"You do?" Elizabeth stopped and stared at him, seeing him anew. "Tell me."

"Oh ... another time. Today, it's about your new business and well, you're alive." And he opened his arms.

Elizabeth hesitated for just a second, and then sank into him, and let the warmth, and security he offered envelope her.

All thoughts of romance slid to the back burner as Cooper relived the scene in his mind of almost running her over.

He trembled and she pulled back. "Hey?" She looked deep into his eyes and saw fear, hoped to see romance. "You didn't' hit me. Understand? You saved me."

He closed his eyes with a shrug.

"Come on, we're getting some food!" And she tugged at his hand. "We're going to take your mind off this accident thing! I'll cook for you!"

He followed her back to the brown stone.

"Pop in a movie, I'm making us dinner." And Elizabeth pointed to a basket full of DVDs. "Something light ..."

He pulled out a Marks Brother Marathon.

"Perfect! I think there are three movies on that. And no matter where we pick it up its good." As he fiddled with the TV, Elizabeth pulled open the pink bubble fridge praying there was something, anything in there. She found Swiss, and cheddar, and half a loaf of Roman Meal bread--rather stale.

And then Elizabeth remembered there was a Mickey and Minnie sandwich griller in one of the cabinets. She'd make grilled cheese!

The sandwiches were hot and gooey crispy Mickey and Minnie faces oozing with cheese. Once the sandwich maker was hot she was able to grill off several in rapid succession. She carried over a platter loaded with sandwiches, a roll of paper towels under her arm. "Hey! It's ready!"

Cooper was slouched on the floor laughing at Margaret Dumont and Groucho, the almost accident shelved. He looked up as she approached. "Whoa! I can't believe you!" He snagged a sandwich and bit in sighing. "Perfect. It's an art. A great grilled cheese sandwich is an art!"

Elizabeth gave a slightly embarrassed laugh. "It's not me at all. It's the sandwich maker--can't miss." They worked their way through the stack of sandwiches, Cooper inhaling them like popcorn, Elizabeth forcing herself to eat as slow as possible to cut down on the calories.

When the platter was nothing more than crumbs and grease Cooper sighed. "What's for dessert?"

Dessert? The man wants more food? Oh   , he just ate five sandwiches and he's still hungry! Water! All I have is water! Tap water! "Uh, Auntie Clara probably has a   pound cake. I can run up and snag us a couple slices." This appeared to be the right answer if his silly grin meant anything.

Grabbing her keys, Elizabeth split out the door, and started to race up to Auntie Clara's. Several knocks got no response. "Wouldn't you know it, she's out." And then remembering the four flights she'd just chugged up, Elizabeth sighed. "I should have called and saved myself a trip up here."

But then she jangled her keys. There was probably cake in there ... there usually was. "And if Auntie Clara had been home she would have insisted I take some so ..." Carefully Elizabeth fitted Auntie Clara's key in the lock and turned the knob.

"Auntie Clara?" Just to make sure she wasn't dozing. As Elizabeth called out she headed to the kitchen. Sure enough, under a layer of tin foil sat the perfect Bundt cake oozing

⅃ The scent alone was intoxicating when she peeled back the foil. Grateful she'd only eaten one sandwich, she whacked off two generous pieces.

The dining room clock chimed, startling her, the knife clattered to the floor. "Silly, there's no one here." But Elizabeth wandered into the dining room. Just in case.

No one.

Of course.

But Elizabeth spied a scrap book on the dining room table.

Open.

"Maybe I'll just take a quick peek."

The page was covered in magazine clippings of furniture: an oak pedestal table, four upholstered dining room chairs, with castors, three book shelves, also oak. One circled in gold pen. A desk with endless cubby holes and generous drawers.

"Why these are the kinds of pieces I would like for the shoppe- -exactly what I'd like." Elizabeth flipped forward but the album was blank. She flipped back. Paint chips. One sea foam green and one Robin's egg blue, circled, again in gold. From a uniform catalog, pictures of white coveralls, denim shirts, bandanas, combat boots.

"The Auntie's uniforms ..." But didn't this seem a little odd, Auntie Clara scrap booking in such detail. Elizabeth went back in the book even further and found a sketch of a shoppe front. It had obviously been labored over.

The front had been erased in part. It looked as though a bay window had been added, with tiny panes of glass. It looked an awful lot like her shoppe right down to the bathroom and stock room.

"How very sweet of Auntie Clara to keep such detailed records of—well--everything she'd been doing." She thumbed further back. There were pictures of the garden at the apartment building. Many pictures, clipped, it appeared from garden catalogs. "How odd, she could have just taken photographs ..."

But the clippings had been carefully glued in among sketches. Elizabeth had no idea Auntie Clara was so adept with a sharpie. She had the front of the brownstone down pat. There was a sketch of a fountain.

Imagine that? A fountain! But it had been crossed out. Thank God, mucking a fountain would be icky.

Elizabeth sat engrossed, reading backwards. The scrapbook showed her little flat before and after. Obviously Auntie Clara had decorated prior to her arrival and yet it appeared to have just all been there. How had Auntie Clara known what she'd love, as she did so love the little apartment?

The oddness of magazine clippings vs. photography started to nag at her. The mini pink appliances were from an ancient Sears and Roebuck catalog. The chaise in the bath she loved so, from Architectural Digest.

These pictures had obviously been put in the book quickly, almost sloppily as the origins of them were still intact. Gone was the tidy trimming. These had ripped edges with Sears and Arc. Digest still visible.

She found an ad for Mini Coopers. She'd gotten to love her pink Mini and couldn't have done better on her own. "How very odd ... how could Auntie find these things when photographing them would be so much easier ...?"

Elizabeth sat down, not even realizing she'd been standing, leaning over the scrap book. She was afraid to turn another page. Afraid of what she'd see. It was almost as though ... certainly not.

Impossible, actually.

Very impossible.

Yet somehow it seemed, well it seemed as though Auntie Clara was scrap booking things before they happened. No ...No way! And yet ... She started to flip more when she heard someone at the door.

"It's Coop. Are you okay?" The door was ajar, he wandered in. She sat at the dining room table, her hands on her head, her head down on a scrap book. "You didn't come back ..." He was at her side. "Lizzie, I did hurt you didn't I?" She was rocking back and forth.

"No—no--no, I'm okay." But she didn't raise her head. "Honest." Then she sat up. "Well maybe not okay but it has nothing to do with falling."

"Well ..."

She pushed the scrap book at him. "Unless falling through the rabbit's hole is possible."

Cooper squinted. A scrap book. She wanted him to look at a scrap book? One of Clara's scrap books?

"It isn't possible ... is it?" This she almost whispered.

"Lizzie, what are you talking about?" He was leafing through. "This looks like your Auntie has been keeping track of your life."

"Manipulating ..."

But Cooper looked skeptical, if anything he looked at Elizabeth as if she was crazy. "Not your Aunt Clara. Why she's the sweetest old lady I've ever met."

"Controlling ..."

"Lizzie, from what I can tell she's simply kept a scrap book of you and what you've been doing. Thoughtful, that's what Aunt Clara is."

"Or wanted me to be doing," Elizabeth winced as she said this. She really did love Auntie Clara so. She wasn't even sure how or why these ideas were formulating. Still, she couldn't seem to stop them.

"What do you mean?" Cooper could see she was serious--almost glazed over.

"Look ... look at the furniture."

"Yes--quite nice."

"It's for my shoppe."

"But your shoppe is empty.'

"And I haven't found any furniture yet." Elizabeth twisted her hands.

Cooper squinted, "What do you mean?"

"Well we talked, the aunties and me. About what would be nice. They said they had a lot in storage--old pieces."

"And ..."

"Well, they described these pieces." She worried her bottom lip.

"That's a coincidence I'm sure."

"Okay," Then Elizabeth sighed, "I'm being foolish. But don't you think it's odd they found pictures to look like what they said they have?"

"Well, they are old. And have time on their hands. Lots of time I suspect." But Cooper considered. "Do you think they've ordered this furniture and well, stashed it for you? You know, not wanting you to know they've spent all that money on you."

Elizabeth considered, "I don't know. They can be devious. I honestly have no clue how much money any of them have. They never seem to be scrimping." She was thoughtful but still clueless.

"Well why don't you wait and see if any of this furniture appears, you know, from storage."

"We better get out of here." Elizabeth looked around nervously.

"What about the cake?"

"Oh yeah, the cake."

5

"So Lizzie, do you have time to look at our odd bits and pieces of furniture today?" Auntie Clara was dressed for an outing, in a herringbone suit with sturdy heels.

Alarm shot across Elizabeth's face, "Uh sure Auntie. I was going to hang out at the shoppe today and paint the sign and see if UPS brings anything from the trade show."

"Then we better get going." Auntie Clara was excited for Elizabeth and wanted to just keep the ball rolling.

"Should we call Auntie Blanchie and Auntie Bertie?" Now Elizabeth was nervous but stuffed it down.

"Uh, they're going to meet us there."

Mini storages were the same across the country. Chain link fence, junk yard dog, weeds growing ramped, and yet everyone's loved belongings in metal cubicles. Elizabeth was shocked when she and Auntie Clara drove out into the country and pulled up to a red barn out of a Norman Rockwell painting.

Auntie Blanchie and Auntie Bertie sat in a limo with a driver from the retirement center. Elizabeth started to raise an eyebrow but her attention was yanked to the barn. Suddenly the doors were thrown open by a uniformed man, and Elizabeth got a glimpse of what looked like a furniture warehouse at High Point or owned by Sotheby's.

Elizabeth jumped out of the car and rushed in, the Aunties in her wake. There was an aisle of mahogany china cabinets! Biedemeir end tables jammed next to old English hunt boards! It looked like a clearing house for Kittenger or Baker or ... the rich and famous.

Elizabeth ran her fingers over a glossy chestnut dining table, practically drooling. She danced up and down the aisles until she found the oak--golden and very 1930's. There was a rectangular table--perfect for projects, a side board she could use for a coffee maker, shelves--so many book cases and shelving units!

Auntie Clara was right behind her with sticky notes. "Just tag whatever appeals to you dear."

Elizabeth was so excited she felt like a child at Christmas, all thoughts of the scrap book forgotten--flown from her head. The scent of lemon wax and old money seemed to permeate the endless barn.

She had to refrain herself from getting too greedy. After all, it was a very little shoppe. Still she wandered the aisles just taking in all the grand furniture feeling like she'd just won the vintage furniture lotto.

"Oh Auntie Clara--a desk! Look at that great desk! All those cubby holes!"

Auntie Clara handed her a sticky note and grinned.

It was several hours before they finished. Blanchie had the fore thought to bring a floor plan, Bertie carefully sketched in each piece Elizabeth chose.

Elizabeth hugged Auntie Clara, "You Aunties really are my faerie god mothers!"

"You're happy then my dear?" Blanchie asked; a bit tearful herself.

"Happy! I feel like I've won the furniture lotto!" Then Elizabeth paused, "Are you sure? I mean, are you all sure you don't need any of these pieces? There's an umbrella stand I think would look great in your foyer Auntie Bertie." And Elizabeth picked it up and held on to it.

"Oh don't give it a thought dear," Auntie Clara began. "Why, we've been done with this stuff for ... years. We're thrilled to have some use for some of it."

"But Auntie Clara--we should have a sale, an estate sale. You could turn this into some nice cash."

Blanchie panicked, "Well that's an idea dear, but we really don't need any extra cash." And Bertie and Auntie Clara nodded, rather frantically. "And well, once it's gone, it's gone. And I have a granddaughter and so does Bertie. Someday they may need some furniture. And you Lizzie, one day you'll have a house."

And a husband, Blanchie added mentally. "And we'd be thrilled to see some of our pieces have a new home. A young home."

Blanchie was so convincing, Elizabeth relaxed a little, "Well, I still feel guilty picking out so many pieces."

"Nonsense my dear, why you'd just have to buy things, you know new fixtures are so ..." Blanchie fished around her mind.

"Commercial," Auntie Clara supplied.

"Exactly. And scrap booking is so personal and old fashioned. These pieces will be perfect."

"Homey," Bertie added.

"And how nice for your customers ..."

"And for us when we come scrap booking," Auntie Clara finished.

Elizabeth got a faraway look in her eyes. "Yeah, you can tell my customers stories. Stories about meals on this table and ... and work done at this desk--and things you collected in these shelves. It'll be an ice breaker and well, it'll be your home away from home too."

And as Elizabeth dabbed at a wayward tear the three aunties squinted their eyes and mentally groaned.

Arrangements were made for delivering everything, and Elizabeth headed to the shoppe to work on the sign and wait for UPS, while mentally arranging. The desk certainly would be perfect right there. And she pointed and then giggled.

One of the big tables would go in the window, so the Aunties could watch whoever came or went while they worked on their own projects. And so Elizabeth mentally placed it all to a piece, now anxious for the fittings to be there.

Elizabeth was dabbing glitter on her sign and her mind drifted to Cooper. She didn't know what to make of him--great looking, no question, in a reckless sort of way. And at times she caught that kind of arrogant look in his eyes.

But at other times, when he wasn't paying any attention, he seemed careful, almost studious. Maybe tender.

She thought about the panic when he thought he'd hit her, or almost hit her, and that out of control adrenaline look as though she might be more important to him than he was letting on. Or that she might be gone. She didn't know.

She had no clue who had ever touched his heart before, or if he'd ever even opened it up.

"It's too bad relationships aren't so simple you could just ask." And if you could, expect an honest answer. Relationship? Have I referred to him as a relationship? Certainly not and yet ... But her mind wasn't ready to stop it's wandering around the idea.

Elizabeth was fascinated by his arrogance, almost like a moth to a flame. But his tender side, now that, well that was irresistible. What she did know for sure was she was no good at relationships.

Her track record was, well, a train wreck. And didn't they all start out lovely and rosy? And when did the train wreck come? And why couldn't she ever see it coming or for that matter, prevent it?

Her heart had been shattered so many times, she wondered if there were enough pieces left to amount to anything. Or if it was so mended it was almost perforated, ready to shatter again.

She also knew she was no good at picking men. Maybe all those cultures with arranged marriages that she'd always sneered at--maybe they had an edge. "Why if the Aunties picked someone for me ..."

On this note Elizabeth simply leaned back and closed her eyes tired from all the excitement of furniture hunting. "Just for a minute, just a tiny nap ..."

The Aunties sat at an <u>old table at the library</u>, stacks of books practically obliterating them. Copies of 'Who's Who', 'Fortune 500' lists, and most eligible bachelor articles from magazines. Blanchie was up at the Xerox machine.

"Girls I like this mega billionaire, he owns Louis Vuitton and Pierre Deux."

Auntie Clara raised her eye brows, "Blanchie, enough on the fashion. Besides, do you want our Lizzie to move away to Europe?"

Blanchie shrugged and hit cancel on the Xerox machine. "I guess not."

"I found someone who owns 5000 acres of farm land here in Illinois."

"Are you sure Bertie? That could almost be Illinois."

"What about this soap star?" Blanchie looked dreamily at a real hunk of a man.

"Right, an actor, come on Blanchie this is Lizzie's life we're dealing with not a one night stand."

"Gee, a lot of these Fortune 500 guys are geeky." Blanchie was flipping again.

"Geeky is not so bad. Are they single?" Auntie Clara had standards after all. Standards for Lizzie.

"What about this guy who owns the zoo?" Bertie did love animals.

"Well, he would be compassionate."

"Is it a cage zoo or a free range set up?" Blanchie asked.

"I don't know. It just shows him with lion cubs."

"What about a Caterpillar exec? Business mind and all?"

"A chef?"

"Tall?"

"Well tall enough for Lizzie's   ."

"Black hair--like jet?"

"Or that dirty blonde that edges in grey as time goes on?"

Auntie Clara started running her jeweled fingers through her hair. "Girls--maybe there isn't just one perfect man for Lizzie. Maybe we need to make one. Our own."

"Exactly!" Bertie's eyes lit up, warming to the idea.

"But what will we all agree on?" Blanchie looked wary.

"We'll take turns ..." Auntie Clara considered. And they ran back and forth to the copy machine recording men and then cutting them up.

"Black hair." Blanchie glued it down without a face; but Auntie Clara slapped blonde on top of it! All three wanted blue eyes--and why not? They were magical. Other than the sea and sky, what else was blue? Of course blue birds, and blue berries, and blue iris weren't even thought of.

Their dream man started to take shape. He held a brief case, and a hammer, and eventually a Santa sack that they loaded careers, and hobbies, and trades into.

"Jeans, Clara? Come on, give him something better. We want him to have good taste?"

"They're designer jeans. Ralph. And there's something better than Ralph?" Auntie Clara peered over her nose at Blanchie.

Blanchie shrugged, being a big Ralph Lauren fan herself. "I guess not."

"Besides, we don't want him too pretty, now do we?"

Bertie was snipping wildly from a dictionary!

"Bertie! We can't cut up library books--tape that back in and drag that to the copy machine!" Auntie Clara shook her head and tossed her the scotch tape.

Shamefully, Bertie lugged her big volume to the Xerox machine.

A man took shape in front of them made from a huge collection of scraps. Elizabeth watched in her dream, almost as though she were invisible. "I knew it!" But she only thought it and continued to watch.

"Are we ready to past him into the book?" Blanchie asked as she slid the paper they were working on over to the open scrap book.

"Wait!" Auntie Clara held a little clipping of a bulldog. "He needs a pet."

"Clara! You don't even know if Lizzie likes dogs, mind bull dogs! Just because you like them Clara ... shouldn't we leave something for them to figure out?"

But as Blanchie was chastising Auntie Clara, Bertie was slipping some cut out money in his pocket.

"Enough! We're ready!" Blanchie handed the Elmer's to Auntie Clara as she tipped up one corner of their perfect man. Glue slid under and they pushed it around.

"Manners! We forgot manners!" Bertie protested.

"Honey ..." Blanchie placed a gentle hand on her, "We can't give him everything. We can't play God."

And the difference was? A few accessories? Elizabeth was horrified! But Auntie Clara was closing the book and giving it a little tap tap tap with her jeweled hands. Or was she using that huge blue topaz ring? Elizabeth couldn't see. Couldn't tell.

Carefully Blanchie and Bertie reopened the scrap book. The composite man now appeared to be animated. He rolled his shoulders as if stiff, stretched out his arms, letting his sack, brief case, and hammer go.

He pushed a blonde lock of hair out of his eyes and then focused on the aunties. Suddenly his entire face came to life! He smiled. It reached the depths of his sea blue eyes, crinkling the corners.

Then he spoke, "Ladies ... thank you."

But before they could react, he jumped off the page, and with a farewell wave was out the door.

"But ... but ... but!!!!!" The aunties protested in unison! All that was left was the glue bottle, odd snippets of scrap and the book.

"Did you put a picture of Lizzie in that sack?" Blanchie's elegant composure long gone as she ran her bejeweled hands through her elegant coif.

"I--I--I don't remember ..." Bertie was crying.

Auntie Clara had run out the door, huffing and frantic!

Elizabeth was speechless! Shocked really! Beyond shocked! She tried to call out! Or was it scream?

And then she was awake.

Back in her shoppe.

Her paint brush had crusted dry.

Her sign 'Creating Memories' was still in front of her.

She rubbed her eyes, freaked. A dream? It had been a dream! Surely only a dream.

But before she could concentrate on the elusive craziness she heard the squeal of air breaks and saw a delivery truck out front. "My furniture!"

And with glee, raced to the door.

The dream forgotten.

"Over here, uh huh." Elizabeth motioned the men with a gigantic library of shelves. "On that big wall … and the desk …" And she pointed. "Those two long tables here and the round one … uh, in the window." The men unloaded and hauled and Elizabeth pointed. Not a scrape on the freshly polyurethane pine floors. Not a knick on the newly painted walls.

"Perfect."

"Perfect?" The men looked quizzical, used to moving, and removing, and moving again. The bigger the piece, it seemed the more undecided the customer was.

"Yes! Absolutely! Now what do I owe you?" Elizabeth beamed.

"Owe us? Not a thing. It's all been taken care of."

But she slipped them a couple twenties as tips. Those Aunties! As the door closed, the air breaks squealed in reverse, Elizabeth twirled and shouted, "I love it!"

And she did!

Suddenly the empty space had personality! Warmth! The sea foam green was the perfect backdrop for the oak. Elizabeth stood back to admire. "Maybe … maybe I'll duplicate my sign on the wall." She ran to her stock room for her paints.

Once she roughed it in she decided maybe she'd also paint some sayings across the top of the walls--like a border. Sayings about memories and friends and family. Mentally she started to work them out as she painted the open book sign.

It was dusk; the true light was fading, turning golden, magical. Elizabeth leaned back on her heels. The open book on her walls was almost finished. Fingering the charms she now wore constantly around her neck, she looked at the charms she had sketched on her wall book: the basket of flowers, the lamb, the thimble, the Claddagh.

She tried to add more than she had on the outside sign. People could see the detail in here, closer. She thought about Dee, the charm designer, and wondered when she'd see her charm order, and if she'd ever see Dee again.

Elizabeth added a sprinkle of gold glitter to the scissors she'd painted, contemplating all the new merchandise on its way. She looked around, her heart bursting at the seams at the shoppe taking shape in front of her.

Her shoppe.

How very odd it was not to get up every morning and drag herself into the ad agency, fearing the latest tantrum. Instead she bounced out of bed every day, expecting the unexpected, and loving it all. And it was unexpected, from a slice of Whiskey Pound Cake with Auntie Clara to a barn full of furniture.

The furniture ... Elizabeth ran a hand lovingly over the round table. Then her mind slid back to the scrap book--the page full of furniture. Did it look like the furniture in the scrap book? She wasn't sure. It was oak, and chunky, and well, it could be ... or not. The desk with the cubby holes ... was that in the scrap book?

Now it was getting late, feeling late, and Elizabeth realized she was tired. She started to tidy up her paints, turn out the lights.

The furniture from the scrap book danced in her head. She should just let it go. Let it go and enjoy the new furniture, and her turn of luck. It didn't matter anyway. Besides it couldn't just come from a scrap book to her, so why was she getting so worked up?

Let it go.

Breath.

Let it go.

As Elizabeth headed home she slowed down. "Maybe I'll just drive by the barn ...just to reassure myself." Reassure myself of what I'm not sure. She headed out a country road she was sure she had been on. Yep, there's Dink's, the Cape Cod diner she remembered passing, this way up. Chinese lanterns swung in the air above picnic tables, people sat out drinking pitchers   and eating what looked like colossal burgers.

This was the right way. Now past the apple orchard, MacTamara's, and then the old wind mill. She laughed at herself as she checked off the landmarks. Now down a crooked little lane past some grazing sheep and one more corner ...

But when Elizabeth turned the pink Mini around the corner there was no red barn. There was a tiny farm house with ornate ginger bread. A golden light shone from one window. A couple of sheep grazed in what would be considered the front yard. But there was no barn.

Red or otherwise.

Elizabeth slowed down, cramming her neck and then went on. "Maybe ... just maybe it's a little further." But further down were some grazing cows. The countryside rolled like a primitive painting, but there were no buildings.

No red barns. She turned around and took the next street, then the next, ultimately ending back at the farm house. "This has to be the lane. This has to be the spot."

She turned her CD player on to keep grounded. Jim Hart sang sadly of days gone by, people and places.

Rolling the Mini to a stop in front of the farm house, she just sat there. "Maybe I'm wrong." But the feeling of déjà-vu nagged at her. She saw the front door open and an old lady wearing a bib apron headed toward her.

"Now I've done it. I've gone and scared someone." And Elizabeth worried her bottom lip.

"Help you?" The old lady was actually very friendly, not the least bit afraid, rather grandmotherly.

Elizabeth stammered, "Oh, I'm sorry. I don't know what I was thinking. I wasn't thinking. I was, well, I just had the wrong address, and I was trying to get my bearings." She pushed back a stray lock of hair, nervous, embarrassed.

At this point an old man in coveralls came out to see what was going on. "Problem Ruthie?"

"Nope--girls lost that's all."

Elizabeth felt she better say something and start the car. Why wasn't she starting the car and leaving? "I was, well I was looking for an old red barn. I was out here earlier and I well, I thought this was the spot."

The old woman frowned, looking off into middle space. The old man spoke, "Well there was a red barn here once--long ago." And as he leaned toward the car, Elizabeth's mouth dropped open! She swore it was the caretaker at the furniture barn--just trade coveralls for a uniform.

Couldn't be ...

"Uh ..." Elizabeth had nothing concrete to say. So she gaped a bit.

"Yep--gone. That barns gone," And he said it like he meant it. "Come on Ruthie, Green Acres is coming on."

Green Acres? Re-runs? That barns gone? The red barn? My barn?

"I'm sorry--so sorry. I must have gotten it wrong." And Elizabeth rubbed her eyes.

"Very wrong missy, good night to you." And the old man and woman headed back up the walk.

"Wait. Can we talk? About the barn? About ..." But Elizabeth's words echoed to an empty night.

They were gone.

And as she stared, the golden light from the single window blinked out. Elizabeth turned the key and put the car in reverse. "Sleep, I need sleep."

6

Sometimes Cooper wondered why in God's name he had so
many interests. He was as at home at his desk at the car dealership as he'd been behind the wheel of a race car. He could
wander at a park or mingle at a club.

He loved rock and roll, sultry blues, and a gentle ballad. Right
now Lee Lessack was singing a heady duet with Michael Feinstein
about this being the best part of his life. About a secret word meant
only for him.

Cooper closed his eyes and let the words carry him off. Maybe
this was the best part of his life … When Lee Lessack and Michael
Feinstein sang of seven generations asking you to just do one better
he thought of his grandfather.

And the dealership that now occupied almost all his waking mo-
ments. The fascination with ordering, and selling, and repairing--it
was a world unto itself--a world that somehow people needed, to move
from place to place.

In style.

Cooper had never been a status man, absorbed with things, or
fashion … had he? But BMW's, and Range Rover's, and Jaguar's were
more than status and fashion. They were quality … and luxury. And
maybe quality wasn't a luxury at all; maybe it was an approach.

To the best.

In someone.

Made by someone who understood that.

Cooper liked, no loved, the cars at his dealership. But he also understood them. Understood they were isolated, brilliant art.

In the form of a machine.

He stretched and knocked a brass hammer off his desk he used as a paper weight. Where it had come from, he had no clue. It had just been on a stack of papers when he took over. Cooper picked it up, and felt the weight in his hand. It was warm, almost alive. And it felt good, the tool of a trade. He put it back on his to-do pile, turning it just so.

Maybe he needed to get out of here for a while? Take a ride. Rev up the Jag. Let the wind blow on his face out in the country.

Cooper was on an open road doing just that before he knew it. He clicked on his radio and surprisingly heard the strains of Jim Hart this time, singing about bringing back romance. The road his Jag ate up was now rural.

Country.

Deep.

One he hadn't been on before. Trees were older, bigger. Like a child's drawing of a tree, covering the paper--such a change from Southern California. And he realized in a flash he didn't miss California at all.

He drove past an orchard 'MacTamara's U Pick/We Pick' and pulled in on a whim. An elfin girl sold him a sack of crunchy apples called Honey Crisps. Biting in he discovered she was true to her word, as he was assaulted with crisp and sweet fruit all at once. Thanking her, he headed back to his car, past an old Victorian house.

Bed and Breakfast.

Obviously part of the orchard. A great golden dog wandered toward him, another was asleep leaning against his car door. "Honey

Crisp! Brae Burn! Come!" A boy; couldn't be more than eight or nine years old, whistled for the dogs from the porch. "Sorry mister." And the dogs raced to the boy's side and slobbered as he hugged them.

For just one split second Cooper was that boy, loving those dogs, feeling the warmth of them panting on his face.

A dog.

His mother had hated animals, and his father had no time. Cooper vaguely remembered being a boy and wanting one so bad--something of his own. To love.

When he was racing, he'd never considered indulging in one, since he was always on the move. And a dog had always smacked of commitment, responsibility. Things he seemed to avoid. Things he now did every day, naturally.

Those dogs didn't look like anything but warm sloppy hugs, their huge brown eyes looked like understanding, and love.

How could he have ever thought otherwise?

Cooper drove on, eating his apple, letting his mind play with the idea of a dog. What kind of dog would a man who sold British cars own? A British dog, of course. But not a King Charles spaniel or a skinny wimpy dog. No, a real dog. A man's dog.

He toyed with this idea as he drove. Tried it on. Saw his faithful friend asleep under his desk, an occasional soulful eye open, adoring. Waiting for a moment of his time, or just a look from him reassuring the animal he was in fact his.

Roads turned to lanes, small, winding; trees growing over, forming a canopy. Through them he saw sheep grazing, contented, unphased by the passing of his car. Their creamy white wool and black velvety looking stockings dotting the landscape--a contrast to the city or beach life he'd spent so many years at.

It was peaceful, gentle, almost just their very nature eeking out all his pent up stress. He spotted a black one among a flock and swiveled his car, caught by the charm of it.

A breeze kicked up, he could feel it playfully on his face. He felt a million miles from everywhere. Relaxed. Almost comforted. His apple finished, he drove on aimlessly.

And then he stopped.

He didn't know why.

The house was small.

Battered, weathered, forgotten.

A farm house.

Like in a painting ...

With gingerbread, and a winding path to the front door; narrow tall windows with peeling green shutters, and a chimney that had a crook in it, like a candy cane. Cooper laughed. Maybe it was Hansel and Gretel's house, and the chimney was in fact ginger bread, and a wicked witch was inside stoking up her oven.

But this house was friendly, comforting--nothing witchy about it at all.

Thinking nothing of it, he got out of his car, and walked to the front door which was rounded on top, maybe a little gothic. He hadn't really retained that architecture class he'd taken, when he'd been studying a bit of everything ...

He rapped and the door pushed open. Calling out, he heard his own voice echo. No one answered. He walked through a front parlor, passing a rose chintz sofa peeking out from under a dust cloth; to the back kitchen. A scarred table sat in front of criss cross organdy curtains looking out to the back.

To a red barn.

Gleaming in the sunlight, its pristine paint looking just like it had been lovingly given a fresh coat. Holly hocks grew near the huge doors, doors big enough to use as a garage for his cars.

As the thought washed over him a black sheep walked in front of the door, pausing and staring at him. Mesmerized by the velvet face and almost human eyes, he reached to the glass, as if he could touch it from the kitchen. The movement broke the spell, and the little black sheep darted off, its tiny bell tinkling. The ringing came through the glass, magically.

Cooper ran back through the front door and around the house, looking for the sheep. Elusively it was gone. He stood in grass that desperately needed mowing, the barn looming ahead. "Should I look inside?" But as the thought entered his head, black clouds appeared, thunder rumbled, and the heavens started dumping rain.

Instinctively he ran for his car, to put the top up. He almost beat the rain from back yard to front as he raced to his Jag. The top finally snapped in place, he lovingly wiped the seats down with the inside of his jacket. Now chilled, he started the engine.

The rain tormented, where just minutes before the sun had flooded warmth and blue skies. Reluctantly he knew he should try to beat the storm and head home--to the dealership.

To his little apartment over the garages.

To his rescue.

By the time he hit the hard road, it was a drizzle; when he reached the highway, he noticed the pavement was dry.

7

Elizabeth opened boxes with glee. As fast as UPS Jeff could bring them, she would rip in like a child at Christmas! Scrap books were priced; stickers were on cup hooks on the wall, bottles of glitter glue in baskets and still more arrived!

The Aunties were in heaven! They were camped at the round table in the bay window sipping tea, and helping put price tags on merchandise.

"What's that?" Elizabeth eyed a pile off to one side, of assorted scissors, glitter, background papers.

Bertie cringed. "Oh you noticed ..."

"Noticed? Auntie Bertie, that pile's as big as a bushel basket!"

"Well, it's me stash ..." And Bertie bit her lip nervously, "I mean, we've done without all these luxuries for so long that ..."

And Elizabeth's laugh rang out like tiny bells. She simply kissed Bertie on the top of the head and went back to work. There was a kitten and puppy section that had tiny chairs and a small table where little children could sit and mess about.

The oak shelves were all chock full by category, lovely, tempting. The bridal, engagement, and anniversary area was like its own little store--soft, fluttery, and romantic.

It made Elizabeth's heart skip a beat when she put it together and still gave her a twinge whenever she walked by it. A good twinge.

Scissors were on racks with paper to demonstrate all they could do, as cutting just wasn't cutting any more.

And the charms.

They were center stage. Elizabeth had tried to duplicate Dee's creative display idea and had them in tea cups by category. She also had ribbons so you could wear them, and planned on adding bracelets.

And why not? Dee was right; the charms were dear enough to be worn. Her own charms swung from a ribbon around her neck. Her good luck charms. She felt the weight of them bobble now and again, and it made her smile, and took her back to the trade show, and the charm booth, and Dee.

Jinx, from Fairchild's, stuck her head in the door. "Hey, how's it going?" Her eyes darted wildly, trying to take it all in. Jinx knew she hadn't been officially invited in yet but she couldn't stand it. She felt this was like her own little pet neighbor. And she felt she'd been the one to push the empty shoppe on Auntie Clara and Elizabeth.

But to Jinx's best recollection she just couldn't seem to remember it having so many cute appointments. Like the bay window. But certainly that wasn't new ... even though she walked past it a million times on her way to the bank or post office. Still. Jinx wanted to see in.

"Good, very good Jinx," Auntie Clara kept right on putting little price tags on some stencils.

"Well, can I, er, come in and look around?" Jinx's curiosity was uncontrollable.

"Now dear, when we're ready, we'll be ready," Auntie Clara went to the door and patted Jinx like a spoiled child. "We want the element of surprise. We're nearly there."

"But ..." Jinx knew these old ladies were far tougher than she was. "Well, I'm going to celebrate when you're finally done!" And Jinx left. Not in a snit, but still not happy to be left out.

"You know girls ..." Blanchie started idly, "That's an idea. We should, well, celebrate when we're ready. You know, throw a party--a grand opening party!"

Bertie and Auntie Clara's faces lit! "A party! Why what a great idea!"

Elizabeth couldn't imagine the work of a party on top of all the work they were now doing. It sounded exhausting, draining, not to mention expensive. "Uh, I don't know. I mean it would be a lot of work ..."

"Nonsense."

"And we hardly know anyone to invite ..."

"More nonsense."

"And ..."

"And nothing Lizzie! We'll have a party! We'll get Jinx in on it. And she'll spread the word!"

"You mean a big party?" Elizabeth started twirling a strand of her hair, nervously.

"Of course a big party!" Blanchie joined in, "Is there any other kind?"

"We'll throw it wide open! Why think of all the people we'll meet; potential new customers!" Bertie was rubbing her hands together. Auntie Clara was nodding in agreement, already planning.

"We'll have Colette, at the Patisserie, make us cookies that look like open books, like your sign," Bertie was starting to make a list.

"And invitations, that look like scrap books. You could design those Lizzie." Auntie Clara knew what kind of things bated Lizzie's imagination.

Elizabeth nodded slowly, grasping the idea of designing invitations over the party. Yes, she could do that. That's what she did best. The card could open, like a book and ... The wheels turned as she tuned out the party plans.

Somehow party planning, and invitation designing, took center stage over pricing. Around six o'clock Bertie finally admitted defeat. She plopped down in one of the chairs on coasters and slid around a bit like a five year old. "You know girls, I think we need food. I'm not used to all this work!"

Auntie Clara had finished the jumbo size bag of M&M's, except for the blue ones. "Not natural." They lay in a pile on the table. "Me stomach is calling for food!"

Elizabeth hated to stop; she had the rough sketch for the invitation almost done. A scrap book; of course, but she'd sketched the shop front and the Aunties. "I guess we could break. I drove past a roadside diner called 'Dinks'. It looked good."

"Diner food ..." Blanchie squinted.

Elizabeth wasn't sure if this was the beginning of a snub turning into a full fledged whine. Blanchie was rather particular.

But it took another turn with Blanchie, "I love diner food. Takes me back to New York City ..."

Elizabeth raised an eyebrow in question but got no further answer as they all started to wrap it up.

Dink's was packed. A weathered Cape Cod turned roadside burger joint, on a grassy yard. Picnic tables were filled with people having a great time, Chinese lanterns swung in the trees above, tacky and fun. You could smell deep frying as you got out of your car.

A stocky man with shaggy hair pulled back in a tail, wearing an apron that read 'I'm Dink' came out as they were heading in. He held a tray over loaded with what looked like onion rings shaped into loaves of bread!

"My goodness!" Auntie Clara let slip.

"My goodness is right darlin! Welcome to Dinks! These are me onion loaves!" And he headed off to a picnic table of eager diners. The screen door had metal bands across it that said 'Eat More Beef'.

Laughing, and already in a good mood, the odd foursome headed in. Blanchie fussed at her hair, "I'm not too old for this er, establishment, am I?" She certainly didn't want to be.

"Nonsense Auntie Blanchie!"

At that an equally elderly woman in another butcher apron greeted then at the door. Her apron read 'I'm never retiring!' She was granny round and her eyes sparkled. "Welcome to Dinks. I'm Biscuit."

Auntie Clara smiled, loving the name, and felt right at home.

"Will ye be havin' a booth or table?"

"Did I pick up a Scottish accent?" Auntie Clara was ready to clap her hands.

"Aye, ye did!" And Biscuit gave her full wattage, her crinkly eyes merry; she pushed back a wisp of silver hair that had escaped her bun. Auntie Clara practically hugged her. "Highlands!" Biscuit proclaimed.

"Muthill!" Auntie Clara matched, wondering if Biscuit had any idea where that was.

But Biscuit seemed to know it was near Stirling, and with that Auntie Clara felt a friend was made.

Bertie got a wistful look on her face, "I'm from up on the A93, just past Balmoral.

"Ah, the good Queen's country."

Blanchie, who was from Edinburgh, always a city girl, put in, "It's all Queen's country."

Biscuit looked at Elizabeth with a question mark.

"New York City," Elizabeth said shyly.

But Biscuit threw an arm around her. "Then you'll fit in just fine me dear." By this point they were at a round table, dead center, under a wagon wheel chandelier.

Pandora came over with a pad and introduced herself as she took their drink orders.

Biscuit came rushing over, "Now don't let our girl here fool you. She's Mrs. Dink!"

And Pandora blushed to the tip of her nose.

"And a bride at that!"

"Well hardly Biscuit."

"It's been nary long since you nearly ran over Mr. Dink and then not much longer before ye ran off with him," Biscuit explained and Pandora smiled in defeat.

At this point a weathered silver haired, drop dead man came out of the kitchen with the requisite butcher apron on. His apron simply read 'Roast Beef'. "Now lassies. I hear too much chatter and no orders." Then he did a mock bow to the group. "Ladies." And his grin was devilish. Time hadn't slowed it a bit.

They all got a little flustered, immediately under his spell.

"And it'll be four roast beef sandwiches then and an onion loaf."

There was no question mark at the end of his words.

"Jingles!" Biscuit reprimanded.

But the Aunties and Elizabeth laughed, "Righty then. How can we say no?" Bertie grinned as she spoke for the group.

"Ah, a lassie from me own shores." Jingles winked at her but headed off back to the kitchens.

Music wafted out over them. Piano with a bit of an edge, country yet somehow soothing. Elizabeth looked over in the direction it seemed to come from.

Pandora caught her eye. "That's Jim Hart. Ever hear his stuff? Great musician turned friend. Sometimes he has his pals playing with him. Looks like tonight he's alone--either way it's good music."

Auntie Clara and Elizabeth both stared, "Jim Hart? Our Jim Hart?" They said it in unison. But Pandora only laughed.

"You've heard of him?" Pandora asked with a twinkle. She and Dink liked his music so much she was sure everyone had heard of him. Still ...

"Heard of him? Why my Lizzie plays him on the sidewalk as she weeds and he's been blaring at us, though right nicely, while we've been pulling together the scrap book shoppe."

Elizabeth nodded in agreement, "And he got me here from New York City. Well not him exactly. But his music did. I swear it kept me going through some of those boring states." And then she laughed at herself, "Well maybe not boring, but boring from the highway ..."

Pandora laughed and called out, "Hey Jim, come over here and meet a table of your fans!"

And the women all got rather flustered when he actually did. But Jim turned out to be shy and rather darling, or at least that's how the aunties saw him.

Elizabeth saw him as shy or maybe just quiet and rather drop dead in that almost bigger than life way, not 'darling'. Though Elizabeth had a feeling she knew what the aunties were going for when they said darling. "You look like your music," She blurted out, and sure enough he did have a shy side as his ears got red, and he did a slow blush.

Followed by a slow smile.

Jingles came bounding back out of the kitchen. "You ladies hitting on my piano player?" And they all laughed. Jim said a few kind words and headed back to play. And the ladies settled back down.

They looked around and saw Dink bringing out two ridiculously gigantic frosted glasses dripping with ice cream. He set them on a table in front of a young boy and a tiny girl. Lifting his hands like horns, he started to moo at them, and laughing, left them cheering and mooing back.

Jinx caught sight of the Aunties, and Elizabeth, and walked over. "Black Cows--you know: Root Beer and Vanilla Ice Cream. It's rather a staple here." Jinx pulled up a chair. "Can Jefferson and I join you? It's a bit crowded tonight." Not waiting for an answer, she waved Jefferson over.

"Bart and Annie have been coming here for ages." Jinx indicated the serious little boy and the golden curl haloed girl.

It could hardly be ages, Elizabeth thought, they didn't look older than seven and maybe five.

"Their folks own MacTamara Orchard. Best apples this side of Michigan. You'll like them, the parents that is--Randi and Angus and the apples."

Elizabeth was sure the couple was Randi and Angus and not the apple varieties but still ... But she was sure she'd like them either way.

"We, we passed that orchard the other day when we went to look at some old furniture," Elizabeth remembered thinking it was picture perfect. Norman Rockwell picture. She'd wanted to stop, well not stop then, but come back some time.

Then she was too anxious to just see what furniture the aunties had stashed.

"They actually run the orchards with Angus' brother Jamie, and his wife Josie. I'll flag them over to meet you. They also run a bed and breakfast." And Jinx was up, gesturing wildly at a stunning blonde, and a quiet brooding dark fellow. By the time introductions were made, and five year old Annie had curled up in Blanchie's lap, fascinated by her many strands of pearls, Jinx had explained about the scrap book shoppe.

"And we're actually planning a grand opening party," Auntie Clara announced. And why not? These people, well, she wanted them to be her people, and Lizzie's people. "And of course Jinx, we need your help."

And Jinx beamed to be an almost insider. And she was in a way since it was Jinx's encouragement that got them even looking at the empty building.

"Mommy, can we go?" Annie was now jumping up and down rather like a spring toy. Randi looked helplessly at Elizabeth.

But Elizabeth was amused. She was rarely around children but thought how hard could it be? They're cute and bouncy with energy. All good. Well, at least this one appeared to be …

"We'd love you to come. Jinx will get me your address and well, yes, we'd love it!" Auntie Clara spoke for Elizabeth and why shouldn't she? Auntie Clara was single handedly running things, whether Elizabeth knew it or not. Well, not exactly single handedly. She had Blanchie and Bertie right alongside her.

Still Auntie Clara was a take charge kind of gal and she knew if the shoppe was going to be a success they all needed to reach out to any warm bodies that showed an interest.

And Randi surely had friends, friends who would also become customers. It was one thing to clean, and decorate a shoppe, even fill it with merchandise, but the real trick was to get people in the door.

At least once.

After that first visit Auntie Clara felt confident they'd be hooked.

And Elizabeth was both charmed and a little intimidated by the speed at which she was somehow making friends.

"Yeah! Yeah!" And Annie ran back off to her Black Cow as a party of its own took place. Bart was standing on his chair surveying the restaurant, and Annie was wildly waving to the aunties trying to explain to her brother about the party they were going to be invited to.

The scrap booking party.

The party was announced, the roast beef sandwiches were devoured, new people were met, and Jim Hart, Elizabeth's go to music, was there in person. The night didn't seem to be able to get any better. And Elizabeth had Auntie Clara to thank for it all.

"Dear, I got a call from, er, the owner of the BMW dealership, you know, where I take me Rover," Auntie Clara just tossed out.

Elizabeth raised an eyebrow but kept opening boxes. The shoppe was littered with UPS deliveries.

"Anyway, they'd like, well, were wondering that is, I mean since you are an artist and all …"

Elizabeth put down a stack of kitten and puppy stickers and faced her aunt, "Just say it Auntie, whatever it is."

It was rare that Auntie Clara fumbled over her words.

"Well, I know you're busy with the shoppe, and the lawn, and all." Auntie Clara looked a little nervous.

Elizabeth wasn't quite sure why Auntie Clara wasn't getting to the point. The point of whatever it was. "Not so terribly busy Auntie." But she did need to mow. Maybe tonight …

"Well, they are looking for a new logo--the dealership that is--updated so to speak. You could design one. You know, for their stationary, and their ads, and their sign or whatever …" There, Auntie Clara had gotten it out. She snuck a look at Lizzie but to her utter surprise saw it was a great suggestion, not a pull on her time.

Elizabeth perked up. This was her bailiwick. She loved these kinds of projects. Then she hesitated, "Uh, what kind of restrictions?"

"Restrictions dear? Why none. Just dream something up." Restrictions--Auntie Clara had forgotten to ask Cooper if there were restrictions.

Cooper had been eager to propose the idea, and finally confessed to Auntie Clara that Lizzie thought he was a mechanic, and well, he wasn't ready to tell her otherwise.

When Auntie Clara had objected he objected louder. "You don't understand, as a race car driver I had fans, not dates; women in love with my fame. Lizzie seems to like me, I think. I've never had that. I don't want her to be mesmerized by my owning that dealership, by power or ... or money."

Auntie Clara sighed, her heart squeezing for the young man. "But me dear, one day for sure she'll have to know."

But Cooper said nothing.

"Well, Auntie, what do they have now at the dealership?" Elizabeth pondered.

"Now? Why Lizzie, nothing really. You've been there. It's just a boring sign that says BMW, Range Rover, and Jaguar. Anything would be an improvement." It had even bored her so she knew it was bad.

"Oh yeah, I remember seeing it. It didn't say Mini Cooper." Elizabeth thought it was an over site. A sloppy one not to mention one of the more popular, or at least affordable cars, they represented. It had made her feel not wanted there.

But of course it was the Mini dealer also. And Elizabeth didn't think she'd trust her darling car to just any mechanic.

"See, you could incorporate the Mini in it." Hopefully not the pink Mini. "And of course they'd pay you," Auntie Clara tossed that out hoping it would help. By the light in Lizzie's eyes Auntie Clara thought maybe she'd struck a good note.

Pay ... extra money ... Elizabeth sighed. Yes, she had free rent, if she kept mowing, and dead heading, that is, and well, a small, very small, pocket change small salary. And the shoppe of course, would make money, after it stopped consuming money that is, and was, well, open.

"Uh sure."

"Sure?"

"Uh huh, it'll be fun." And Elizabeth knew it would be--she loved one of a kind projects. And from the looks of the old sign she really could do no wrong. Anything would be an improvement. Chances are she could wow them.

Auntie Clara let out a breath she didn't even know she was holding. She could report back to Cooper with success. A go. And Elizabeth was very talented, and when Elizabeth set her mind to something, she worked at a rapid rate.

Why, it would be easy, breezy, Parcheesi for her to do. And of course Elizabeth would have to eventually spend more time with Cooper, which Auntie Clara assumed was his plan along.

And hers too.

Elizabeth looked around the shoppe. She could easily work on free lance projects here while customers shopped. Distractions were just part and parcel with her old life at the agency. She could still help, even teach, and have an art project going, even have a free lance project setup, and get to it in between whatever.

Her mind almost worked better in a busy setting. And if her customers saw it, and asked about it, great, it would be her own little advertising for her side line.

And who knows, maybe some of her scrap book customers would want her to design something. Wedding, birthday, anniversary invitations ... She could help them make favors and place cards. After, all, scrap booking didn't have to just be in a scrap book.

Down in her basement flat, Elizabeth worked deep into the night on the car dealership. After scrapping about a million attempts, her mind drifted to Basil Herrington and his very art deco dealership: classy cars; classic logo.

So much of what she had seen day in and day out in New York had been very deco, bold, clean lines. Her mind started puzzling together deco looking images.

In another part of the apartment building, up near the very top, Auntie Clara was burning the midnight oil. She sat at her dining room table; an old Tiffany dragonfly lamp pulled forward illuminating her scrap book, a glass of lemonade and Pimms by her right hand. Her own sandwich forgotten, crusting up a bit. The lamp cast just the ever prettiest beam of light on her scrap book.

On Elizabeth.

Auntie Clara paged through the progress she'd made--Elizabeth had made--since they came together. She ran a wrinkled papery hand lovingly over the page with the pink 1940's appliances from the Sears catalog. How sweet they looked in the basement flat. Cozy, almost cartoonish, almost make believe.

And of course Lizzie had been tickled by them--and fooled. But they'd been the perfect look. The retro, 'I've been down here forever' look.

Auntie Clara rubbed her eyes. Almost make believe? They were 'make believe'. The Sears catalog was proof, wasn't it? And what looked like an old chaise lounge in the bathroom. Old? Auntie Clara laughed.

The furniture company had duplicated that very 30's looking chaise right down to the faded fabric. The million—dollar--I look-- old fabric. Fooled Lizzie it had.

Could have fooled anyone. It looked exactly like something Auntie Clara would have had up in her attic--if she'd had an attic. It was replicated to have that look. She'd just hoped it hadn't smelled too new. But it was fine.

And what about the garden out front? The only true part was that it had been a wreck. Ferguson, the grounds keeper, had really passed ... on. And left the yard a mess, and it continued to get worse. Okay die. It all continued to die--when he died.

But originally when Auntie Clara had 'purchased' the brown stone she hadn't planned on a garden out front, or even landscaping. Hadn't thought of it in her excitement. As a result when the brown stone became 'available' it didn't have any real plants to speak of. Or character.

It did have Ferguson, he came with it, sort of a gift with purchase. So Auntie Clara was pretty sure he was near his expiration date then. He seemed ancient even to her. Of course she'd been very fond of him, and he did putter around doing whatever odd job popped into his mind, though it wasn't usually gardening. And he had a mind of his own ... as if he wasn't quite real.

Well ...

It was the magazines that got her wanting a garden out front. All those lush magazines she'd see at the grocery store. All those plantings, and color combinations. And of course those shows on the House and Garden channel didn't help much either. They just fueled her desire for a few flowers, a few flowers at first.

Then maybe flower beds, or borders, or both. And maybe some shrubs, with top knots. Okay, topiaries.

A plan, a design plan.

As much as Auntie Clara thought the brown stone was the real deal, well, it needed landscaping. And with no real sense of color or design she tapped into Lizzie. After all she was a commercial artist.

But Lizzie's life was on a downward slide. And Auntie Clara knew it wasn't turning around by itself. How could it? The poor girl had too much going against her and no real guidance. Okay, no guidance. She was just bumbling along. And not very well. Auntie Clara had rationalized to herself that Lizzie needed her.

And of course Auntie Clara needed Lizzie. Being old was rather nice. No one questioned her eccentricities—ones she'd had all her life and were sneered at for. No, in old age, they were over looked, accepted, even thought of as 'cute'. Not that Auntie Clara wanted to be cute, but still, she felt free to do as she liked.

Say as she liked.

Certainly dress as she liked.

True Auntie Clara ran out of steam, well okay, got tired. But it was nothing a toes up in the afternoon couldn't fix. And she didn't have to really be anywhere at any special time. Punch a time clock in life so to speak, so if Auntie Clara was a little run down now and again it was okay.

She usually perked back up. Sure sometimes it took a fist full of Flake bars from Jinx's store or an extra wink with the TV lulling her, but on the whole she was healthy and just fine.

But Auntie Clara was lonely. Of course she had Blanchie, the faded fashion maven, and true friend. And dear Bertie, her out-doorsy alter ego pal. They were the best. Constant. And they understood what it was to be her age. They were. No explanations needed. No sorry looks. They accepted because they were right where she was.

There was comfort there.

Comfort in her pals.

And Auntie Clara seemed to know everyone in the community: Jinxy dear over at the shoppe, and Jinx's quiet husband Jefferson. Jefferson was still always kind and helpful to her despite his introverted ways and tight schedule. And Charlie and Colette at the Patisseries, so young and full of spirit with that just starting out wham that kept them hopping about. And that passion of being newly married that seemed to fuel their whole business.

No, Auntie Clara felt she was part of the community.

Maybe it was those young couples that caused the ache Auntie Clara couldn't seem to get rid of, she wasn't sure. But it was there sure enough, big and loud, nagging at her, complaining that she didn't have her own, her own Jinx and Jefferson, her own Colette and Charlie.

Her own family.

But of course she did. She had Elizabeth. Well, Lizzie to her. Always had been Lizzie, even when her mum moved away. And of course took little Lizzie with her. Lizzie had been her one real shot at a granddaughter.

Granted she was a great grand niece but in Auntie Clara's mind it was all the same. It was her little person to have tea parties with, and buy fluffy dresses for, and share a cocoa or a story.

No, Lizzie surely had been meant for Auntie Clara. For her to love. And she had loved her--still loved her. All those years, long after Lizzie and her mum moved away.

To the city.

New York City.

It wasn't that far. Not really. But for an old lady it wasn't just a hop and skip on the local bus. The bus no one seemed to ever take. The one the community called the 'big lonely'. Sidetracking, Auntie Clara sure hoped they didn't drop that bus …

No, New York City was a cab to the airport, and a plane ride, and another cab--all that jostling and odd smells and rude people. And a hotel.

And a chance that Lizzie would have any time for her or that her mother would even let her. And then she'd have to do that whole cab plane cab thing again, in reverse.

And as Lizzie got older, well Auntie Clara knew in her heart that her time for taking a little girl for a manicure or an ice cream had passed--passed her by. Lizzie was older. She wanted to do older girl things--with her pals. Date, run around, and experience all that was new, and fresh, and exciting.

And she, Auntie Clara, was old. So she'd just kept one eye out on her but never interfered. Never took that cab plane cab combo out to see her.

That didn't diminish the longing though.

Not at all.

So when Auntie Clara felt Lizzie needed her she knew it was time. Her time.

It was just that simple. And when Auntie Clara had explained it all to Blanchie and Bertie they thought she was crazy. But as Auntie Clara persevered with her plan they thought they wanted a little bit of that crazy for themselves.

Because they understood.

They understood because they were old, they had no one right there, and what Auntie Clara wanted was exactly what they wanted.

Did they have the nerve to take Auntie Clara's bold steps? Not really. But they sure as heck were going to enjoy Lizzie as if she were their own. It was, for all intensive purposes their chance too. So they helped Auntie Clara plot, and figure out the finer details.

Fine tune it, as Bertie kept saying, "Clara dear you need to fine tune this. You have one shot at it, and you need to make sure it all runs like a well oiled machine." And of course Bertie had been right. She usually was. So Auntie Clara labored over the details, and when she was ready she simply sent off that faded lavender letter, and well, sat back.

Auntie Clara fast forwarded, past the Mini Cooper, and the early stages of Lizzie moving to Wind Star, and to the shoppe. Auntie Clara loved that little business so ... She ran a finger over the bay window and a tear started to leak.

Just one.

Absently Auntie Clara brushed it away but another took its place. She'd always wanted to be a shoppe keeper. "In the trades," As her own mum had called it. In a tiny village.

Where everyone knew everyone else.

A family, so to speak, made up of businesses, each having a specialty, each unique to the others. And as a whole, needing each other, and also, as a whole, attracting people to them.

Auntie Clara suddenly remembered her own child hood when she was shy, wanting to be the bold one, the leader, but always afraid to take that first step. She'd played shoppe while her friends played with doll houses. Auntie Clara's was a shoppe made of a shoe box. With a piece of glassine for a bay window, she'd lovingly and painstakingly fashioned.

Her tiny shoppe held different things, depending on her age or mood. Once it was a pet store selling only rabbits, once a doll shoppe.

As Auntie Clara got older, she turned it into a dress shoppe selling the latest frocks. She would cut them from the Sears catalog. So many of her childhood toys came and went, but her little shoe box shoppe had stayed up on her closet shelf.

Still a dream.

Until now.

Auntie Clara's breath came too quickly and so did her pulse. Oh no! She started freaking and trying to calm down. "What am I doing? Does Lizzie even want to own a shoppe in a remote village? Am I forcing her? Controlling her? Is this my dream? My dream I'm living through Lizzie?"

And as the thought took hold and started to grow it frightened her. "What am I doing?"

She felt her heart race, and tried to take deep breaths, calming breaths. Breaths to get her grip back. Auntie Clara closed her eyes and sighed, heavy with the reality she was facing. She was sure it was okay to help Lizzie, okay, maybe manipulate was a better word, when she was sure it was for Lizzie's own good. After all she loved Lizzie.

Always had.

But this ... this was what? Who's good was this for? When had Lizzie expressed an interest in being a shoppe keeper? She was an artist, a commercial artist. And Auntie Clara knew in her own heart that it was she who was the wannabe shoppe keeper ...

Auntie Clara fell asleep at the dining room table, fear putting a black cloak around her. She dreamt it was opening day at the shoppe. Banners and balloons covered the front. Crepe paper dangled off the sign like a child's party.

The Aunties were in their finest; the displays packed, and change was in the vintage cash register. They'd even put in over sized pots out front over spilling with flowers. They almost had a ribbon cutting but decided it was, well, a bit much. Excitement tingled in the air, and a small crowd had gathered, waiting for the opening.

The Grand Opening.

Everything was ready. Ready to go.

Suddenly a Grey Hound bus pulled up front, its air brakes squealing. Lizzie raced from nowhere, a duffle bag over her shoulder. She still wore her grand opening little dress they'd talked her into. She swiftly kissed the Aunties as she fled out the door.

"But ... but ..." They all protested. Too shocked to say more.

"I'm going back to New York. To the City!" And Lizzie hopped on the bus and was gone.

Auntie Clara woke with a start. She'd put her head down on the dining room table and it had slipped, startling her. Or maybe it was the dream. The Tiffany light still glowed warmly, but a sickly cold had crept over Auntie Clara's skin. Her palms were clammy. She looked over at her drink but decided against it.

"A dream--just a dream. Nothing but a dream ..." But as she looked down at the scrap book the fear gripped her heart. "It's one thing to control me life, but Lizzie's ... I've made a mistake--a terrible mistake." She went to rip a page, the latest page, but couldn't. Looking at the pile of wedding dresses she'd clipped from Today's Bride, she crumpled them in a heap, and swept them in her waste basket. Wedding dresses she envisioned Lizzie in.

At her wedding.

To Cooper.

Sadly, slowly, with a heavy heart, Auntie Clara closed Lizzie's scrap book. She couldn't throw it out--wouldn't. It had been a part of her life now for a very long time.

A big part.

She got her aqua step stool from the kitchen, and lugged it to the dining room. Carefully Auntie Clara climbed the two steps, clutching her Lizzie book. She reached up, and slid it on top of her china cabinet, out of her way.

Out of her line of sight.

And maybe out of her mind.

Well, of course not out of her mind. It was, after all, her creation, her pet, her baby. Something she fiddled with every day. But maybe if it wasn't quite so handy ... Auntie Clara climbed back down the aqua step stool and just stared.

Then carefully and with a heavy heart she lugged the step stool back to the kitchen.

"I'll let her be. I will." This was a brave step, a new step. "I'll let her do whatever she wants. I'll, I'll just consider what I've done as raising her. Yes, I've raised her this far. And now, like any other young person, she'll have to be on her own—graduated--launched."

It was a momentous thought, but hadn't she given her sweet Lizzie every opportunity, every extra? Auntie Clara fretted, facing something she never thought out loud. "I'm old. She'll need to be on her own one day ..." And she gave one last sad look at the album on the china cabinet, and trundled off to bed.

The shoppe looked ready. Money sat in the cash register, all in its little slots. Bags sat ready to be filled. The windows had been Windexed again, and shone like diamonds. Colette, from the Patisserie, had been by earlier with her scrap book shaped butter cookies. The caterer was due any minute with finger food.

"Where's Lizzie?" Blanchie straightened her silk skirt for the millionth time. She'd had her hair touched up and it glowed.

Bertie was all decked out in what could only be described as a cocktail dress for a very old lady. On top of it she wore a cute little apron that read 'Creating Memories.' Her work apron. So the world would know she wasn't just shopping or simply lingering. She was working. She was part of the team that created this darling shoppe, and hopefully created memories. And Bertie was ready for all the excitement to begin.

Auntie Clara wore her best citrine jewelry and her worst scowl, remembering her dream.

"She's changing. She'll be here."

"On time?"

"In plenty of time," Auntie Clara answered confidently. But the confidence rang hollow. I hope, she thought. Oh, I hope so. There was plenty of time, guests wouldn't be there for another two hours, but the Aunties had a motto: 'be prepared' and that usually meant 'be early'.

And today was no exception. As a matter of fact, today was more important than ever.

The caterers came bustling in, and suddenly it felt like a party. The aromas of rich buttery tid bits filled the air. Blanchie turned on the CD player to their favorite Jim Hart CD. It had a bounce about it.

Happy.

Exciting.

Just like they felt.

Elizabeth shook out her long hair. She'd curled the ends, just a bit, for softness. Her dress was pink, short and flirty. Was it too much for a scrap book shoppe grand opening party? Elizabeth shrugged. It was, after all, a party.

Her lucky charms dangled from an extra long pink velvet ribbon she had attached them to. She spritzed her favorite perfume and added just a touch more lipstick.

She picked up her presentation for the BMW dealership. It was ready and in her opinion, stunning, simple, yet classic--and classy. She had used a deco font and had simply stacked the car names, one on top of the other. Then she angled around them in bold curved lines.

Elizabeth meant to start the sign with BMW but somehow her loyalty to her pink car got the better of her. And after all, it was the child, so to speak of the group. As she'd played with the lettering, she finally made the word Mini in all lower case and then switched to upper for the Cooper. Under this she'd spaced Jaguar, then BMW and based it all over Range Rover. It was simple, elegant really.

And sharp.

On impulse she picked up the story board covered in tissue and slipped it in a portfolio and took it with her.

When Elizabeth arrived the Aunties were pacing, nervous. She threw open the front door, a spring in her step. "I hear there's a party going on!" And grinning, rushed in.

They opened their arms, all glad to see her. Auntie Clara fought back a tear of relief.

"Now, now, come on. Let's open the sparkly! A celebration! We-- my Aunties and I are opening a business!"

And possibly for the first time Creating Memories was openly referred to as all of theirs. Not just Elizabeth's--but all of them. And the words felt like magic themselves.

Elizabeth left the portfolio on her desk, and popped the champagne cork, while noticing the Aunties had brought all their gorgeous old Waterford crystal! Imagine! For strangers! And at a party where people might leave an empty glass just anywhere... The thought was so decadent Elizabeth just grinned, rather foolishly at their generosity.

Carrying a small tray, she handed them drinks, "To us and our marvelous imaginations, and all our hard work--to scrap booking!" And she raised her flute in salute.

The Aunties mocked her gesture but all drank. And all seriousness disappeared in the bubbles and the party truly began.

To the auntie's relief Jinx and Jefferson were the first to come with Biscuit and Jingles, from Dink's Diner, in tow. Dink wasn't far behind with his bride Pandora. Larson, the town lawyer already had a plate loaded and was inhaling the tasty tidbits, chatting up the crowd.

Jinx beamed at all the progress, not quite believing how truly wonderful the shoppe had turned out. She pointed out things she'd never seen before to Biscuit as though she were an old pro and had been in dozens of times.

Bertie listened, amused, and touched, understanding wanting to be part of it all.

Biscuit had picked up a shopping basket, and was making her selections as though it was a going out of business sale, and she better hurry, and decide before it was all gone. But of course it was a grand opening.

And to Blanchie's trained eye, going very well.

The next time Auntie Clara looked up, she saw Lizzie surrounded by people and heard the warmth of conversation, the tingle of laughter, and a stray cord of Jim Hart.

Auntie Clara nabbed a shrimp puff and nibbled, relaxing for the first time all evening. She could hear people oohing and ahhing.

Little Annie, who Auntie Clara had met at the diner drinking a Black Cow, had picked up a shopping basket, and was loading it with Hello Kitty stickers. Her brother Bart had golden retriever stickers, and a bottle of Snapple, one in each hand. Auntie Clara smiled indulgently.

Bertie was working the cash register, letting Lizzie socialize.

And Blanchie was holding court like the grand dame she was, and as though this were a society party caught in time, not the opening of a tiny shoppe.

Jamie, Angus' brother, and his wife Josie were shopping. Josie had stencils of herbs and wild flowers. "I have a botanical business," Josie told Auntie Clara. "These will be perfect! It's at the orchard. Stop by some time." Then Josie took in a gulp of air, "MacTamara's U Pick/We Pick orchard, out on the black top."

Auntie Clara thought she would file that for the future, already curious.

Auntie Clara looked around at so many faces she'd never seen before. Faces she was pretty sure she would get to see again. And know. Everyone was friendly, in a party mood and excited.

Excited about all the merchandise.

And she gave a secret thanks to Jinx for helping with the guest list.

It was getting late and Cooper was closing a deal on a dozen Jaguars--a corporate deal. It meant a lot of business and he almost didn't care. He was missing Lizzie's party--her grand opening party.

When the last detail was finally ironed out, he practically kissed his clients, following them to the door. A quick trip of the lock and he was on his way.

Flowers! The florist box was on his desk! Cooper ran back in and grabbed it, grateful he'd thought to order some. He could have had them delivered but he'd wanted to bring them himself.

There were three gardenia wrist corsages for the Aunties. He imagined they'd blush and possibly fuss when he presented them. The flowers for Lizzie were Freesias. He wasn't sure what made him decide on the tender yellow blossoms. Maybe the fragrance ... He didn't know.

He found a space close by and carelessly abandoned the Jag as he raced to the shoppe. Golden light poured out the bay window along with music and laughter. He opened the door to a huge crowd. Not sure what he expected, he suddenly felt shy and self conscious with the florist boxes.

Lizzie was helping a small blonde child, showing her how a pair of scalloping scissors worked. She looked like a fashion model in a hint of a pink dress, her colt long legs ending in even taller heels. Her cognac hair swaying as she bent to help the little girl.

It touched him and he wasn't even sure why. He'd seen her looking stunning many times. Still ...

For some unexplainable reason she looked up and their eyes locked. Little Annie continued snipping paper but Elizabeth just stared.

Cooper wore a dark suit, contrasting with his sun drenched blonde hair.

Elizabeth stood, abandoning Annie, forgetting the child completely and slowly headed his way.

He just stared, didn't move. Or speak.

Auntie Clara watched from a tall stool near the cash register where she'd been resting, her feet dangling, smiling to herself. Biscuit was paying for some cookie stickers, and followed her glance. "Oh me," And they both sighed.

"I know," Auntie Clara conferred. It was obvious. Obvious to anyone who was looking.

"You made it," Elizabeth knew that sounded stupid, but for the life of her, she couldn't come up with anything better.

"I, I well, I was caught up at work." He knew it sounded like an excuse, and not a very good one.

Elizabeth gave him a quizzical look, after all he was a mechanic, and it was evening, Saturday evening.

But before she could question him or think about it he spoke, "You look ... magical." And then he blushed. My God, am I fourteen? But for some odd reason, she looked spectacular! Had he only seem her in cut offs? Hadn't they been to dinner?

She gave her head a little toss and laughed, sending her glorious hair swinging along with the trio of charms. He spotted the glint of silver dancing across her front and reached gingerly for it.

"My good luck charms." She was so used to saying that, it never dawned on her it sounded superstitious. It wasn't, of course, it was just sentimental. Okay, maybe a little superstitious, but definitely sentimental. They represented, well, everything.

The velvet cord they hung on was long, and he clasped the charms like prizes. "A car, a book, and a bell. You know this looks more like my car than yours."

"The designer gave me these. People put charms in their scrap books." And as she said this, he came back to earth, and of course the shoppe, and the party.

Reluctantly he let the charms go, falling from his hand. Suddenly he was aware of a million people, sounds, music, and scents of food. He forgot he had the florist boxes under his arm.

At this point, the Aunties, unable to resist, huddled near.

"Ladies ..." And of course they blushed like crazy. "I brought you something." He opened the first florist box, and produced three smaller boxes with the gardenia wrist corsages.

The gesture was too much for them. They swooned, and ooed, and got teary eyed.

The florist had been right with the wrist numbers, or he'd be awkwardly pinning the traditional ones on them. And he was absolutely sure he didn't want to do that.

Blanchie's eyes glistened over, "A gentleman if ever there was one. And gardenias--our favorite."

Bertie turned a sideways glance at Auntie Clara. "Did you ...?" She hissed.

But Auntie Clara shook her head no in disbelief.

Once all three Aunties had their flowers on, Cooper handed the last box to Elizabeth.

She was already beyond impressed with what he had done for three elderly ladies. She tipped up the lid and the fragrance abounded. Freesias. Pale yellow and delicate yet punched with scent. She drew the box up and buried her face in them.

This was the second time Cooper had brought her flowers; the first time when he ran over her flower beds. But she wasn't thinking of anything but the moment.

Cooper slipped one tiny cluster from the bunch and tucked it behind her ear, caught in her glorious hair. The contrast was breath taking--to Cooper.

Time stood still, just ever so briefly, then little Annie, chasing Bart, barged into Elizabeth. Cooper went to catch the little girl and suddenly he was back at the party. He placed a hand on Annie's blonde head, "Slow down now princess."

But little Annie just pouted and ran off.

Elizabeth felt slightly embarrassed and maybe a tad self conscious.

Auntie Clara had taken the florist box and headed off to look for a vase.

"Let me show you around."

Blanchie was at the cash register, it seemed people wanted to shop and party. The caterers were fluffing up the picked over platters, the bar tender was popping another champagne.

Cooper looked around, amazed. What had been a vacant store front with a few pieces of furniture was now an exciting business. And Lizzie and three old ladies had pulled it off! He looked at all the merchandise, fascinated by the odd scissors that pinked, scalloped, zigged, and zagged. And then at templates, stencils, background pages, stickers, and of course albums. The assortment was mind boggling. When had scrap booking turned into art projects? Not to mention big business.

Lizzie was busy showing the charms to a group, explaining how you could incorporate them in a themed page or wear them. Her own glistened on the ribbon around her neck. Cooper watched, fascinated as she animated. She obviously loved her business. And so it seemed did her guests.

The evening wove its magic and Cooper could see all the signs of Lizzie's venture taking off.

It was getting late, party goers were dwindling and he was hoping to take Lizzie home when his cell phone rang. The evening turned from serene to panic. He spoke just four words into the phone. "I'll be right there." A possible break in at the dealership, and he was flying out.

He ran into Blanchie at the door, "Uh, tell Lizzie I had an emergency at work and had to run."

And he was gone.

The very elegant Blanchie stood very still. She'd seen a look on Cooper's face she hadn't seen in a very long time. The look they used to call smitten. Blanchie had no clue what they called it today, none what so ever. And it was all clouded over with regret as he raced out. Reluctantly she headed for Lizzie, who was saying good night to Randi and Angus, and their kids.

Little Annie had declared she wanted to live in the scrap book store, quite vehemently, and that she wasn't leaving. Randi was expressing her embarrassment but Elizabeth was touched.

"Annie, you can come back. We'll sit over here," And Elizabeth indicated a place at the Aunties table in the window. Annie's bottom lip quivered, as she looked over at the table. "That's the Auntie's table, and they also own the scrap book shoppe."

"They do?" Annie looked around for the elderly business women.

"Uh huh--they know more about scrap booking than anyone I've ever met. Why their scrap books are practically magic!"

"Magic? Magic scrap books?" Annie forgot angry and was now excited. "I want to learn how to make a magic scrap book!"

Bertie stopped with a drink mid way to her mouth, Auntie Clara dropped an empty platter of finger food, and Blanchie just felt tired, very tired. But she still listened, carefully.

"My dear ..." Blanchie stepped in, "All scrap books are magic. And we'll teach you how when you come back."

"You promise?" Annie did the cross your heart thing. Blanchie just stared and then it sank in, and she crossed her own heart, and nodded. "And my friends?"

Dear God, it'll be Pre School, but Blanchie nodded again. Annie threw her sticky hands and pudgy arms around Blanchie's knees in a hug. All dignity finally melted and Blanchie reached down and scooped her up into her arms. "My little dear, why you'll be our mascot. We'll keep an honorary spot always ready for you."

Annie had no idea what any of this meant but she did know it was good. She gave Blanchie a smacking kiss and shaking her blonde curls said "Deal!"

The MacTamara's finally left, Annie appeased, and the Aunties, and Lizzie were alone. The party food picked over, the drinks gone. Plates and glasses littered the tables along with balled up napkins. Auntie Clara closed out the cash register; Bertie tripped the lock on the door.

"Girls ..." Blanchie began, beaming but exhausted, "Well done! Great party, and if I'm not mistaken, many new customers and friends!"

And it felt successful! They all felt it! Displays were picked over but not trashed, and they all had a chance to write up a sale, use the new shoppe bags, and tissue, and actually help customers make selections.

"It's fun!" Auntie Clara declared, "I didn't expect it to be so much fun!" Her satin party shoes were tossed aside as she padded around in her stockings.

"And everyone seemed so taken with all our merchandise," Elizabeth grinned, her own heels abandoned. Then she looked around. "Oh, I guess Cooper left."

Wincing, Blanchie felt awful, "I meant to tell you dear, but then little Annie had her melt down. He said he had an emergency at work, and he flew out of here. He did look sad to leave though," Blanchie added that as an afterthought, seeing the light go out of Lizzie's eyes.

"An emergency at work?" Elizabeth shook her head. It was, after all Saturday night. But she took a breath and decided not to let it ruin her perfect evening. People had shopped! Actually shopped!

As if reading her mind, Auntie Clara said, "I know I was surprised too! They seemed to like everything."

"Like?" Blanchie was having one last glass of champagne. "They loved everything! Why I think you are going to have to re-order charms! They went like crazy! People couldn't buy just one!"

"And the stickers!" Bertie piped in, "People acted as if they'd never seen stickers!"

They all tidied up and talked nonstop, but Auntie Clara put it best, "I think me dear, I think we are launched!"

Just before they all dragged out, Auntie Clara spotted the portfolio on Lizzie's desk. "Is this what I think it is?" She asked hopeful.

"It is Auntie Clara--I don't know why I brought it here, I could have run it upstairs for you. It is self explanatory, and well, I hope they like it. And you, I hope you like it."

Elizabeth drove home, tired yet excited. She went to pull off the tiny pink dress and her hand caught on the sprig of Freesia. Carefully she removed the blossoms and wandered to the kitchen for a drinking glass. Filling it with water, she slipped in the flowers. The fragrance seemed to come alive. Carefully she set it on her bedside table.

And fell asleep.

Dreaming of Cooper.

8

The shoppe was nothing short of a miracle. It seemed there were always at least two or three customers browsing, and a couple at one of the tables working on a project. The Aunties were spending more time there out of necessity, between unpacking new merchandise, and running the cash register.

Bertie seemed to have developed a knack for displaying new merchandise; Blanchie led small informal classes with elegance. Auntie Clara sold. Her own personality was so contagious that everyone loved to be around her. And that old adage, sell yourself and you can sell anything seemed to be written about her.

"Are the Girl Scouts coming after school on Wednesday?" Bertie asked Lizzie.

"Uh huh, but I think there will only be twelve this time." They were making a page with all the Girl Scout sayings on it, trimming it with stickers, buttons, and ribbons. It was for their creative badge.

Their leader had decided twelve to fourteen pages, each one a different theme, would qualify for a badge. "We need to come up with some more themes for those pages."

"I know maybe we should stretch out those sayings and only do one per page?" Elizabeth tossed out.

"That's as good as anything. But aren't they motto's not sayings?"

Lizzie shrugged, she was clueless. She hadn't been a Girl Scout. She'd been living in New York City. "We can vote today to see which one goes first."

And Bertie looked relieved. After all, it was a lot of children with even twelve, and there would probably be other shoppers. And children's temperaments not only ran the gambit but fluctuated in seconds. The phone rang, disrupting their plans.

"Lizzie, it's Cooper ..." Blanchie passed her the portable. For some reason they hadn't seen each other since the grand opening party but managed to talk every day.

Elizabeth took a deep breath and picked up the phone.

"Lizzie ..." Cooper never called her Elizabeth. He hesitated just a bit. He wanted to let her know he'd be gone for a couple of weeks.

She didn't know him well enough to ask where he was going, did she? Regardless, he didn't volunteer any information. An awkward pause followed. How would she ever get to know him better if he had all these emergencies, and now he was going to be gone? Maybe he didn't want to get to know her better ... and yet, she thought of the Freesias long gone save the sprig she'd pressed in her scrap book.

"But I'll call you," It sounded lame even as he said it. Why don't I just say I'll be in Europe for a car expo looking at new models, new trends? After all, she does seem to care for me regardless of my job status. Maybe it wouldn't change if suddenly I escalated from worker bee to King bee? Was there even a King bee?

She gave him some luke--warm response, and Cooper hung up knowing in his heart what this relationship needed was nurturing not distance.

Elizabeth just stared at the phone. Leaving? She could hear Blanchie and Bertie in the background. They sounded as if they were trying to recite the Girl Scout pledge. But they sounded far far away. A tear slid down her cheek, releasing just a drop of the pent up regret she felt.

"Lizzie?" From the little fridge she'd felt they needed, Auntie Clara was handing her a Diet Pepsi. It was cold, the effervescence waking up her mouth, tingling down her throat, bringing her back. "Me dear, don't worry." It was as though Auntie Clara knew.

Elizabeth nodded half heartedly and then put her mind back on the Girl Scouts.

"Should we have snacks for them?"

But Auntie Clara shook her head no, "Maybe Snapples, at the end. We don't want a mess," And looked around at all the perishables.

"Why don't I make some cute labels for the Snapple's and we'll give them to the girls as they leave?" Elizabeth wanted them to feel it was a special outing. And she wanted them to want to come back, to do another page.

Auntie Clara nodded and they headed to the stickers and ribbon.

The fact that Cooper was gone flitted in and out of Elizabeth's mind at the oddest times. She was busy, too busy--too busy to dwell. The Girl Scouts were now regulars along with many of their moms. Blanchie was teaching Memories 101. Such a silly name, Elizabeth had originally thought, but for some reason, everyone seemed to like it. Blanchie had eighteen in her class every Thursday.

It seemed Elizabeth, Auntie Clara, Blanchie, and Bertie never had time to work on their own scrap books; there was just so much to do at the shoppe. Details that needed their attention and general sweeping up and tidying that simply had to be done every day.

And new merchandise. It just kept coming in refilling the bare spots, keeping the shoppe chubby with goodies.

It was early one Monday; Auntie Clara was running the vac. "That glitter gets everywhere." Bertie was opening UPS, Blanchie was next door getting coffees and Elizabeth was reworking the giant cork board she'd put on the wall.

The board held a new scrap book idea from back ground pages and stickers to buttons, ribbon and charms. Today's was a trip to the city! Elizabeth had put in a playbill and a menu from a fancy restaurant she'd printed off on her computer. She added part of a walking map, a charm of a tall building and ...

The phone rang. While still wondering what else to add, Elizabeth grabbed it absently. "Creating Memories, this is Lizzie, er Elizabeth."

And then she froze.

And listened.

"Are you sure?" Was all Auntie Clara and Bertie heard her say? Auntie Clara stopped the vac discreetly and edged closer.

"Can't one of the others do it?"

More pauses.

"Collaborate? I can't collaborate! The only person I ever even came close to collaborating with was Bob!" Elizabeth thought of Bob at the old agency. How he'd stopped seeing her after she got fired.

After another silence Elizabeth spoke, "Oh, he wants to collaborate with me? And the client really wants me back?"

Elizabeth looked around the shoppe--her shoppe. "I ... I don't know. I mean, I've made other plans and well ... Yes; I could come for just this project. The Granville Auction House had always been my favorite job." She twisted a strand of her long hair, and Auntie Clara bit her bottom lip.

Bertie sat down, collapsed really, staring off into middle space. She knew. Knew it wasn't good. Bertie strained to hear more of Lizzie's conversation.

"Tomorrow? Well, I guess I could. Hotel? Well, yes I'd need you to put me up somewhere. How long? Oh not long ... well, can I get back to you? No? No? You need an answer? That is a lot of money. Yes, yes I guess I could be there. A ticket at the airport? In my name?" And Elizabeth listened intently for the rest of the details.

Elizabeth clicked the phone off and jumped up in the air, "They want me back!" She practically hollered, "My old agency! The one that tossed me out like ... like old garbage without so much as a 'thank you very much'! They want me back! Well, the Granville Auction House does! Imagine? For a promotion! And a new image! And they want me!" She swung her arms out, all but twirling.

At this point Blanchie returned with a tray of coffees, "Chocolate raspberry mochas girls!" Blanchie saw Elizabeth dancing wildly! "We're ... we're celebrating?" Trying to catch the spirit. Then her eyes moved to a sitting Bertie, her head down in her arms, and then Auntie Clara, whose face was ashen, save a stream of tears.

"Lizzie ... Lizzie ... Lizzie just got a call."

"A call? Yes?" Blanchie still clutched the coffees. She needed more information. How long had she been gone? Minutes, simply minutes.

"From her old agency," Auntie Clara barely got it out.

"In New York," Bertie added, as if they all didn't know where that agency was ...

"City," Bertie added the city part, because she was too freaked to know better.

"That's right Auntie Blanchie!" Elizabeth came over and smacked a kiss on her cheek. "I'm going back! To the city! They want me back! To work on the Granville Auction House!" And the smile practically covered her face.

"Going ba ... back?" Carefully Blanchie set the coffees on the counter, loosened the silk scarf around her neck, and took in a deep breath.

"Back where?" Of course Blanchie knew where. She felt the knife stab to her heart that Auntie Clara was feeling--felt it herself, and was sure Bertie did too. "Oh my dear, are you ... sure?"

"Auntie Blanchie! They want me back! After the way they treated me!"

"Exactly dear ..."

"But now they must realize it was a mistake! They'd made a mistake, a horrible mistake!"

Auntie Clara continued to weep silently.

"And you'd well, you'd consider leaving?" Blanchie was now knotting the end of her scarf. Crumpling the silk up, and tying it, and untying it.

"Tomorrow! I have a flight at 9:00 am!"

"But ... but ... the shoppe dear?"

Finally Bertie came to her senses, "And the Girl Scouts? They'll be here; they'll want you to help them." It was all she had.

"Nonsense! You can help them," Elizabeth was beaming, oblivious, "You're better at stencils than I am and Blanchie explains far better and ..."

Finally Auntie Clara's glaze cleared, replaced by what could only be called anger. "You don't understand! This is your shoppe! And you're considering leaving?"

"I am leaving ..."

"Abandoning! Abandoning us!" Now Auntie Clara was shouting.

Elizabeth stopped. Her happiness froze. "I'm er ... I'm not abandoning you ..."

"And you call it?" Bertie snuck in not trying to hide the sarcasm.

"I'm--well, I'm simply going back. You don't understand. This is my agency--the one that fired me. And now--well, now they need me!" Elizabeth tried to sound sweet but she knew she sounded defiant. She couldn't help it. She headed to the door, she had to pack.

Auntie Clara's voice was now a whisper, "We ... we need you."

But Elizabeth wasn't there to hear. Physically she was on her way to pack. Mentally she was already gone.

The driver took Elizabeth to the Hilton and deftly carried her luggage. The concierge was expecting her. The suite reserved by the agency was ready and waiting; her new home away from home.

The fruit basket looked like a prop from an old movie. The bed looked crisp, turned down. The desk had an internet connection. The mini fridge had little bottles of liquor to celebrate.

By herself.

She longed for a diet Pepsi...

Elizabeth left her luggage, flipped her hair, and grabbed her brief case. She had a hard time finding that briefcase back at her little basement flat. She'd packed it, well, never expecting to use it again. It had been over the pink bubble fridge in a cabinet, next to the glasses with maps of the states. The glasses she'd used with Cooper, when he'd first taken her to dinner.

After trashing her garden.

Cooper ... She hadn't called him. Was he still out of town? She stopped for just a second wondering. Wondering what he was doing, where he was, and of course, why she hadn't heard from him. Or for that matter called him herself. They'd had what she was pretty sure was a great connection.

Pretty sure.

There was a closeness yet with a zing. Not necessarily sparring, well okay maybe a little, but also an unspoken understanding of each other. At least she thought so. Was she so insecure or was she just inexperienced that she didn't know, know for sure? With a sigh she realized maybe a bit of both.

Funny she should have a thing for a mechanic ... Not that she ever pictured herself with a certain type before. She hadn't. She always figured that was up to Mother Nature, and she would just go along for the ride.

Because she didn't know what type she'd like. Oh she'd learned what type she didn't like but that usually had nothing to do with his career choice. It was how he acted and how he treated her.

Maybe Auntie Blanchie was right in her theory of asking more ... and getting more--asking to be treated better by simply expecting it, and acting better. Well, Cooper certainly treated her better, better than anyone else she'd ever known. And even without the comparisons, just better. True he teased her, but he also respected her.

It wasn't that she felt good around him, which went without saying. She felt like herself. The self she wanted to be, saw herself as. Not able to put it in words she just sighed, realizing she missed him.

And did he miss her? Think about her? She had no clue--none what so ever.

Cooper had certainly teased her about her silly car. Well it was silly. But she could refer to it as silly in a tender way. She wondered if it was safe in one of Auntie Clara's garages. Of course it was safe. It was Wind Star.

But didn't a car need to be driven now and again to, uh, keep the oil moving through it or something like that. She had no idea. She was clueless. Had she left her good sunglasses on the dash? She was pretty sure she had. And her favorite pink Burberry scarf was on the back seat. Well back bench, still for her it was a back seat. She might need that scarf ... and those sunglasses.

Elizabeth's mind drifted to her garden ... When had it become 'her' garden she wasn't sure? It wasn't hers at all. It was Auntie Clara's, and management, whoever management were. The unseen people, or company, that continually had flowers delivered for her to slave over.

Then she laughed. Why it was hardly slaving. It had been fun, no, exhilarating to put the flowers in. True the prep work had been rather back breaking, or at least monotonous. But when the ground was cleared, and the flowers delivered well, it was different then--exciting really, if she could call gardening exciting.

Coming up with her own little plan, and then getting them planted had melted the time away.

In a good way.

A fun way.

And the end results really were quite magical. Hard to actually believe it was the same shabby stoop she first saw.

When she came home.

Then she stopped herself. It wasn't home; it was Auntie Clara's brown stone. But a tiny corner in the back of her mind knew it felt like it. Felt like home.

Regardless, her garden was a hit, even Auntie Blanchie and Auntie Bertie seemed to love it, and after all that work she couldn't let it just slide into oblivion like Ferguson had. After all Ferguson had died ...

Who would mow it for her? She couldn't picture Auntie Clara huffing and puffing with the mower, or even getting it out of the back shed. Should she call Jinx? Would she have time? Did she even know Jinx well enough?

What about the geraniums? They needed dead heading on a regular basis, and the marigolds, she planned to save some seeds ... for next year ...

But Elizabeth pushed this all aside as she hit the lobby, bounced back in the car, and the agencies driver whisked her to the agency.

Back.

To work.

🐚

Auntie Clara unlocked the shoppe. Bertie was late. Blanchie had a hair appointment. Auntie Clara was alone. Coffee. She should head over to the Patisserie for a coffee.

But first she needed to turn on the lights, put the money in the cash register, and turn on the CD player. Where was the CD player? It always seemed as though music just drifted out at her. Soothing. Cheerful.

They needed a coffee maker. There wasn't time to leave and get something.

She opened the little fridge and pulled out one of the Diet Pepsi's Lizzie was so fond of. Untwisting the lid, she sipped; cold, fizzy, almost biting. The caffeine seeped into her system. Auntie Clara really wanted a hot mocha coffee to sooth her awake, not a cold sparkling bang.

Finding the CD player, she turned on Jim Hart. He sounded sad today, singing about changes and things lost. His words blended with his piano, and rolled over her. At first they made her feel worse, if that was even possible. Then she decided maybe he made her feel just a tad better. A tad.

She sat.

On a tall stool.

And dangled her feet and let her mind drift.

To New York City.

To Lizzie.

How was she doing? Where was she staying? Oh yeah, some hotel. Did she miss us? Of course she missed us. Didn't she? Well I miss her. So does Blanchie and Bertie, though they don't want to talk about it.

Again. And again.

Slowly Auntie Clara got up and started the routine of readying the shoppe to open. There was a box from UPS no one had gotten to yet; she hefted it onto a work table and sliced open the top. Stickers. Amazing how heavy a carton of stickers could be ... She got price stickers to price the stickers and laughed at the irony.

These were wedding stickers. Little brides, bouquets, diamond rings ... Auntie Clara wanted to be using them in her Lizzie scrap book, or on invitations for a shower or a luncheon ... for Lizzie and Cooper. She wanted to sprinkle them around her flat to remind her of an upcoming wedding.

An upcoming wedding, which only raced around her mind, and not in reality--not even close. The future bride was gone, and for that matter no one had really heard from the man Auntie Clara referred to as the future groom. Cooper.

Auntie Clara sorted the stickers by style, putting all the diamond ring packets in one pile, ditto for the bouquets, and on to the veils. And as she sorted she got sadder.

How could she ever have gotten all this so tangled up--tangled up in her head? How could she have wanted a situation so much that now it just ate at her? And she knew it wasn't a situation at all.

It was Lizzie.

Lizzie living here, being nearby, running a store here, marrying here, settling in here ... So Auntie Clara could see her whenever she wanted. Talk to her whenever she wanted.

And of course love her.

Auntie Clara started to work and her mind drifted to Blanchie's stream of accusations.

"How could this happen? How could you let this happen? What have you been doing? Why haven't you been working on your Lizzie scrap book?" Blanchie had been adamant, accusing, blaming.

Auntie Clara was afraid to tell her; confess.

"It's never failed us before! Clara! What did you put in her scrap book that got mis ... misinterpreted?"

"I ... uh ... I ..."

"Spit it out Clara McGillicuddy!"

"I ... I didn't do anything!"

"Oh yes you did!"

And then Auntie Clara broke, "No ... no I didn't. I, well, I haven't been working on Lizzie's book ..." There, it was out. She said it--barely. But it was out. Finally out.

"What? Not working on Lizzie's book? What are you talking about? After you found the gardenia corsages, what did you put in next?" Blanchie was fuming, and Auntie Clara was a little afraid Blanchie might pop a blood vessel.

"I, well, I didn't put in the gardenia corsages." Auntie Clara's sigh was loud. Couldn't help it, didn't want to. It was all too much for her--way too much.

"Of course you did!" Blanchie squinted at her. A look Auntie Clara had actually taught her. Now, used against her.

"No, no I didn't." Auntie Clara fumbled with the words. She felt a bead of sweat on her own brow and her own pulse kicked in. She needed to sit. And breath. In and out. In and out.

"What are you talking about?"

"Cooper, he did that by himself." Even Auntie Clara had been shocked. Really, they just didn't make them like Cooper any more. But there he was, so she supposed they did ... Looking like to-day and acting like yesterday ... Her mind was rambling--rambling away.

Poor Cooper.

No Lizzie.

Poor me.

"Impossible! Unheard of!" Now Blanchie was just out and out shouting. Her elegant face was not only red; it was beginning to get contorted with rage.

"Maybe, but he did," Auntie Clara was resigned now, resigned to Blanchie's rant.

"Is it the shoppe? Have you been too busy? You're behind?" Blanchie demanded.

"Uh no. Well yes. I mean, the shoppe does keep me busy--all of us busy. It's just ..." The shoppe was exhausting, to put it mildly, fun but exhausting. She'd had no idea ...

"Well?" Blanchie softened; strong arming Clara had never worked.

"Oh Blanchie," Auntie Clara wouldn't crumble, "You have to understand."

Blanchie looked nervous--felt nervous. "You haven't lost the knack?" Oh my God, Blanchie felt a bead of perspiration on her perfectly made up face. It was on her forehead where the tension headache was starting to bloom. Explode.

"Oh no--I mean, I don't think so ..." Auntie Clara owed Blanchie an explanation. After all she'd dragged Blanchie and Bertie both into this project.

The Lizzie project.

Blanchie didn't push her; but it cost her. She could feel the heart burn starting.

"I don't know how to explain ..."

Slowly, Blanchie spoke, "At the beginning Clara dear, at the beginning."

Auntie Clara plopped down on a chair and started to tell Blanchie about the toy store she'd made as a child, the one she actually still had, on the top shelf of her closet. How it had been her dream to run a shoppe. How it had even changed over the years as she changed. But it still remained.

A dream.

Always a dream.

Her dream.

"And now its Lizzie's dream Clara," Blanchie soothed.

"Is it?" Auntie Clara raised one penciled eyebrow. She knew it wasn't--not at all. Lizzie's dream was at her agency, back in New York. New York City. Far far away.

"Well of course it is," Now Blanchie was getting a shade impatient. Just a shade.

"But we don't know that ..." Auntie Clara had a look in her eyes Blanchie had never seen before.

"Of course we do," Blanchie squinted.

"No, we told her to open a shoppe. A scrap book shoppe. She didn't even pick the type of shoppe to open. We picked that for her." There, Auntie Clara said it. Clearly, she hoped. Still it was out there now.

"Suggested--we suggested," Blanchie was firm.

"Yes we suggested. And so did Lizzie's scrap book." Auntie Clara took a deep breath, a clearing breath. "No one, and I mean no one, stands a chance against the three of us when we suggest something. And you know it. We each subtly tackle from a different direction--from our strength. It's a pretty sure thing. Then add in Lizzie's scrap book; oh Blanchie, she didn't stand a chance." Her bottom lip quivered, just a little.

"So ..." Blanchie squinted. More squinting.

"Lizzie--she's me blood. I don't have much family left. And she's ... well ..."

"I know dear, she really does remind me of you--then." Blanchie was off in middle space somewhere. All traces of yelling at her friend now set aside. She saw Clara as she had been. Really still was, just in a slightly different package.

Okay older.

Auntie Clara nodded and swiped at a tear, wishing she was tougher, just a little tougher. "I took her ... her freedom away Blanchie. Are those her dreams? I have no clue. They're me dreams. They're mine." And then that single tear multiplied and suddenly all that pent up fear, and sorrow, that was starting to drown her poured out.

Blanchie produced a Chanel scented hankie and started to dab, carefully, slowly. Finally she took Auntie Clara's face in her hands, "Oh Clara--I didn't know. I really didn't."

"Blanchie, I normally never ever feel guilty when we do, what we do. But ..."

"Oh Clara ..."

"And I don't know what to do." Auntie Clara whispered, "I really don't. Shouldn't she be able to do--whatever? Whatever she wants?" Of course Auntie Clara's face said it all.

And Blanchie knew she was right--very right. Sadly and slowly Blanchie nodded yes.

"But oh Blanchie ... I miss her so."

And Blanchie cried right along with her.

9

Bob met Elizabeth at the door of the agency, "Missed you Elizabeth." He looked slick, sharp, professional, handsome. But did he go to kiss her? Hug her? No.

"Great suit Bob. Thanks." Elizabeth expected to feel more. She felt glad to be back. She felt ... she felt she should feel a little more zing. Still she was glad to be back.

Bob ran a hand through his dark combed back hair. A style that took chiseled good, no great, looks to pull off. "I'm glad you're back," He said the words. They didn't ring true but at least he said them. He knew she was the key to this project. So he said them and was nice.

Nicer than he really knew how to be.

Kinder than Elizabeth had expected.

Relief washed over her; after all they were going to be working together—collaborating--on this project.

"Your old desk is still there."

"Really?" Elizabeth hadn't expected that. She hadn't been replaced? Maybe they really were just cutting back. They walked together back to the artist's cubby holes. The scent of artists paint was as familiar as her own cologne. The hum of computers, the music of the agency glided over it all.

One of the partners waved, "Glad to see you back Elizabeth," And kept walking, as though she'd been on vacation--far away. To a place she could never have imagined. And she had a very developed imagination.

"We're meeting with the auction house in the morning. I've laid out their old art and some ideas I've had," Bob was in work mode already.

Good. She wanted to get to work. Elizabeth nodded and started to leaf through papers. "And a list of what they're looking for?"

But he didn't answer.

Maybe he hadn't bothered to ask. To find out. He always had his own ideas. Still ... The Granville Auction house was special to her.

She wanted this to be special. She didn't want them happy. She wanted them thrilled. She wanted them to love what she did for them because it was just what they wanted ...

Bob handed her a folder. Their hands brushed and she remembered when they'd dated. It seemed like a long long time ago. How could that be? How long had she been gone? Long enough to learn how to use a lawn mower and open a shoppe.

Hmm.

The lawn.

The shoppe.

Elizabeth pushed it aside and started to make notes on the list of requests. A logo. For an auction house. Updated. Old but somehow new. The wheels started to turn. She skimmed the list down to a notation for a commercial. Fun! T.V. spots were always exciting, granted challenging to turn the flat art to 3D, but something that always got her pumped.

It did seem like old times.

The receptionist ran out for salads, and Elizabeth and Bob kept working. They had a million ideas between them, they just needed to narrow it down and then clean it up.

Though so far she hadn't heard one that sounded too exciting from her or Bob. It was a million versions of same old, same old.

And Elizabeth was pretty sure this was not what the Granville Auction House had in mind.

Not even close.

"We can work over dinner," Bob sounded like old times.

"Great," She kept working, not even looking up.

"I'll stop by your hotel." It wasn't a question, just a statement.

Then Elizabeth stopped. It would be so easy to get room service and spread out all their work in her big suite.

Near her big bed.

"Why don't we meet at Reynolds?" She suggested a restaurant with big tables. Close to the hotel. She wasn't ready to pick up everything where it had been. Not even close to ready. And she realized that chapter of her life was done and buried.

"Okay." Bob hesitated as if he wanted to say more but stopped. He finished with, "Then I'll see you at Reynolds."

Their dinner was uneventful as was their pow-wow to jump start the Granville Auction campaign. Bob's ideas were all rehashes that Elizabeth had heard a million times. They were slick, quality, but well, unexciting.

She struggled to keep up, eating absently, bored to tears. What was she eating? She couldn't tell you--something low cal and dainty. She was thinking back to her roast beef sandwich at Dink's Diner. And the onion loaf, deep fried onion rings molded into a loaf, like a loaf of bread. Hot, sizzling, greasy and outrageously good.

"Well, we'll start again tomorrow," And Elizabeth escaped back to her hotel. She walked along the short distance just to let the night air clear her head. It was sticky out. The night air was thick, hard to breath. Her allergies were starting to come back. She swiped at a watery eye and kept walking, fishing in her hand bag for a Kleenex.

Walking past designer's stores with famous logos--her old haunts, her old favorites. She forgot to look in the windows. Her feet hurt. Why was she wearing such tight shoes?

She didn't know.

The hotel loomed ahead impersonal but still her home.

For now.

As Elizabeth slid out of her suit, and into an oversized T shirt Jinx had given her, she stared in the mirror. The T shirt read 'Congratulations on creating Creating Memories'. Obviously Jinx had had it made at Kinko's, but still Elizabeth had been thrilled to tears. And she cherished it, and hadn't wanted to leave it behind.

She sat on the edge of the bed, swinging her legs like a child, her mind swinging back. Back to Wind Star.

"I wonder how the shoppe's doing. I wonder how the Girl Scouts are getting on. What page they're on? Had they run out of mottos, and were borrowing ones from the Boy Scouts? If Auntie Bertie has taken over my display bulletin board?" And of course she felt Auntie Bertie had a knack. A good knack for design and a good eye.

Still it was one of her pets…

"Is there enough merchandise? The racks would look unprofessional if they weren't full." The kitty stickers were low when she left. And Elizabeth was pretty sure they needed more charms. She wondered what was selling and what was sitting … These thoughts raced around in her head, exhausting her.

Her dreams were no better. She was back in Wind Star only the Aunties had gone corporate. They'd sold franchises, hired a manager and were tied up in meetings, their old Chanel suits dug out of moth balls. This was so horrifying it woke her up.

"I'll just pad over to the little pink fridge for a Diet Pepsi to calm me down." But when she switched on the bedside light she realized she wasn't in the little basement flat at all.

She was in a hotel. In New York. And there were no Diet Pepsi's, just tiny bottles of rum and scotch. The scotch made her think about Auntie Clara's Whiskey Pound Cake. She could really go for a slice, okay hunk.

And a Diet Pepsi.

Days wore on with Bob suggesting the usual campaign. He might as well be Darren on Bewitched, Elizabeth thought dryly.

The first week bled into the next. Elizabeth had a routine of getting coffee in the hotel lobby before walking the short distance to the agency.

The streets that had always fascinated her seemed noisy, crowded. The air was thick, hard to breath. Why hadn't she ever noticed that before?

The stores were either garish or sophisticated; there didn't seem to be much in between. Why hadn't she ever noticed that before? There was nothing whimsical like Jinx's store Fairchild's--nothing unexpected. It was as she had left it and for whatever reason it now seemed a tad flat.

Of course it wasn't flat. This was New York City. The City. The most exciting place in the world. Well the United States for sure. She really didn't know about the world. The world, well it was the world.

Accidently she stepped into something squishy. It stuck to her heel, and she had to run her foot back and forth on the pavement to rub it away. As she looked down she was actually relieved to see it was an éclair.

Probably someone had accidently dropped it, or found it too sugary, and just tossed it on the sidewalk. And she'd walked in it. Walking on, she gave her head a slight shake.

Elizabeth rounded a corner and realized she missed her car--her silly little pink car. She knew it was safe in the garage at the apartment building but still … didn't it need to be driven? Cooper would know …

Cooper.

She hadn't heard from him.

Nor had she called to tell him she would be gone … how long? She didn't know and hadn't gotten that far. He had her number. She knew her cell was in her Burberry purse--it was always with her and it was faithfully plugged in at night to re-charge. But why? It hadn't rung and she hadn't used it.

Before she could dwell on it she was at work.

They seemed to be getting nowhere on the Granville Auction House account. How much time had they spent just getting nowhere? Her Aunties were action women. They would have scoffed at this progress, or lack thereof.

Everything Bob suggested was bold, contemporary. It went without saying it was also stale and boring. If she squinted she could have taken the words Granville Auction House out and put in just about anything else. This wasn't art. This wasn't design and it certainly wasn't right.

Somehow when Elizabeth thought about antiques, and after all that was what the auction house was all about, she thought about sipping tea on cabbage rose china with Auntie Clara.

And Auntie Bertie unwrapping a platter of chocolate chip cookies on an old Meissen plate, or serving her famous tuna casserole in an old silver chafing dish.

And Auntie Blanchie wearing strands of pearls, and her over--ringed fingers, regardless of her outfit.

Old things and old people. Things they had lovingly never stopped using. Never given up, because they were elegant, and dear, and theirs. Things that had ignored the latest trends, the new color schemes, and just continued to be perfect because they were personal. They were not things; they were a part of their lives.

They were who these people were.

Basil, with his comb over, and bow tie. Funny bow ties were back in and yet she was pretty sure Basil had not started wearing them to follow a trend. They were him as much as Blanchie's pearls were her.

And his vintage cars that he kept just to decorate the show room, because he loved them. And he wanted to see them every day. And share them with who ever came in. Because he knew they would see in them a glimmer of what he saw and loved. They took up valuable square footage in his show room because they were important. Important to him.

That was it!

Elizabeth laughed out loud!

But before she could say a word, Bob beat her to it. "Maybe we should knock it off for today. The well is dry ..." And he gave her a look that said he had no clue why management had brought her back.

Knock it off? Why she just had her brain storm!

Fine.

Great.

"So we'll see if either of us can come up with anything Monday." It was Friday and Elizabeth had the feeling Bob wanted a long weekend. Well ... she could use a long weekend too.

Fishing out her cell phone she called Basil at Herrington Motors. "Basil ... its Elizabeth McGillicuddy. You sold me a Mini Cooper ..." Did he remember her?

"Yes of course, Clara's niece. Lizzie, how lovely of you to phone."

She realized she missed being called Lizzie. "Basil, I need a favor, and well, I wanted to swing by and see you. I'll er take you to dinner." He sounded excited. He had to have time for her. She hoped he did.

But Basil was old. Very old. He had lots of time.

Hanging up she made her plan. She scurried into an antique store. It wasn't quite lunch time so she felt confident she could accomplish her mission without too many crowds of people clogging her up.

The rose china turned out to be Royal Dalton. She selected a cup and saucer, tea pot and dessert plate. Wincing at the prices, she set them on the counter. She found a yellow straw hat with faded red streamers, a clump of artificial cherries, and a feather, and added it to her pile. The cherries and streamers seemed to go with the china.

She handed over her Visa, wondering if she could be reimbursed at work. Then she didn't care, and scurried to her next stop.

Baldacci's deli had wedges of cheese, delicate little fancy cakes, and fruit. She added a willow picnic basket, and last minute grabbed a carton of strawberries and a Battenberg table cloth. So far, so good. Lugging her purchases she hopped on a bus for Brooklyn.

To see Basil.

He was in a pin striped shirt, red braces, and red bow tie. The comb over was perfectly lacquered in place. He was ... perfect.

"Lizzie! You know when you called, I never think of you as Elizabeth ..." He held out his arms and in an awkward gesture, Elizabeth fell into the hug. "So you're back in the city then?" He raised a grey bushy eyebrow.

"Well, the agency needed help with a difficult account."

"The agency that fired you?" Now the other eyebrow went up and Elizabeth wobbled from one heel to the other, embarrassed. Still ...

"Well yes--that one."

"And Clara? You've left Clara then?"

"Uh, well not for good ... just uh for a bit." Oh God, he thinks I've left Auntie Clara...and I have! "Anyway, back to this difficult account. I er, well I was wondering if you would help me."

Walking over to the old silver Bentley convertible, she made her plea, "I want to photograph your car, and you, and well, I brought a picnic I thought I'd spread on the back seat. You see, the account is an auction house--the Granville Auction House.

And so far the man I'm working with, my co-worker, is stuck on modern. Somehow all that modern seems wrong. An auction house says to me my Aunties having tea on their old china." And she started to unwrap her purchases.

As she spoke she placed the Battenberg lace cloth hanging down on the back leather seat and then propped open the picnic hamper.

"My Aunties, well they love their old things but I can imagine if they felt they needed to part with anything they'd want to do it right, with class, at an auction house."

Now the tea pot peeked out of the basket, the cup and saucer sat on the cloth. Two small cakes and a few strawberries were placed on the dessert plate waiting ... Waiting for a Victorian woman to appear.

Instead, the straw hat was brought out of her shopper and was now leaning against the basket, the contrast making it look all the older. A wedge of cheese and a few pears could be seen peeking out of the basket. You would have thought the car was in Windsor Park, so perfect was the effect.

"Lizzie...this makes me want to ... well, it takes me back. Back in time." Basil's look was far away.

And she respected it.

Elizabeth twirled! "Fabulous Basil! Now wait until I shoot a few pix." Digging her camera out of her purse she began snapping. She clicked off photographs with Basil in the Bentley, and without him, and every angle conceivable. After a bit she sighed, "I think I've got it! Let's look."

"Look?" Still not used to digital cameras, Basil shook his head in amazement. Elizabeth sat in the front seat next to Basil and flipped the camera to view. "Amazing! Lizzie! Simply amazing! Why I'd pay an ad agency big bucks for these!"

Elizabeth laughed. "Hey, consider it a gift. I'll make you a disk and some copies. This could be your Christmas card!"

"But there aren't any of you ..."

"Well ..." Still laughing she handed Basil the camera, and swung her long high heeled legs over the open window. "Just aim and click!" She gave him full wattage, tossed her luxurious mane of hair, and teased Basil about a second career as a photographer!

"Too bad Clara can't see these pictures ..." Basil indulged in a little melancholy.

"Why she can. We can down load them, and Email them to her! Easy, breezy, Parcheesi!'"

But Basil looked skeptical, his bushy eyebrows drawn together.

So she gave him her best smile. "I'm sure your computer has everything on it ..." And she cocked her head toward the main desk.

"Well yes but ..." He hesitated ever so slightly.

She understood. She was behind her younger crowd. It just happened. Didn't have to but it did.

"Well then?" Elizabeth didn't want to tease him.

"Well, you're here. What will Clara email it to? And even if we did Clara wouldn't ..." Basil stumbled on his words.

"Basil! Auntie Clara and her pals are all computer savvy! She'll flip when she sees these pictures. She's on line all the time researching something!"

"She is?" His voice became tiny, reedy.

"Uh huh! You could be emailing her! She'd love it! Come on!" And she grabbed his hand and tugged him to the counter. And she saw a light in his eyes.

Twenty minutes later all was down loaded and sent off. "Now these are on your hard drive Basil, so you can send them, or print them, or just pull them up and look at them. And if you forget how to do it call me. I'll talk you through it."

Then an idea flashed. "When I get back to Wind Star, I'll take a slew of pictures and send them to you--pictures of everything. Where ever I am, the Aunties, Creating Memories. We'll stay in touch with just a touch of the computer keys."

"So you're going back?" He asked it so innocently it caught Elizabeth off guard.

"Uh ..." But she didn't answer. She didn't know.

Basil picked up the slack. "Why don't we go out to dinner and celebrate! We can collaborate on the copy!"

"You mean it?" Elizabeth returned to the here and now, Wind Star tucked back in to a little nook and cranny of her head.

"Absolutely! Let's pack up your goodies! I'll call the limo!"

"The limo Basil?" And Elizabeth just shook her head because it sounded so outrageous and ...fun.

"And why not my dear! I do own an auto agency! If we don't travel in style after all, who should?"

And she laughed and started to pack her props. "Let's leave all this food here. You have a fridge back there somewhere don't you?"

And they were off.

The Granville Auction House not only loved Elizabeth's proposal, they adored it.

And her.

"You're a genius!" What better three words could she want to hear?

"It's exactly what we wanted but of course had no idea until we saw your photographs!" And as they laughed, Elizabeth blushed. They'd started serious, tentative, even doubting that there would be anything that they would like. They were expecting things they just knew they'd have to accept, because they needed something.

Anything.

As Elizabeth flashed her photos on her lap top, and passed hard copies around, they collectively sighed.

Boredom melted, their attention riveted. They wanted to see the next one and the next.

She didn't say anything; she just let her work speak for her. And besides, she didn't think she needed to.

There was something about the photos of Basil they particularly loved. He was so genuine. Someone they could have met a million times in their dealings at the Auction House. He was key. He was what it was about. He made it personal. If this very dapper relic of a man could trust Granville Auction House ... well ...

They stared at Elizabeth in a new light, some of their mouths gaping. She understood. She got them. She had taken a red pencil and underscored their very deepest thoughts. Thoughts about why they got into the auction business. Thoughts about why they loved the auction business.

Even Bob got on board, being smart enough to tag on to a winner. And try as he did to take credit, the powers that be at Granville Auction House knew without a doubt where the ideas had come from. Bob didn't care. He was willing to take whatever he could get. And he figured he could pawn it off as his back at the agency.

The final product ran the gambit from newspaper ads, TV commercials, bill boards, in house signs, stationary, and business cards. Basil, and his Bentley, became the symbol for all that was elegant and old. Suddenly the word old mingled with the word elegant.

Granville Auction House became the symbol for confident caretakers of all Basil and the Bentley represented. It was class and it became status--instant status to have the privilege of Granville placing your loved possessions.

And it happened quickly, as all good advertising is meant to. Suddenly Granville Auction House became the 'it' name. Prominent obits in the paper were followed by even more prominent auction announcements. People flocked to them. Even in death they wanted that touch of elegance and status.

The guardians of all precious were seen at museum gatherings, restaurant openings and 'A' list social events. The press the auction house received from just being seen out and about was almost as good as their advertising. Party planners included them, society hostesses sought them.

And Elizabeth was their pet, often convinced to join the status celebrations. She was instantly the golden flame that had ignited the Granville's. No amount of modesty could tone down their appreciation for her.

And it was at one such gathering at a chic restaurant that Mr. Granville Senior took Elizabeth aside, "My dear, I want you to think ahead. I don't know what that might mean, but I want you to build on this theme. We are so thrilled with your work; we don't want to lose you." He said it sincerely and she was touched by his words.

Elizabeth blushed humbly, "Mr. Granville, you won't lose me. I love working on your ads. I can ... well, I can relate to old things."

"Are you still camping at that hotel?"

"Guilty," She was embarrassed to admit it.

"We need to find you a home. A real home."

But when he uttered these words, Elizabeth responded before she could even think. "But Mr. Granville, I have a home. A cute little retro flat ..." And then she froze. Froze before she could say ... "In Wind Star." Suddenly she missed Auntie Clara. She pushed aside her crème brulee, wanting a thick wedge of Whiskey Pound Cake. She put up a brave face but one stray tear leaked out giving her away.

Mr. Granville was the arch type of all grandfathers. He took a breath and let it out in a sigh, "My dear, maybe you need to think about going home."

Elizabeth bit her bottom lip.

"To your own world," And he paused before he added, "Again."

She had been moving at such a fast pace she just kept pushing thoughts of Wind Star, Auntie Clara, and Creating Memories out of her mind as she dashed out the door.

"Tell me, my dear, what do you do at home?"

Elizabeth looked nervous but the encouragement in Mr. Granville's kind faded eyes edged her forward, "I own a scrap book shoppe--Creating Memories."

"Really?"

"Uh huh. Well, actually, I co-own it."

"Oh."

"Oh no, it's not what you think. I co-own it with three elderly ladies. My Aunties! They're scrap bookers, my mentors, my ... well, they're my family."

"I see."

And she was sure he did.

"You know Mr. Granville, each of them is unique. I could see Auntie Blanchie, who is very elegant and owns more jewelry than Tiffany's, running her be-jeweled hands threw a treasure chest of pearls and jewels. It would be a wonderful photograph for you to promote jewelry auctions. Why she wore a triple strand of pearls when she painted my shoppe!"

"No?" Even Mr. Granville was shocked.

"Honest! And she has designer clothes from the nineteen twenties and the nineteen thirties that would make your mouth water! Why her closet is like a peek into a wardrobe of an old black and white movie!"

Then Elizabeth laughed, something she hadn't done in a long time. "And Auntie Bertie has more first editions than most museums. I'm going to send you a photograph of her at her old desk with her steaming cocoa, wearing her plaid robe, surrounded by leather bound first editions."

Mr. Granville was captivated as Elizabeth went on, "And and ... Auntie Clara! Well, she makes this Whiskey Pound Cake that just melts in your mouth. And she always has one made, and I swear they are never on the same cut crystal cake stand. She has more china than ... well, than the Queen of England!" And her grin was just this side of a young child's enthusiastic happiness.

Mr. Granville was grinning foolishly, picturing it all. He slipped an arm around her.

"Elizabeth, I don't see why you can't free lance from ... from where ever this is! I might be even tempted to visit and meet your Aunties. That is, if you could guarantee a Whiskey Pound Cake!"

And Elizabeth swiped at a stray tear, only this time a happy one.

Elizabeth's boss was thrilled! He insisted on lining up other difficult accounts, offering sums of money that staggered her. One was for a tire company, another for canned peas. Something about insurance. A mega hospital wanted help. A new look. She took the files back to her hotel, and collapsed on the king size bed.

Tires were a hard sell in a city where most people took one form or another of public transportation. Tires? She had no clue. Tires were simply something on a car. Not only did she not have a clue, she could care less.

And peas.

In a can?

She didn't eat things from cans. Not to mention peas. No. She, again, was blank. And again, didn't care.

And hospitals depressed her. She lived in fear of her Aunties needing one. No, she couldn't get inspired to work on a hospital account.

Boring.

It was boring.

Elizabeth could possibly squeeze her brain into action. Maybe a hot shower and she could let her mind drift to tires, and peas, and those antiseptic hallways with gloom and doom around every corner.

As the scalding water sluiced on her tired shoulders, her mind did drift a million miles from tires, and peas, and infirmaries.

To Wind Star.

To Creating Memories.

To her Aunties.

And to Cooper.

10

Cooper signed off on his condo. He was back in California after spending a couple of weeks in England at Range Rover and BMW. The condo finally sold; one more chapter of his life he could put away.

He took a sip of iced Starbucks as he walked along the beach. The sun felt good beating on his shoulders, his hair already was streaking gold. It needed a trim. The sand worked its way between his toes leaving damp footprints. He was following another set; only these were dogs paw prints.

"It would be nice to walk the beach with a dog." And then he remembered the old farm house he'd seen in Wind Star out in the country. Out in the country? Ha! Wind Star was all country! But he saw the street tunneled with old oaks, and the rolling farms with gentle sheep, and grazing cows.

And the red barn--the one he thought he could keep some of his vintage cars in. And the porch--he saw himself on the porch--with a dog. His dog. A sappy faced bull dog. Tan or speckled or brindle ... he was sure they called that bull dog color brindle. Well, sort of sure.

And Lizzie. Sunning herself in the yard, pretending to garden, in her miniscule cutoffs. Dozing, half way between reality, and sleep. Her hair would be tied up on top of her head, with some haphazard bits dangling on her shoulders.

Lizzie …

It had been a long time since he'd seen her. His trip to the UK had stretched to over two weeks and now he was in Malibu. Why wasn't he home?

A young girl about ten years old skipped by, her sloppy tee shirt skirting a damp suit. Her long legs danced in the waves. Suddenly she stopped, and turning back and whistled. A Heinz 57 mutt raced from nowhere, its shaggy hair matted with water, caught up with her.

She could have been a young Lizzie, right down to her waist length auburn kissed hair.

Before he could really decide if she resembled Lizzie, she and the dog were gone, over a dune and out of site.

He kicked at a mound of sand, sending the silver grains flying. "I wonder what she's doing? How her scrap book shoppe is going?" He'd thought of her once while at Heathrow, and bought her a bag full of British stickers; Big Ben, the typical red phone booth, pillar boxes, the Union Jack flag, and famous castles.

He had wished then that she'd been with him to see the newest cars, tour the countryside; snag some fish and chips, maybe tuck into a cozy bed and breakfast. But she hadn't been, and he'd basically worked while there. The most frivolous thing he'd done was buy her the stickers when he was leaving.

And day dream about her …

He kept walking.

A couple of bikini clad teen girls walked by giggling, "Are you someone?" One with blonde ponytails asked brazenly.

"Uh yeah," Cooper shook his head, "I'm someone."

The other girl jiggled up to him and looked at him suspiciously, "She means someone famous!"

And then Cooper just scowled indulgently, pitifully.

"You look like someone famous," She went on boldly.

"Sorry," It was the best he could give and kept on walking.

"Too bad, we could have had some fun!" They called out after him and suddenly he remembered all the groupies he'd had as a race car driver. He used to refer to them as adoring fans but in his heart he knew they were no different than these girls.

His relationships had always been shallow, when they got so far as to be a relationship that is. Mostly they'd been one nighters. Usually, no absolutely, no reason to go for two nights. And as soon as they were gone he never thought of them again.

Until now.

Until Lizzie.

Lizzie sure wasn't an adoring fan or groupie! For the longest time she'd been hostile! So what if he'd run over her garden, pimped her little pink plaid car, and ogled her long legs in cut offs? He just never encountered a woman not ready to drop everything for him.

He was a poor conversationalist--he knew it. He'd never developed that skill. Never needed it. He didn't care what most girls had to say, and never wanted to encourage them telling him whatever it was they rattled on about.

Until Lizzie.

Cooper found her gardening attempts fascinating, her love of the Aunties endearing, and her ambitious tackling of a small business inspiring. And he wanted to talk. It was as if the flood gates were finally opened. He wanted to tell her about his racing career, and his Grandfather, and his childhood, and the dealership, and his love of nature, and quiet, and his love of cars in all forms and ...

He wanted to call her.

How long had it been since he last talked to her? Had he even told her he would be overseas? Of course not. Then he would have had to tell her it was for business. And then he would have had to tell her he owned the dealership--because mechanics didn't go to Range Rover in England.

And if he told her would she turn into a groupie? A money groupie? Or just turn away? He shook his head and kept walking.

11

"Clara, what in heaven's name are you doing? We're going to open in half an hour!" Blanchie tsked. Auntie Clara tried her best to give her a dirty look but kept right on working.

Cutting.

And gluing.

The table in the bay window at Creating Memories was littered with Auntie Clara's mess. "Well we are a scrap book store. If someone comes in, isn't it obvious I'm working on a scrap book?" Auntie Clara had a tone going. Slight but still a tone.

Blanchie frowned but put cash in the register, cracking open a roll of pennies, and then started to straighten out a pile of stickers.

Auntie Clara was cutting out more people from her old Sears and Roebuck catalog. She had a small stack she hadn't glued in yet. It was getting late, why was she being so finicky? She flipped over six people, ran a stream of glue down each and plopped them on a page. In a row. Next to several other rows.

Blanchie wandered to the table and peered over her shoulder. "Oh my God Clara! What are you doing?" Auntie Clara ignored her and kept working. "That's your Creating Memories scrap book isn't it?"

Auntie Clara begrudgingly nodded.

"Why are you putting rows of people in it?" And then she stopped horrified. "Clara!"

"Well, business has been slow, you said so yourself. You know if people come in they fall in love with our merchandise and buy. And we, well we have to keep up until Lizzie gets back. We want the shoppe to survive don't we?" Auntie Clara was frantic. Frantic to not let Lizzie's retail venture fail. It had to be growing, thriving when she got back.

If she got back.

"Clara! Give me that old Sears catalog! Those people look like they're from the nineteen forties!"

"They are." Auntie Clara stuck her chin out but kept working.

"Clara! For God's sake be careful! Why couldn't you at least use contemporary looking people? Why ... these people look like a throwback ... maybe even a forgotten conservative religion!" Blanchie grabbed the catalog and went to toss it on the desk.

Auntie Clara reached in her tote and pulled out The Enquirer. "Can't let Lizzie down. We need customers." And started snipping and gluing like a crazed woman.

There was a rattling at the front door that startled her. Auntie Clara only managed to put two more people in her scrap book before she heaved herself up and headed to the door.

They were in line! Waiting to come in. They wore gabardine suits, and felt hats; sun dresses with shoulder pads, and brimmed straw hats. Some even wore gloves. Gloves! Some of their hose had seams!

Blanchie let out a small shriek as they streamed in. Auntie Clara just stared in wonder. Why she'd forgotten how fabulous some of those older fashions had been.

"Welcome! Welcome!" Auntie Clara put on her best retail smile, "Welcome to Creating Memories." Then she added, "I'm Auntie Clara, and we are a scrap book shoppe. Let me show you around." Okay, Blanchie was right, maybe they didn't even know what scrap booking was. But they were milling around chattering and filling shopping baskets, intrigued by the whole concept.

Blanchie was ringing up the register as fast as she could!

Why one lady paid her with silver dollars! Probably worth a fortune! The customer had an alligator handbag with the little reptile head and shoes to match! Her suit had a mink collar with the tiny feet and legs dangling off the edges.

Even Blanchie hadn't seen that style in a very very long time.

A woman in a red and white striped sundress and matching red straw hat was next. Her espadrilles were laced up her ankles in crisscross red grois grain ribbon ending in bows! Blanchie cringed!

Auntie Clara had just snipped models from her old catalog with no regard to season! The woman behind her had a one piece maillot swim suit, terry beach robe and platform sandals! There was no time to panic or holler at Clara …

Bertie had been down at the Patisserie getting them all mocha lattes and muffins. She wandered back in with her waxed bag and tray of drinks, eyeing the customers nervously. She hadn't done it … thank goodness.

Bertie was blamed for most mishaps, not that this was a mishap. Still it looked, well, not right. She angled her way to the check out desk and set down the goodies. "Blanchie …"

"Don't ask dear. Just help. Please, I need bags from the stock room." Blanchie's perfectly coifed hair was starting to fall apart. Her red lipstick had been chewed off. She was afraid the next thing she'd be biting her lovely red painted finger nails.

Auntie Clara was chattering with a couple little girls in smocked dresses with lace ankle socks and Mary Jane's. Their hair was in pig tails, tied with bows that matched the dresses. Their manners matched their clothes. Auntie Clara was explaining stickers to them.

The door chimed as Jinx walked in. She stopped dead in her tracks! She was with a woman with a note pad. They both just stared in disbelief! Auntie Clara spotted her and nervously headed through the crowd.

"Ms. Clara …" Jinx began but didn't really know what to say. Of course she forgot to call her Auntie. Jinx stared in awe and almost forgot why she'd come in.

Finally the other woman who had come in with Jinx spoke up. "I'm Catherine Schable from the news paper. Jinx has told me about your shoppe and I thought I'd do a little article ..." The newspaper woman was looking around in wonder at the other shoppers. Wondering where they could possibly have come from.

Blanchie and Bertie were working the counter, Auntie Clara started to stammer.

Jinx slapped her head! "Why Ms. Clara, you're having an event! And everyone's in costume! How clever! Creating Memories and dressing nostalgic!"

And as Jinx spoke Auntie Clara just nodded and the reporter scribbled on her pad. "Now I can give you more details on the shoppe, if you like. We can go to the Patisserie for a coffee, where we can talk."

The din of shoppers was too much for them to talk over, and the reporter nodded as Auntie Clara steered them out the door. Once seated at the Patisserie the newspaper woman exclaimed, "Brilliant! And yet I saw no publicity for it!"

"Oh well, we just sent out a few post cards and people responded like crazy." Auntie Clara blew on her coffee, desperate for caffeine.

"And those costumes, so authentic."

"Yes, yes they seem to be and of course we're, er giving a prize for the best."

"Even children ..."

"Well, no one likes to dress up more than children." Auntie Clara fidgeted and then just started to drink her coffee, hoping to change the subject. And not burn her throat.

The reporter finally finished her notes and Auntie Clara claimed she had to get back.

"How had these people come?" Jinx asked innocently enough.

Well, Auntie Clara knew how. The real question was, when they were done shopping, how should they leave? Auntie Clara didn't even care where they went ... Rushing back, she squeezed in and headed to a rack of stickers and found what she was looking for. Her scrap book was behind the desk.

She ripped open the sticker package, flipped through her scrap book and stuck in a bus. Giving it a quick tap with her citrine ring, she closed it back up.

Sure enough the squeal of air breaks could be heard, and an old city bus pulled up. Blanchie looked up squinting at her. "Clara …"

"Well … I had to do something." The vintage people clutched their shopping bags and started to load the bus while others continued to shop and wait to ring out.

As if things couldn't get any worse, the door chimed, and as Blanchie, Bertie, and Clara glanced up, in walked Nicole Kidman and Keith Urban!

"Why honey, look at all these old fashioned scrap books …" Nicole began, "And people." She looked around in awe, as if on a movie set, then reached for a basket and started to gather up stencils, stickers, glitter …

Bertie was stuttering, but Blanchie was hissing to Auntie Clara. "You've gone too far! Too far! Where did they come from?"

Auntie Clara just glanced over at the cut up Enquirer next to her scrap book. Silhouettes of the famous couple were all that remained. The actual stars were there, at Creating Memories, shopping.

"You're just lucky your vintage Sears people won't recognize them!" But Auntie Clara was escaping Blanchie's wrath and going to greet her new customers.

"Welcome. Welcome to Creating Memories." And she held out her bejeweled hands. "I'm Clara, Auntie Clara. Make yourself at home."

Nicole clasped them and giving that famous full wattage smile said, "We were just passing by." Sure enough, behind the bus full of Sears and Roebuck people was a tour bus. "And I said to Keith, look at that little shoppe. I think we have time to stop. We're just on our way back to Nashville, and decided to take the country roads."

Nicole went on about the tour or where ever they'd been, Auntie Clara only half listened, keeping an eye on the door for fans or customers. Real customers. She tuned back in. By this time Nicole had a basket stuffed with goodies and Keith had an armful of albums.

Nicole was scooping up the charms as though they were pop corn. "I don't know how you did it, but everyone is just treating us like, well, regular people. Thank you." And she handed off her basket to Blanchie to ring up and kissed Auntie Clara on the cheek, possibly so used to Hollywood types she never commented on the other customer's unusual clothing.

Keith unloaded the albums and turned to Blanchie, "You don't know what this means to my wife. Do you ship? We may call you for Christmas gifts."

"Ship?" Bertie found her tongue, "We ship. We deliver."

But Keith took the delivery part as a joke and laughed at her as he picked up a couple of business cards. Keith now held all the shopping bags, and Nicole was thanking them, "You ladies are remarkable."

"Aunties--we're the Aunties," Auntie Clara put in, letting out a breath.

"Aunties then, I feel privileged to meet you. I'll call for more."

And they were gone.

The tour bus pulled out with the bus full of Sear's and Roebuck models. Blanchie, Bertie, and Auntie Clara looked around. The shoppe was a wreck! There were things everywhere. The tidy stack of tissue behind the counter had skidded to the floor as they rushed to wrap.

The bin of shopping bags held one last sack. Stickers were off their hooks, albums people had decided against were stacked on the tables.

"It ... it looks like locusts have attacked our shoppe!" Bertie was practically in tears.

But Blanchie and Auntie Clara just started to laugh and finally Bertie joined in. "Oh girls ... I never ..."

"Knew your own potential Clara!" Blanchie finished as she sipped a now cold latte. And they started to pick up the mess and restore their darling shoppe.

Auntie Clara missed Lizzie so much it became an ache. An ache she carried around. Every time the door opened at Creating Memories Auntie Clara jumped sure ... sure Lizzie was back. But in her heart she wasn't all that confident. As a matter of fact she was pretty sure Lizzie was never coming back.

And Auntie Clara didn't know what to do. It was a helpless feeling she didn't think she'd ever had before. It shadowed everything she did, every conversation she had with Blanchie and Bertie. She wasn't sleeping. She was off her Cadbury's chocolates.

Even her beloved shoppe had a shadow cast over it, though she was usually too tired to even notice. The shoppe had a shadow, so did her life. Auntie Clara's heart raced, or slowed down to a pokey beat.

She was just this side of desperate and she knew she was driving her best friends crazy.

Cooper got Lizzie's voice mail. "Where is she?" But of course there was no answer. He hated to leave a message. He'd call the shoppe; she was probably there anyway.

"Creating Memories."

"Oh, hi, this is Cooper. Is Lizzie there?" He was impatient. Now that he had made up his mind to talk to her he was anxious. Ready.

"Cooper dear, this is Auntie Clara. Nice to hear from you. Where have you been?" She was proud of herself being so polite when what she wanted to do was holler at him. She'd convinced herself a million times he could have kept Lizzie in Wind Star.

"England and California," He actually was still in California but he was too impatient to give details.

"Oh lovely dear. Lizzie's not here." There Auntie Clara said it.

"She's not answering her cell phone. When will she be back?"

Auntie Clara hesitated, and then her normally cheerful voice started to crack. "Well dear, I don't know. I just don't know." And then she hung up.

Cooper stared at the dead phone. Not there? And Aunt Clara didn't know when she'd be back? And did she hang up on him? He redialed squinting at the phone.

"Creating Memories."

"Er hi, it's Cooper again."

"Cooper--lovely. This is Blanchie." Auntie Clara was beside herself. She had refused to answer the phone and trundled off to the back room for a Diet Pepsi.

"I'm looking for Lizzie." What happened to polite formalities? He'd scrapped them!

"Oh dear. She's gone," Blanchie sighed. She felt old, very old.

"Gone?" Surely this old woman was joking. How could she joke when he was so desperate?

"Yes gone. She, well, she went back to New York City. To her old agency." Blanchie could barely say it. She looked over at Clara and prayed she wasn't being overheard.

"Yes, we're running things our selves. No we don't really have a choice but well, we are managing." Then Blanchie laughed, just a little, "We're tired. We're all surprised what it takes to well, actually run something."

Cooper chuckled. No kidding, "Try running a car dealership." Small talk continued until Cooper reined it back in, "I tried Lizzie's cell, and well, maybe she didn't have it with her. Or on. No, no I didn't leave a message. Yes, I know I disappointed her. Hasn't Aunt Clara told you Lizzie thinks I'm just a mechanic?"

He listened patiently as Blanchie stormed him. "Are you ever going to tell her?" Blanchie finally demanded, "She'll find out, you know. The truth always eeks out."

And he swore he could see her raise a scolding finger up to him, over the phone lines, as if he were a young boy. Cooper shuddered despite the warmth from the sun, and the heat of the sand under foot.

Find out? It never dawned on him Lizzie would find out. Of course it also never dawned on him he wanted to keep seeing her either ... At least not at first.

"Women don't like to be lied to Cooper ... and evasion is its own form of lie. Just think about it." Blanchie had her say. Well as much as she thought Cooper could or would take.

Cooper hung up and thought maybe he ought to get to New York. He could stop and see Uncle Basil. Basil had always been sharp. Very sharp. Maybe Basil could tell him how to tell Lizzie. Because suddenly he realized Miss Blanchie was right. He had to tell Lizzie, that is, if he wanted her in his life. And he'd finally figured out it wouldn't be much of a life if she wasn't.

Yes, Miss Blanchie was right on all accounts. He should have told her right off the bat. Now it was going to be ... he wasn't exactly sure what. Harder for sure. And it might also be his undoing.

He'd catch a plane. Go from California to New York and Basil would tell him how to tell her. But as he made plans, a nagging little voice said- -just tell her.

"Blanchie--that was Cooper wasn't it?" Auntie Clara couldn't stand to be left out of the loop even though she'd refused to pick up the ringing phone.

Blanchie gave a single nod.

"He misses her, doesn't he?"

Again a tiny nod.

"What's he going to do?"

At this Blanchie gave an elegant little shrug. When Auntie Clara got that impatient worked up look, Blanchie just held up her hands. "Clara. It's up to them. It is. I don't know what he'll do. Or her for that matter," Blanchie sighed deeply.

Her feet were killing her. If she was going to continue to tend shoppe she hated to admit it but she needed sensible shoes. And she did intend to; it was fun and stimulating. And ... tiring.

"Besides, we have a business to run ..." And Blanchie went back to the books.

Auntie Clara looked at her sideways and lifted one eye brow. Her wispy silver hair looked like an angel's halo but her expression was pure mischief. "You're right Blanchie." And mentally added as an afterthought, about running a business. She loved it too.

"As a matter of fact, I have to run a few errands. I can bring back sandwiches." And Auntie Clara jiggled her car keys, and put on her sweetest smile. "Can you and Bertie hold down the fort?"

With that UPS Jeff came bustling in rolling his two wheeler stacked with boxes. "Christmas time ladies!" He joked. In fact it was getting on December soon enough and Auntie Clara was sure the boxes were loaded with Christmas stickers, holiday stencils, velvet albums, papers with jolly Santa's, and frosted ornaments. But she kept going, determined with her mission.

"Young man, you are always a joy--a virtual joy to us old ladies!"

Jeff laughed as Auntie Clara signed his electronic pad.

As they left together Jeff asked, "Where's your cute little boss?"

"Oh you mean me niece Lizzie?"

Jeff nodded.

"She's on her way back," Auntie Clara said it with finality.

Back in her apartment Auntie Clara climbed on her aqua metal kitchen stool. Carefully. Falls were the kiss of death to old people. She hated to stand on the top but gingerly took the last step, clutching the front of her china cabinet.

She released one hand from the china door and reached up on top. With the tips of her fingers she could feel the album she'd tossed up there.

The Lizzie album.

Slowly and carefully, she climbed down and rushed to the kitchen, opening drawer after drawer until she found her hot dog tongs. With prize in hand she climbed back up. "God don't let me fall ..." Auntie Clara held on to the china cabinet with her left hand and with her right, clutching the tongs, fished around.

When she found the album she opened the tongs up and clamped down. Inch by inch she pulled the album toward the edge. Finally she felt she could grab it. It was so thick she really needed two hands.

Terrified, she inched her left hand up the cabinet until she reached the top. With both hands, she grasped the album and slid it to her. When it was over her head, she locked her knees and started to lower her arms and the album. When it was finally at waist height she let her breath out, and carefully began the three steps down.

With the scrap book finally on the dining room table Auntie Clara sighed, "I need a wee nip," And rushed to the kitchen for her cake whiskey. Armed with her drink, Auntie Clara sat and opened Lizzie's book. She looked at a basket full of magazines and started to flip through. "What I need is a picture of Lizzie ... why don't I have a picture of Lizzie?"

Before she could really plan, she cut out a picture from In Style of a model that looked a lot like Lizzie. "Hairs right ..." She muttered. In fact it was long, flowing and Lizzie's color. Ready to paste she stopped, "No ... this would only bring a Lizzie look alike to me. I must have a photograph ..." She found a shoe box of pictures and started sorting like crazy.

The best she could come up with was a snap of herself. Then the light bulb went off. She cut it out and glued it in.

With a black magic marker Auntie Clara started to draw. First she drew a little cloud over her head. "If I get a wee bit sick she'll come back ..." Then Auntie Clara dotted in what looked like rain. Finally she circled puffs around the entire photograph.

And then she put her head down, and passed out.

Blanchie and Bertie were starting to worry. No sign of Auntie Clara. And no sandwiches. They'd eaten their emergency Milano's--three bags--and were reluctant to go to the Patisserie and ruin their appetites.

But by four o'clock they had a sneaking feeling Auntie Clara wasn't coming.

The shoppe was crowded with customers when Jinx strolled in. "Aunties ..." As she had finally started to call them. "I need a break; Jefferson's watching the store ..." Jinx looked around. "Where's Auntie Clara?"

There was a mom with two little girls at a project table seriously concentrating, a couple of women were browsing, and a few more were in line at the cash register.

Blanchie looked up from her sale, "Dear, we don't know. She left hours ago and well ..."

"We're worried," Bertie called out. And she tried to hide the fear she felt. They were, after all, very old.

Jinx raised her eyebrows. These ladies were no spring chickens, anything could have happened.

"We think she stopped at her apartment but she isn't answering the phone ..." Blanchie's perfectly made up face was cracking when she frowned.

"I can go over and check. I mean if you want me to." Jinx didn't really want to go back to her shoppe. And she was terribly fond of Auntie Clara.

Blanchie produced a key, and wrote down an address, and Jinx was off.

"Probably fell asleep in front of the TV." But still she drove like a maniac.

The old brown stone was charming. From an era Auntie Clara herself came. Jinx fled up the walk, and started to search the lobby for an elevator. But all she saw was a wide set of marble stairs. The key said '400'. She started to fly up the stairs. By the second set she was down to a quick walk. By the third she was winded. By the fourth she was exhausted.

There was only one door. Jinx was either too tired to see others or Auntie Clara had a gigantic apartment. Slipping the key in she called, "Ms. Clara ... Auntie Clara, its Jinx." No response.

Then Jinx saw her.

Slumped over the dining room table! Jinx rushed to her side and tapped her shoulder. Nothing.

Jinx felt Auntie Clara's arm. Cold. "Oh no! Auntie Clara! Auntie Clara! Wake up! Come on Auntie Clara!" Was she breathing? "911! I need to call 911!" She punched in the numbers, and then called Creating Memories. "It's Jinx! I found her but she's passed out! I called 911. Can you meet us at St. Francis?" But Jinx didn't wait for a response, the paramedics were there strapping Auntie Clara on a gurney.

Jinx followed in her car, freaked. Dead? Auntie Clara couldn't be dead! Not Ms. Clara! Auntie Clara! Where was Lizzie? Someone needed to call Lizzie. Jinx punched back in the shoppe number and caught Blanchie, "Call Lizzie," Was all she said.

The doctors were puzzled. Auntie Clara's heart seemed okay, just slowed way down. Of course Auntie Clara was breathing, but just barely. She was on oxygen but just minimally responding. Blanchie, Bertie, and Jinx stood around her bed. "What did they tell you exactly Jinx?" Bertie asked for the millionth time.

"They were vague. I don't know. Doesn't vague mean they don't know?" Jinx wiped her brow, pushing back a stray curl. Then she wondered why she was saying that. Was she trying to frighten these old ladies? Weren't things bad enough as they were? She took a deep breath and shot up an arrow prayer.

Blanchie held Auntie Clara's hand, "Clara, now listen to me. Snap out of this dear--we have a business to run. We need to keep it running until Lizzie comes back."

Lizzie? Auntie Clara heard her name deep in her fog. Oh Lizzie, come home. But what had she done? Auntie Clara couldn't seem to move her hand in Blanchie's. Or wiggle her toes. Or ... or get up. I've gone too far. She wanted to cry, and felt the pent up pressure but couldn't seem to. She couldn't seem to do anything.

"Did you call Lizzie?" Jinx was afraid to ask but did anyway.

"I left word on her machine ..." Blanchie was crying now, "Will you keep trying Jinx?"

Jinx got up to go but Bertie held her back, "Tell us again. Where you found her?"

Jinx strained and thought, "In her apartment." She'd already told them this.

"Yes dear." Blanchie and Bertie said in unison encouraging for more. Hoping for more.

"Well, she was slumped over the dining room table. There was a little metal stool on the floor, as if it had fallen. And she didn't respond when I called her. She was cold ... so cold."

But alive, Jinx thought. Thank God alive. Why did she mention the cold part? Why wasn't she being more sensitive? She was too panicked to remember her manners.

"What else Jinx?"

"Oh I forgot, there was a tumbler that had spilled. Brown liquid. Smelled like maybe whiskey. And I mopped it up with a towel. Afraid it would hurt her beautiful table."

"She was drinking? In the middle of the day?" Blanchie and Bertie exchanged a look.

"I think I got it all off the table," Jinx went on, hoping she had, "But I'm afraid it maybe ruined her scrap book."

"Scrap book ..." And then Blanchie and Bertie started to cry.

Elizabeth listened to the message again. Auntie Blanchie was frantic. Auntie Clara was at St. Francis hospital. But Blanchie didn't know what was wrong. Elizabeth called the hospital. "Yes, I'm a relative. I'm her niece. Her great niece. Oh. Oh I see."

But she didn't see at all. What were they saying? They didn't seem to know what was wrong. Why didn't they know what was wrong? They were the doctors, the pros. Elizabeth tuned back in, and tried to listen.

They were not saying what was wrong only that her aunt was frail and unconscious. They were talking in generalities.

About her Auntie. Auntie Clara.

"If you want to see your Aunt, I suggest you come quickly." Now that was a horrible response! One that left Elizabeth freaked. But one she understood. She called her agency, "Emergency." She didn't know what else to say, didn't have time to go into details.

She called Granville Auction House. "I need to go home; my Auntie is in the hospital ..."

She called the airport.

And then she called Basil.

12

Cooper wandered around the busy streets. It was chilly; after all it wasn't Southern California. The sidewalks were slushy. Had there been snow? He'd lived in California so long he thought of winter as simply crisp air, busy shoppers, roaring fires…

He'd moved to Wind Star in the spring. True, he occasionally saw the weather channel but it all looked so remote and temporary. And wasn't snow supposed to be white? This was gray. Dirty. Little mounds up against bus stops and newspaper machines were sooty, crusty, dirty.

And it was cold. Not so much the air, though it was brisk. But his feet. In the slush. He looked around. What did other people wear that kept the wet icy chill from seeping into their feet?

Cooper passed a bevy of young girls with suede boots and short micro skirts. They had on trendy little jackets--one was trimmed in pink fur. Their boots had heels. Tall heels. They were giggling and oblivious to the weather.

The Salvation Army lady had on a hardy over coat, and matching scarf, and was cheerfully ringing her bell. Two little toddlers wearing fluffy snow suits, walked by with their mother. They seemed oblivious to the cold.

He needed a coat, a real coat, not this thin leather jacket, and maybe a sweater. Sox. He had on a pair of old deck shoes, no socks, worn jeans, and a tee shirt. His leather jacket would have been closed but the zip tab was long gone. Besides he knew zipped it would look dorky. Still, he was cold.

Where was Lizzie's hotel? Cooper swung his leather carry-on to the other shoulder and kept walking.

The door man wore a uniform. Like in a 1940's movie. Cheerful, yet formal, but not cold looking--as in freezing. Cooper rubbed his hands together thinking about gloves and walked in.

"I'm looking for Lizzie McGillicuddy." Now why did he sound like a bounty hunter? Should he add--to visit?

The shark behind the desk never looked up. "We have no one here by that name." She was scanning a computer screen.

Cooper was sure he had the right hotel ... "Elizabeth. Try Elizabeth!" Oh yeah.

The shark scanned again, this time with a scowl, and a small nod. "That's better." He sighed.

"We had a Ms. Elizabeth McGillicuddy. She has checked out."
"What?"

"She has left us sir." Now impatience seeped into her voice. He could hear her click off the computer. A sign she was done--with him. Still he stood. Finally she spoke, "Kindly step aside sir."

A line had formed behind him and he hadn't even noticed.

Gone? Lizzie was gone? To another hotel? Did she get an apartment? Move in with someone? That last thought sent a little shiver down his already cold back.

He left and started to walk, finding himself in front of Barney's. He wandered in and bought a heavy jacket, and gloves, and a scarf. A sweater, he'd buy a sweater, and then come up with a plan.

On the way to sportswear he found sox and bought a pair. He must have looked like a beach bum with his golden tan and sun streaked hair; something the current just swept in. He didn't care. He also didn't care what the snotty sales associates thought every time he bought something and put it on.

"The shoppe! I'll call Creating Memories!" But all he got was a recording. It sounded like Blanchie; old, dignified--announcing their hours. Why weren't they open? It was …11:30! "Basil! I'll call Uncle Basil!"

"Mr. Basil has left town sir."

"I'm his nephew."

Then the receptionist paused, softened, "Unexpectedly. To Wind Star."

Wind Star? Uncle Basil has gone to Wind Star? He racked his brain for the name of Lizzie's agency. In all the conversations they'd had, surely she'd mentioned it. Hadn't she? It was near … maybe he would recognize it if he saw it listed in the phone book.

Surprisingly Barney's had a lounge with phones and more importantly phone books. He sat on a cushy leather sofa and started to look. There were tons. He narrowed it down to five that had a familiar ring and started calling.

Luck was with him on the third call. "Ms. McGillicuddy does work for us. Yes. But she seems to be out of the office. An emergency. In Wind Star."

He hung up and hopped in a cab headed to LaGuardia.

Auntie Clara knew she'd gone too far. If only she could get back. She was walking on a velum colored road. No, it wasn't a road at all, it was smooth; it was paper. No, it was more than paper, it was a page. A page in a scrap book. But where was she?

She stumbled and looked down at golden rocks blinding in their brilliance. They were covered in glitter. Or was that glitter? Gigantic glitter she'd tripped on?

"I'm in a scrap book?" And Auntie Clara laughed, "Darnest dream I've ever had. Now wake up. Come on. Wakey wakey," She told herself. Still she walked. She was at the apartment building now.

And the front was a tidy little garden with a couple of mop head topiaries and pots of geraniums. Red. She so loved red geraniums. Always reminded her of the Grand Hotel on Mackinac Island.

Auntie Clara walked to the next page. Ah yes, the shoppe. How hard they'd all worked to get it just so. She started to run now through the aisles but paper seemed to ripple under her feet. Catching her breath she tried to slow down.

She was at the old barn with Blanchie, Bertie, and Lizzie selecting furniture for the shoppe. Suddenly furniture started closing in on her, following her down the barns aisles. High boys, and china cabinets, led by wing chairs, and massive armoires were pulling up the rear blocking her from going back. She started to head for the barn doors, slightly out of breath.

Could that furniture all be following her, pursuing her? She picked up speed, seeing the massive barn doors just ahead. End tables and library steps had now joined the race. Auntie Clara pushed hard against the doors, her breath burning in her throat as she heaved. The doors gave way, sunlight streamed at her blindingly.

But she ran! The case goods charged. She was almost knocked down by a set of bookshelves. Grasping wildly in the air, she kept pushing forward.

The grass in the pasture was tall, uncut, making her progress slow. She saw Lizzie's little pink Mini. Two sheep were grazing next to it. "Out of me way!" She screamed and made a mad run for the car. Gunning the engine, she stepped on it, and started to peel out. Arm caps from one of the wing chairs were caught in her door, flapping wildly as she drove.

A small end table was wrapped around the radio antennae. She watched in horror as it shook free and flew off into the air. The street? Where was the street? Looking in her rear view mirror she saw the field scattered with furniture--some of it in groupings as though waiting for her return, others lined up, ready to attack.

The tires hit the black top, and she sped away shaking and shuttering. Auntie Clara drove wildly, randomly until she was sure she was safe. "The shoppe! I'll be safe at the shoppe!"

But as she headed toward the quaint tree lined village of Wind Star she stared in horror.

Ahead of her loomed acres of black top and a strip center, gaudy with neon signs, flashing, and winking. She pulled in under metal arches like McDonalds gone bad. The sign read 'Welcome to Creating Memories World'.

"World?" Shivers ran down Auntie Clara's spine. She drove on past a receiving dock, and then came smack dab in front of a small booth.

A surly looking woman with wild gray hair sat behind the window reading a magazine. Gingerly Auntie Clara pulled up. The matron waved her to a stop. "State your business."

State me business? Auntie Clara freaked! This is me business ... "I'm here to go to me shoppe." She didn't mean to sound meek; she just couldn't get anything better out.

"Your shoppe? Lady, are you lost? This is Creating Memories World! Headquarters and warehouses! There are no shoppe's here! We don't even have an outlet store! Did you want to visit one of our franchises?"

"Franchises?" Auntie Clara whispered. But the guard didn't hear her; she was pulling a pamphlet from a file. "You ... you said your head quarters are here? Can I speak with someone?"

"Do you have an appointment?" The woman glared, obviously wasting her magazine reading time.

"Uh no. No I don't. But could you tell me who's in charge? Who owns this?" Because as I headed here I was sure I owned this along with Blanchie, Bertie, and Lizzie. But she just thought this last bit, far too intimidated to say it out loud.

"It is owned by a consortium!"

Now what did that mean? Auntie Clara worried her bottom lip.

"From Japan!"

And with this last bit of information, the guard pulled a shade down over her window and yelled out "good bye!"

And Auntie Clara broke into tears.

"Look Blanchie ..." Elizabeth squeezed Auntie Clara's hand, "I think she's crying!" Sure enough, tears leaked out of the corners of Auntie Clara's closed eyes.

"Quick!" Blanchie directed Bertie, "Tell the nurse there's been some change." Bertie fled while Blanchie and Elizabeth huddled, tears streaming down their faces.

Cooper took a taxi to his dealership. It seemed like ages since he'd been back. Too long. Way too long. And as this missing it all washed over him, he knew he was home, home where he belonged. He felt grubby from his travels, his new wintery clothes still not quite broken in. He wanted a shower, maybe a nap.

But Cooper had a mission. He had to find his Uncle Basil, and find out just what was going on. He would have plenty of time to clean up, rest up later. Hopefully.

His little apartment, over the garages, beckoned but when he stepped into the showroom he was bombarded. "Sir, she's been waiting for you." And the manager angled his head to Cooper's office.

A middle aged woman with a cap of short blonde curls stood. She wore a power suit; a brief case leaned against her chair. She did not look impatient. Just determined. So he figured if his manager couldn't sort it out, he better. With reluctance he headed to his office.

"Rosemary Hills—realtor," She extended her hand.

Cooper took it, wondering if he'd ever seen this woman before. He was sure he hadn't.

"I'm here to buy a new BMW," She asserted. She sounded like she meant business.

He nodded, unimpressed, after all that is what they did. "Joseph my manager can show you our selection." He had to find his Uncle Basil.

"I know what I want." And she produced a magazine ad from her brief case.

"Uh, excellent." Again Cooper wasn't sure why he was needed. A lot of clients wanted the owner to help them, it was just that simple. Somehow it meant more when they made their final purchase. It was, actually, part of the purchase. And for some people he knew it was an important part. He acknowledged that, "We have that exact model and color."

"Could you have Joseph draw up the paper work?" Rosemary now seemed not quite as professional, almost human. She had been there obviously long enough to be on a first name basis with his manager.

He raised an eyebrow but gave a tiny nod. A nod that said you are right. You are my customer and you are right.

"Okay." And he motioned for his manager.

Rosemary produced a cashier's check, obviously she was prepared. There was no haggling, no questioning the bottom line, or pleading for some obtuse discount. She was ready. Ready to drive home her new car.

And he was ready to find his Uncle Basil.

She handed it to Joseph along with a stack of papers. "I actually had an ulterior motive Mr. Herrington," She spoke quieter now, less power woman--more just woman.

He raised that same eyebrow.

"You're buying a car--an expensive car with an ulterior motive?" Cooper still wore his new navy pea coat from Barneys, his one hundred per cent wool sox itched. He was tired. Too tired to be subtle. Yet curious ... he was curious.

Rosemary suddenly laughed, "Well, to tell you the truth, I've had my eye on that car for quite some time."

Cooper let his guard down a level.

And this time she managed a tiny smile when she asked him a favor, "Actually, I wondered if we could go for a drive?"

"In your new car?" Cooper raised an eyebrow.

"Oh no--let them prep it or whatever they do. No, any car. Your car will do." Again matter of fact.

They started out to the parking lot, and as they were seated in Cooper's Jag, Rosemary started directing. Cooper played along. Yes, he was weary but it was a sale--a big sale. And he knew the sooner he went along, the sooner he would be done and could get on with it.

So he played along.

"I want to show you--no sell you a piece of property." Rosemary didn't use her realtor tone; as a matter of fact she was quiet.

Cooper wasn't quite sure he'd heard her correctly. She was staring straight ahead. Gone was the direct eye contact that probably made her a number one realtor. This was ... human.

"But I'm not looking for property," Cooper squinted at Rosemary the realtor. This was the last thing he expected--the very last.

"Aren't you Mr. Herrington?" Her voice was soft. She hadn't meant it to be but it was just how it came out. It probably had more affect on him than if it had been powerful and accusing.

Cooper shrugged a yes. "No really, about the property--and call me Cooper."

Finally Rosemary let her guard down.

They were out in the country. There was a light dusting of sugary snow on the tree branches. Nothing like the filthy slush of New York City--just a sprinkling of glitter.

"It's getting on Christmas Ms. Hills." Cooper was compelled to make small talk. They drove past a tiny clapboard chapel. A few sheep lingered on the lawn. The church sign simply read 'everyone welcome'.

"Next week," Rosemary answered, referring to Christmas. Her eyes also caught the tiny church. For a moment she misted, lost in her own thoughts.

"I well, I got a call--from a client, a new client actually. He wants to sell his house, farm really ..."

A farm? Now what would make this aggressive crazy realtor think I want a farm? Property ... property he didn't have time to take care of.

"And he wants to sell it to you." She was looking out the window, still just a little stuck back at the clap board church.

Cooper jammed on the breaks, "To me?" He'd been in Wind Star a matter of months. He knew a handful of people ... And hardly anyone knew him. Most people hadn't quite realized the car deal-ership had changed hands. He was still, for all intensive purposes, under the radar.

It was too strange, and aggressive, of a proposal--and just a little too personal. And who was this person?

Rosemary nodded, "Up here and turn." She pointed and he start-ed back up again. Why, he wasn't sure. But he did.

"Who is he?"

"Well, that's the strange part ..." And Rosemary hesitated. She knew to be careful. She didn't have her usual hold on Mr. Herrington's personality, her strong realtor's hold. How could she, it was such an odd situation. And besides he was guarded, very guarded. And a little bit elusive. "The request has come from a bank. It is part of an estate."

"You mean your client is dead?" Cooper looked alarmed. He al-most took his eyes off the road but knew better.

"Uh ..." Now Rosemary let a little of her pent up anxiety out, "I don't know. I didn't, well, I didn't challenge it. I was a bit over whelmed by the nature of the request. I was to show you the property and make you an offer. Oddly, when I found out who you were, I real-ized you owned the dealership, and the car I'd been, well, debating about for the past six months was there."

"And here we are," Cooper finished, still wary, still driving.

Finally Rosemary smiled and Cooper softened, "Yes, here we are."

He'd been driving carelessly but started to slow down. The street was tunneled with trees. Even without their leaves, they formed a can-opy. A canopy of frosty and snow covered branches. It was ... well, it was magical.

A tunnel of magic.

He wanted to remember just where this was so he could drive it again. He wanted to see it when the leaves were brilliant oranges and reds of fall and deep dark greens of summer ...

"Just up here." Rosemary was following her own printed directions.

But Cooper didn't need them. He had no idea where they were going but he knew the little farm, and the big red barn in the back was ahead.

"I know it seems rather remote ..." Rosemary was starting her pitch, "But the main roads are close, and as you can see we're just about twenty, twenty five minutes from your dealership." She was guessing, and hoped it didn't seem too far away, too far for her to close her sale.

He was a car guy. Wouldn't mind a commute ... a drive?

Cooper pulled into the gravel drive. Sure enough a couple of sheep stood by the front gate. They had silver bells around their necks. Their bells tinkled as they looked up. The sound reminded him of the silver bell Lizzie had worn around her neck with a couple other charms. She'd told him it was a faerie bell.

The single black sheep was just ducking behind the side of the house. It caught his eye as it disappeared. Cooper wanted to get out and go for it.

Rosemary looked relieved yet hadn't remembered telling him which house to pull in.

Cooper turned off the engine.

"I'll take it."

Rosemary looked alarmed. Relieved--and then alarmed again.

Cooper opened his car door and headed out. Instead of scattering, the sheep went to his side. He walked through the light snow to the side of the house, Rosemary chasing after him. He whistled sharply, not sure why.

The huge barn door was ajar by about two feet. As his whistle cracked the cold air a rustling sound came from the barn. Suddenly an old English bull dog raced out! And charged toward Cooper.

Rosemary froze in fear but Cooper dropped to his knees. "Come here boy." And the dog leapt into his arms, big, and clumsy.

Rosemary watched, still a bit frightened yet fascinated, "You, er, you know this dog?"

But Cooper didn't answer, he just nuzzled the dog.

"There's a rather odd contingency in the offer ..."

Cooper looked up at Rosemary; the dog moved droopy loving eyes up to Cooper.

"The animals come with the property and well, there is a request that you keep them."

Rosemary had been afraid to bring this up. Afraid it would crash her sale hopes to dust. And she wasn't even sure when she'd read it if she'd even get this far. It was after all, an unusual request, though obviously sentimental. Still it was one no one could really enforce, or at least no way she knew of.

Still, it was in her paper work. So she brought it up. Fearful. Hopeful. But to her utter amazement it didn't seem to faze Cooper. He and the dog seemed to already know each other, or maybe they'd just instantly bonded. She didn't know. She really wasn't an animal person.

Cooper was too consumed to ask who'd been taking care of the animals. Last time he'd been in the house it had obviously been vacant ... Dusty, musty, empty. There had been no dog. No dog he had seen anyway.

"Okay."

"Okay?"

"Uh huh," Cooper gave her a boyish smile, "I've always wanted a dog. An English bull dog, actually." The dog now seemed glued to his side. "And how much trouble could some sheep be?"

"Shouldn't we see the house?" Rosemary was still nervous.

They walked over back to the front door and she produced a huge ornate brass key tied with a red ribbon and a small bell. Carefully and respectfully they both removed their shoes. The dog sat on the porch waiting.

The foyer floors were newly sanded pine. Light filtered in from a living room window overlooking the barn. A few odd pieces of furniture lay hidden under drop clothes. He hadn't remembered seeing them, but wasn't sure.

"It comes with whatever is in here ..." Rosemary began, wanting to peek under a drop cloth but knowing she had to stay on track. She was sure she was closing the deal--pretty sure.

The country kitchen was as Cooper remembered it--big, yet cozy with another window looking out at the barn. Criss cross curtains that he'd recalled were dusty and limp were now crisp and bright white. A round pine table sat in front of the bay window seat. He could see himself having a cup of coffee sitting there, just gazing out.

With Lizzie.

The thought hit him like cold water being dumped on him. He not only wanted this house, this property, this barn, this dog ...he wanted Lizzie! He wanted to share it and everything else he had with her. He thought of his tiny furnished apartment at the dealership, his grandfather's little hideaway. His bedroom was the size of a double bed, no more. His view was of the parking lot and cars.

They wandered to the bedrooms. The house was more spacious than it appeared from the outside. More of the refinished floors fol-lowed into the master bedroom. A wall of windows looked out at a stand of pines. He closed his eyes and saw them with twinkle lights for Christmas. An old ornately carved bed painted shiny white peeked out from a drop cloth.

Rosemary sighed as she pulled off the protecting throw. She couldn't help herself. She just wanted to see it. "This is fabulous! And probably worth a fortune ..." This was the type of thing she'd seen in Arc. Digest a million times.

And drooled over.

Cooper agreed, picturing a tousled Lizzie waking up in it. "And you're sure all this furniture and stuff stays?"

Rosemary nodded, "Quite sure." Not sure how and why, but sure what the paper work said. And she hadn't really questioned any of it. The bank, of course was very legit. And so were the lawyers. When she had hesitated they simply said quirky. That there were some peo-ple out there that were quirky.

She felt pretty certain it was part of an estate. Quirky people who were gone? A quirky estate? Finally she'd just accepted the whole mystery and sought out Cooper. She had an address and simply put it in her GPS.

When she was led to the Range Rover/BMW/Jag car dealership she figured it was fate, and time she purchased the car she'd been hedging on, dreaming about.

"And the owners?"

"Anonymous."

He knew it was odd, very odd. Still he didn't question it. How could he? And he knew he didn't really care what the whole odd story was. He just knew right now. The farm house had haunted his waking thoughts, and his head, at night as he slept. And he wasn't sure why. But now he was here.

Again.

"And you brought the paperwork?"

Rosemary nodded, being the ever efficient realtor, returning to the kitchen table and spreading it out.

As they headed back to the dealership Rosemary laughed, "Well you just bought yourself a house!" She was still a bit uneasy but lightening up. And who knew, one day their paths might cross again, they might become friends and she could return.

Cooper grinned, "And you a car!" But then he sobered, "The dog! We forgot the dog! Someone needs to look after it!" How could he forget the dog? His dream dog?

"Shish." Rosemary put her finger to her lips. They both listened. To a snoring sound, mixed in with little grunts and wheezes. Rosemary turned around in her seat and pulled back an old plaid blanket. The English bull dog opened one droopy eye.

"Uh Cooper ... I don't think you'll have to worry about the dog ..."

Cooper looked in his rear view mirror and saw a grinning drooling dog sitting in the back seat. He shook his head grinning himself until he was laughing.

13

Rosemary pulled out in her new car, and Cooper headed to Creating Memories. It was a five minute drive. The front door had a cheery Cedar and Boxwood wreath along with a small hand written sign: 'closed, family emergency'. He wandered to the Patisserie to grab a hot coffee. "You wouldn't happen to know what's happening at the scrap book shoppe?" He asked Colette as she put a lid on his coffee.

"Ms. Clara is in the hospital--Saint Francis hospital. And I think everyone is with her."

He didn't even take the time to ask what was wrong with her, just flew out the door. The race to the hospital was frantic--the receptionist stubborn. Finally he said. "I'm family. I'm her nephew." Well almost. At which point he was given the magic room number.

He skidded to a stop outside the open door. And stared. Blanchie, Bertie, and Lizzie all held hands around Auntie Clara, tears streaming down their faces. His heart started to crack. Auntie Clara lay pale as a corpse. He couldn't even see her breathing. She had tubes coming out of her nose.

And monitors everywhere.

Suddenly he realized time was very fleeting. Miss Clara looked well past her best before date. What was he doing wasting time? His eyes kept darting back to Lizzie. Her silent crying caused little shutters to shake her frail frame. He just watched and didn't hear any one come up behind him. He felt the back slap as he heard the voice.

"Cooper!"

"Uncle Basil!"

"Glad you could get back from Europe, and your trade shows, and away from your dealership." They hugged like the family they were.

Lizzie diverted her eyes from Auntie Clara and stared; her mouth hung open--her tears dried up. Uncle Basil? Uncle Basil? Basil? Her Basil? Dealership? Do mechanics refer to their dealership as THEIR dealership? European trade shows? Do mechanics go to European trade shows?

Even though she was grieving for Auntie Clara, she heard every word.

Clearly.

And just that fast Cooper realized what had happened. "Lizzie … I can explain …"

But she was tearing out of the room.

Cooper fled after her with Basil's echo of "I thought he told her!"

Blanchie and Bertie shook their heads sadly, Auntie Clara momentarily forgotten.

"Lizzie wait! I can explain!" Cooper was the pale one now. Miss Blanchie, of course, had been right--very right.

Elizabeth kept going down the endless hallways, nearly plowing over an orderly. "Explain?" She didn't even turn around, flying past an old man with a walker. "Explain that you lied? There's nothing to explain!" And then she ran.

He caught up with her in the parking lot, sobbing against her little pink Mini. Suddenly he slowed his run down, almost afraid to go to her. Carefully he came forward, and put an arm around her shaking shoulders.

"Lizzie. Please. Please listen to me." She didn't turn. "I was afraid," His voice was low, quiet. "You liked me as a mechanic."

"You lied."

He heard it between sobs.

"I actually am a mechanic--and a race car driver. And as a race car driver women fawned over me because I was famous." He sighed, "Okay, semi famous. But they didn't like me. They didn't even know me. They liked who I was. I couldn't risk that with you. For the first time in my life someone liked me--for me, and would stand up to me. Even yell at me."

He sighed again, "I just happened to inherit my grandfather's dealership. I never intended to keep it. I started to clean it up to sell, and found I liked running it. And then I met you."

She turned, found herself in his arms. "Is that true?" Her eyes were sparkled with tears.

"Every word," He held his breath.

"But ... but were you ever going to tell me?"

He stared.

"Or were you just going to wait until whatever we had just burned out, and you could quietly go away?" She was rough on him because of course she'd hit it on the head--with a hammer.

Shocked by the thought, Cooper was forced to be honest, "Lizzie. Honestly, I never thought I could have the feelings I have. And as they grew I kept thinking now--tell her now. But I couldn't. I just loved what we had. I didn't want to risk it. And then, when I was gone, I realized I love you."

"Love me?" Elizabeth whispered, taken aback.

"Uh huh."

"And you were going to get around to telling me?" Now there was teasing in her voice, tears and anger forgotten.

"I was going to get advice from Uncle Basil." Why was he admitting this to her? Admitting he couldn't figure it out on his own. Because he couldn't figure it out on his own.

"He really is your uncle?" Elizabeth's eyes opened wide.

"Well Great Uncle. But yeah, he is."

"I really like him." And she let a tiny smile slip out. She was terribly fond of Basil.

"Me too."

"He sold me the pink Mini." She remembered when Cooper wondered what crazy person would sell her that little pink Mini. Or even allow it to be pink.

"He should have known better."

"He couldn't say no."

And then Cooper realized no one could say no to her.

"How's your Auntie?" He'd seen her. Why was he asking? Auntie Clara looked terrible. He stroked her hair, brushing a few tear stained strands from her cheeks.

"They ... they don't know. I can't lose her Cooper. I love her so much. And I don't know what to do. Jinx found her, thank God." She started to tremble again because she knew it was close. Very close to being the end of her family. The family she'd walked away from.

"They can't figure out anything--the doctors. They don't say anything because they don't know," She was rambling--couldn't help it.

"Where was she?" Cooper hoped she hadn't been driving. But of course if Jinx had found her she wasn't ...

"In her apartment."

"Maybe we ought to go there and well, look around." It seemed like the right thing to say. They couldn't just go back, and stand there, and watch Miss Clara just fade away. And since no one seemed to know what had happened, maybe they could find something--anything. Anything that might have caused a change.

Maybe Auntie Clara had taken too much cough medicine or ... well he didn't know what. And of course cough medicine was silly, but he was reaching--reaching out for anything.

Maybe she'd mixed up her meds. Didn't you read all the time about old people doing that? Though if he had to admit it she was sharp—awfully sharp. Not the type to mix up her prescriptions.

Still ... As far as Cooper could tell she hadn't been sick ... or had she? Auntie Clara was old, so very old, it could just be death coming to get her... Then he realized he had referred to her as Auntie Clara, thought of her as Auntie. He wanted her to be his Auntie too.

Elizabeth looked lost. Any suggestion was something. And she had run out of them. She'd tried to comfort Auntie Blanchie and Auntie Bertie as best she could. They were so upset they didn't even reprimand her for leaving. They were just grateful to have her back--before it was too late.

She hoped it wasn't too late.

Had she ever thanked Auntie Clara for well, saving her? Really thanked her? Had she ... had she what? She couldn't lose Auntie Clara now. There was so much she didn't know, so many questions she hadn't gotten around to asking her. She needed more. Much more.

And they had things to do together. Who would she get chocolate bars for if Auntie Clara was gone? Who would she share Whiskey Pound Cake with and hot tea late at night with? And the garden? Auntie Clara's little garden outside the brown stone, and the shoppe. What about the shoppe? Auntie Clara loved that shoppe ...

"Maybe you're right." She started to get her keys out.

"Wait. Let's take my car. I uh--I have someone waiting in my car." And he grabbed her hand and tugged her through the lot.

She gave him a baffled look, "Someone? In your car?" But by the time she got the words out he was unlocking the Jag. On the back seat sat a brindle English bull dog, posing. Almost stuffed. Like a prop, with a big silly grin on his face. When he saw Cooper he started panting, and maybe drooling just a little bit.

"A dog? You got a dog? I love English bull dogs!" And Elizabeth reached in to give him a hug.

Cooper watched nervously. After all, he knew nothing about this dog or its temperament. Much to Cooper's delight the dog practically threw himself at Lizzie, and started to make a happy purring sound. Okay, maybe a happy snorting sound. But the dog acted friendly ...

"I can't believe it! My favorite kind of dog ... He's wonderful! And look, he's wearing a collar." And on closer examination she noticed a tiny silver bell looped onto his collar. She softly stroked his big square head, and he looked loving eyes up at her.

"When did you get a dog? When did you get back?" And for the first time in hours, Elizabeth laughed, the weight lifted just a bit, for just a second.

He swung an arm around her. "Oh, it's a very long story. But what about going to your Aunts and we'll talk. I'll tell you everything." And he meant it. He'd tell her about his real job, and his old career in racing, and his childhood on the racing circuit with his dad. And his beloved grandfather, now gone. And Basil, the light of his life, great uncle who treated him like a son.

All.

He wouldn't leave anything out. Right down to the farm house, which he prayed she would like at least a little bit, and about how this very sweet dog had just found and adopted him. And of course how he couldn't live without her ...

The drive to Auntie Clara's was filled with the dog vying for Elizabeth's attention. Cooper swore she talked more to the dog than to him, but it was a relief to see her reaching to the back seat to give his new dog a little scratch, or a rub on the head. And say things to him like don't fall off the seat, and do you need a baby seat?

He laughed because he was sure, well pretty sure, dogs did not get strapped in baby seats. And this dog was solid; he didn't look like he was falling off of anything. The dog oddly acted like he'd known Lizzie his whole life. He started to whine a bit, and when she told him to shush he stopped.

Then she told him how good he was, he made those happy sounds again. For just the very shortest of seconds Cooper felt as if the three of them were just out for a drive, maybe to get an ice cream.

That they were a happy little family just going on an outing.

But once they got to Auntie Clara's apartment they were speechless. The dining room lights were still on, forgotten. The chair Auntie Clara had obviously slumped over in was on its side; possibly over turned when the paramedics lifted her out. Pink Martini's CD Sympathique caught on repeat cried about a shining star falling and falling in love. Chills ran down Cooper's back.

The dog wandered around and then started to howl.

Elizabeth fought back more tears as she neared the table. A single scrap book lay open, black sharpies were scattered around, their lids off, drying up. A bottle of glue lay on its side, pooled on the beautiful old table. Elizabeth automatically started to clean it up and stopped, "Cooper ..." She whispered.

He was at her side as she pointed. Pointed at the photograph of Auntie Clara with the black clouds penned in over her head, and the tear drops of black rain around and on her. Cooper stared. "Strange--very strange. Your Aunt has a rather odd sense of humor."

But Elizabeth wasn't listening; she was scooping up the scrap book. "Come on--get Scrappy. We have to go to the shoppe."

"Leave? Now? We just got here! Scrappy? You named our dog?" But he ran after her. So did the dog.

"Our dog?" But it was an echo as Elizabeth raced back down the four flights of stairs, Cooper, and Scrappy in her wake. They drove like lightning to Creating Memories. Once inside Elizabeth started gathering up packages of stickers. "Help me Cooper."

But he had no clue what he was supposed to pick up.

"My Auntie ... well, she's special," Elizabeth started to try and explain. Explain something she couldn't explain to herself. Still she tried. She rummaged in her desk for a bottle of white out.

"Now I don't really have all the facts; the Aunties are very tight lipped but, well Cooper, they make things happen. I know they do. I am sure, well pretty sure. There are no coincidences in life."

"Well they are pretty ambitious for three old ladies."

"No--you don't understand. They ... they create things." She was concentrating, trying to make decisions. What should she do? What was the right thing? How did she do it? Would it work? How would she know?

"They're artistic?" Cooper scratched his head. They were artistic, that was obvious. All of them. He looked around and thought, of course they are. This was not your run of the mill store. It was very creative.

"No ..." Elizabeth still worked on finding the white out.

"They have magical powers?" Cooper could feel a small bead of perspiration start on his forehead. And another trickling down his neck. What even made him ask that?

"No, oh no ... well, I'm not sure what it really is. Magical powers are pretty strong words. They, well, they put things in their scrap books and then they--well, they happen." She'd finally made the decision in her mind that they indeed did make things happen ... with their scrap books.

How it happened, she was clueless. That was another question. But the fact that things did happen, well there was no denying that any longer. She couldn't get away from it. And she'd had a lot of time in New York to think about it.

Lonely time.

Time when she missed them.

All three of them.

And even though she was no closer to the how, she was pretty sure that yes that was what they did.

Cooper squinted. This was all way out of his realm of reality.

"You know all the furniture in here?" And she waved her arms around taking in the beautiful old waxed book shelves, the lovely tables, her desk, and all the rest. "Well, remember I'd seen it in Auntie's scrap book before I actually found it at the barn."

And he did remember. The night she had run up to Auntie Clara's apartment for Whiskey Pound Cake. And not come back. And he'd gone looking for her. She was sitting at the same table they'd found Auntie Clara's scrap book. Probably the same spot where Auntie Clara had passed out.

She was leafing through her aunt's scrap book freaked out. And to be honest, he was a little freaked out to. But he had tried to cover it. Talk it away. Because of course it was too unbelievable. So he'd dismissed it.

"The barn ..." Was it his barn? The one he was so taken with? Cooper still hadn't digested the house, the barn, the dog. Were they real? Scrappy sure was real. He lay snoring by the door. Of course they were real. He'd just purchased them. Just because he felt a connection to them didn't mean they weren't real.

And the country side was dotted with barns—actually tons of barns. Lizzie's barn was another barn. He was sure of that. Well, pretty sure. He was getting side tracked. Lizzie was talking. He needed to tune back in.

"I think Auntie Clara brought me to Wind Star. I couldn't even remember her ... from my child hood I mean. And yet when I got her letter, it was at a time I was desperate, at the end, so to speak."

"I know that sounds melodramatic and maybe it is, but you have no idea what I was going through. I couldn't find a job; I was running up bills, my apartment was ready to kick me out. I was depressed, terribly depressed, living on Oreos, and gloom. And I got this letter from an Aunt I couldn't remember."

Elizabeth took in a gulp of air, "Auntie Clara was offering me a job, a place to live--a chance to start over. She was bailing me out, and I couldn't even remember her. I had no clue where Wind Star was. I had no clue where anything was outside of New York City. I wasn't kidding when I said I was one of those people who thought the earth ended outside the city limits."

Then with a sigh she went on, "Auntie Clara had put eight hundred dollars in an envelope, and I cried, and laughed. I cried because I swear I had pocket change, that's it. Literally. Maybe a couple dollars in one of my designer bags. No more. And I laughed because she was suggesting I take this eight hundred dollars, and purchase a car, and drive cross country to start over. I couldn't imagine eight hundred dollars going very far. Maybe a couple pairs of shoes ... that's it."

And Cooper raised an eyebrow. She did seem to have an endless array of outrageous shoes. Still he had no idea what women's shoes cost ...

"She told me to go see a friend of hers. A Mr. Basil Herrington and buy a car. In Brooklyn, no less. I had to dig through all my old handbags, and landed up taking public transportation, and paying with loose change. I was grateful I had found enough to get me there.

Of course I hadn't wanted to go--to Brooklyn. You know how I felt about leaving New York City ..."

Then she laughed a little, remembering, "But I was desperate, and her letter was so sweet. The idea of going there, and buying a car sounded impossible. Just one more humiliating thing for me to go through. The money she'd sent me was it. All I had. But I went anyway, to heck with humiliation. Then I met Basil. Well I was stunned. He was so old--very old. But oddly I just liked him so much—I couldn't help myself. He has that twinkle, and well, he is just very dear."

Cooper knew that twinkle.

"Basil assured me there was a car somewhere on that lot for me. I doubted it to the point I felt the whole thing was a joke, a big joke on me. But I knew in my heart I was no one. No one anyone would take the time to play a joke on. So I followed him through the show-room and out into the lot. He has the most spectacular cars I have ever seen."

Elizabeth shook her head. "When we got to the Mini it was sad-horrible actually. Stripped to primer, not at all my idea of a car. But the more I looked at it the more I knew this little car needed me, needed me to save it from this lot of status cars."

Elizabeth took a deep breath, "Of course Basil told me I could have it painted any which way I wanted. And Ray, his paint artist, well he really was an artist, Ray baulked a bit at first but then he gave in and said yes, he'd make it pink. And plaid."

Cooper shook his head as to what that custom paint job had cost his uncle. A fortune. A big fortune. He loved his uncle even more for it.

"Then Basil mentioned that the interior was green and he fig-ured it would match my eyes because Auntie Clara's eyes were green and he just assumed, well he assumed mine would be too. And you know Cooper, I remembered. Just like that."

Now Elizabeth grinned, "I was a tiny little girl. But I knew my eyes were rather strange. No one else had them. And I remembered look-ing up into a papery old face. A kind face. To my very same eyes. And of course Basil had been right. Then I felt guilty about the car and told Basil I was afraid he would get fired for selling it to me so cheap."

"How much did he charge you?" Cooper wanted to know. Needed to know.

"Two hundred dollars."

"What? Uncle Basil sold you that car for two hundred dollars? And threw in the paint job?"

"Uh huh," Elizabeth nodded.

"A good custom paint job could be as much as ten thousand dollars. Not to mention that plaid roof of yours. I can't imagine how much more that would cost. I would put it down for another six." Cooper was shaking his head.

Her car was painted perfectly. And in a color not really found on cars ... And the plaid roof seemed to match those hand bags she favored, and if he wasn't mistaken a tiny little halter he'd seen her wear...

Elizabeth's eyes shot open, "Honestly, I had no clue. None what so ever."

"I'm sure. Or Uncle Basil would never have done it. He obviously wanted it to be special ..." And he was pretty sure Auntie Clara was the reason. The reason he basically bought Lizzie a car.

"I'm going to make it up to him. Pay him back. I'll save up." And she meant it. She didn't want to take advantage of Basil. Uncle Basil.

"So you packed up and drove to Wind Star?"

Elizabeth nodded yes, "I couldn't have done it without that GPS though. I had no clue where I was going or even how long it would take."

"Uncle Basil put a GPS in your car?" And Cooper saw more dollar signs.

"Uh huh. A Tom Tom with John Cleese, you know the Brit from Faulty Towers?"

And he did know. More money.

"I was shocked how the terrain changed as I drove, and I started to rather enjoy it. You know the rolling hills and farms. Wind Star, granted is miniscule, but it has charm. And when I pulled up to Auntie Clara's brown stone I was charmed again. I liked her immediately. Really it was instant. I think we both felt it. It felt like, well, coming home. And she just seemed to understand and care. Of course I had no idea what the job was. When I found out I was the grounds keeper I started to melt down until I remembered what I had left and what I had—nothing."

"So I guess you really were mad when I ran over your flowers ..." Now he felt bad.

Guilty.

Even though at the time he'd just laughed.

But Elizabeth nodded yes with a bit of a shirk, "Seems like ages ago really. Yes, I was, but I got over it." And she remembered how hard it had been digging and scraping in the yard.

"But I think it was all part of Auntie Clara's doing. It certainly toughened me up, and got me out of the bout of self pity I'd been going through in New York. I was too tired to feel sorry for myself. And I was busy. For some reason I didn't want to let Auntie Clara down."

"And my little flat, it's well, it's me. And and ... the flowers for the yard, and of course the shoppe—this shoppe." And she spread her arms around taking it all in. All the love that went into putting it together so she wouldn't have to work for anyone again. "And I think you ..."

"Me? I was part of your old auntie's plan?" Impossible! Cooper started to get angry! Why, he cared for Lizzie because, because ... because he cared for her. And he came to town because his grandfather had died.

"Well, let's just pretend it is possible ..." Elizabeth had filled a basket with stickers.

"Well, if it is ... why would Auntie Clara put black clouds over herself?" But he knew. He knew as he asked the question.

Elizabeth started to cry. It just seeped out, slowly building. Scrappy wandered over and nudged her leg. She bent down to scratch his square head. Finally she whispered, "She wanted me to come back.

To come home. And if she got sick, she knew I'd come ..." And then she sobbed.

"But she didn't know how sick she'd get ..." Cooper was trying to comfort her. "And, that's why the hospital can't figure out what's wrong with her."

Elizabeth nodded as she bit her bottom lip, "We need--we need to bring this scrap book to her bedside. And ... and we need to put things in it to get her well."

Cooper grabbed a handful of stickers, and the dogs lead, and they rushed out. He put the Jag to the test, practically flying. The next thing they were racing down the halls, looking for her room, Scrappy in tow.

Blanchie and Bertie were still huddled around Auntie Clara's bed. They looked up, blurry eyed and exhausted. Uncle Basil was pacing. Elizabeth opened the scrap book and laid it on Auntie Clara's bed next to her right arm. "Cooper--quick start opening stickers and get the bottle of white-out. Auntie Clara, its Lizzie. I'm here. I'm going to fix things. Hold on. Please hold on."

Frantically Cooper dug through the packages of stickers wondering what would be right.

Carefully Lizzie painted white-out over the black clouds. At first the black bled through, fighting her. She kept painting. Then she tackled the rain.

Cooper opened some flowers and started putting daisies and roses by Auntie Clara's feet in the picture.

Blanchie and Bertie watched stunned. Basil watched confused.

Auntie Clara sighed. She felt lighter. A little lighter. As if that heavy weight was subsiding just a tad. She tried to open her eyes but couldn't. She tried to wiggle her fingers, no luck. But then she smelled something. Roses. She breathed deeply taking in their sweet scent. The scent of a garden. Lizzie's garden. Back at her brown stone.

"She's breathing better!" Blanchie cried. Basil stared, afraid to speak.

Cooper put a sandwich sticker by her hand. Maybe she was hungry. Why weren't there any stickers of medicine?

Lizzie peeled off a faerie sticker and put it over the now white cloud. The faerie's little wand was touching Auntie Clara's head.

Cooper was amazed but color seemed to be seeping back in to her face. Just a little. A little was a step in the right direction. He put a sticker of a peppermint by the drawn line that had been her smile. Maybe her mouth was dry from being asleep so long; maybe it tasted bad from all the meds they'd pumped into her. If he hadn't been so frantic he might have felt foolish. He didn't. He felt he was helping.

Elizabeth squeezed his hand in thanks.

He saw her swipe at a tear. He put a dog sticker that rather resembled Scrappy by Auntie Clara's foot on the scrap book page, and suddenly the sheet on the hospital bed twitched. Ever so slightly. Her saw it. So did Elizabeth.

"Lizzie--quick give me your driver's license." He was pulling his out of his wallet. He put them next to Auntie Clara on the scrap book page and she stirred.

"Come on Auntie Clara. I know you can hear us. It's Cooper. Come back. I'm back. Back to stay." He opened a package of wedding stickers, and put a little paper veil over Lizzie's drivers license head, and a top hat over his own. Then he added a bouquet, and a big diamond ring.

"Lizzie--marry me. I love you. Promise to marry me. Auntie Clara come back. We're going to have a wedding. Lizzie's going to stay. I bought the farm house--with the dog. The dog's here under your bed, hiding so he doesn't get caught. We named him Scrappy. Come back Auntie Clara--come back and share this all with us. Be part of it."

A stream of quiet tears flowed down Lizzie's face as she caught Cooper's eye. Then she nodded. She lifted Auntie Clara's hand and placed it over the page they'd created. Auntie Clara's amethyst ring twinkled as Lizzie shifted her hand smoothing it over the collage.

"Clara!" Blanchie was crying, "Clara keep trying." Bertie was sobbing.

And as Auntie Clara's hand slowly moved, her eyes gently cracked open. Just a slit. She tried to smile but just that little movement seemed like such work. Slowly she managed.

Basil went to call the nurse but Blanchie stopped him. "She's coming back. She'll be okay."

Basil wiped his eyes with a dapper handkerchief and then tucked it back in his suit pocket.

Lizzie and Cooper were hugging her and crying. "Auntie Clara--you're back. You got our message! You scared us! We love you so much! I'm back! I'm staying here! I'm going to run our shoppe! I'm going to marry Cooper!"

Auntie Clara's eyes flickered and her smile blossomed. She tried to speak; her throat was dry, so very dry. Cooper slipped a few ice chips in and Auntie Clara's eyes met his with gratitude.

"Auntie Clara! You're back! I love you! Can you say something? Anything? I'm going to marry Cooper!"

Auntie Clara took a deep breath, her eyes now twinkling and her lips parted. She only managed one word, "When?"

14

Jefferson started turning out lights at Fairchild's; the day was over. It was time to leave. Where was Jinx? Was she still down at Creating Memories? He put Maisie and Mrs. Wigglesworth, their red Pekinese, back on their leads and tied them to his brief case by the door.

Jinx came flying back in, her arms full of papers and packages. "I get to help Lizzie with her invitations! She's making them like a scrap book!" Then she looked around, "Is it that late already?"

As Jefferson nodded and the dogs barked, Jinx clicked off the lights, flipped the sign to 'closed' and Jefferson tripped the lock.

Recipe:
Auntie Clara's Whiskey Pound Cake
Ingredients:
2 cups sugar
½ cup white raisins soaked in Glenlivet whiskey
10 eggs, separated and at room temperature
4 ½ cups flour
¾ teaspoon salt
1 teaspoon cream of tartar
3 tablespoons Glenlivet Whiskey
1 teaspoon vanilla extract

Procedure:

Mix the softened butter with 1 ¼ cups of the sugar. Beat until fluffy. If you are lucky enough to have more than one mixer, this is the time to get the other one out. Add the egg yolks. Vanilla and Glenlivet and continue to beat until the batter is light in color and very fluffy.

Add the flour and salt and try not to collapse the batter. Fold in the raisins.

In a separate bowl beat the egg whites until stiff and then slowly add the ¾ cup remaining sugar. Continue to beat until sugar is dissolved. Fold egg white mixture into the cake batter and gently incorporate it being careful not to deflate the batter.

Place batter in two vegetable sprayed and floured bread pans that measure about 9x5x3.

Bake in a preheated 350oven for one hour. Test the cake and when baked, place on a rack to cool.

Glenlivet Whiskey syrup:
¼ pound butter
1/4 cup water
1 cup white sugar
1cup Glenlivet Whiskey
Bring water, butter and sugar to a boil, stirring constantly until sugar is dissolved. (about 5 minutes)
Cool.
Add Glenlivet Whiskey

With a fork poke holes in your pound cake and drizzle in Glenlivet Whiskey syrup. Continue until all is used up. Wrap cake top in foil to prevent it from drying out.

A sneak preview of the next Scrap Book Trilogy:

GRAND
MEMORIES

INTRODUCTION

"Jinx!" Jefferson lugged an over flowing tote bag, and two red Pekinese on leads, up the rose lined sidewalk to their British shoppe Fairchild's. He had a brief case on a long strap over his shoulder. His wife Jinx trailed behind absorbed in a brochure. Her hands free. Well, free of totes, and packages, and all things needed to start the day. Her hands held a brochure. Glossy and pretty.

A brochure from Grand Hotel on Mackinac Island. And not just any hotel; a premiere—resort—caught--in--time hotel. On a tiny little island in northern Michigan. Mackinac Island.

Jefferson tripped the lock; the scent of English soaps and lotions wafted at them, like their own little garden escaping their packages. He clicked the lights, letting the pups run to their baskets. Then he started to boot up the computer. He had cash out for the vintage brass cash register, ready to be sorted into its little slots.

Absently Jinx flipped the sign to open, clicked the C D player to Jim Hart's latest music, and continued to read. Jim's piano music wafted out into the shoppe, filling it with the beginnings of a new day. "You know Jefferson; the Grand Hotel has a Murder Mystery event." She was revving up, "And this year it's in a nineteen twenties theme ..." And she just looked out into middle space far far from her shoppe.

1

At the same time Aunties Blanchie, Bertie, and Clara were opening their own shoppe, Creating Memories, their scrap book store. It was just down the street, in the village of Wind Star, in the middle of the middle of nowhere. The Aunties were, well, of undetermined age, but if one had to make a determination it would be old, very old. The words ninety and one hundred had been bantered around. Of course everyone assumed that was a joke. Still ... they were pretty old.

Creating Memories was a scrap book shoppe they owned with Auntie Clara's great niece Lizzie. Auntie Clara had lured Lizzie to town when Lizzie's own career in New York City had hit rock bottom. Auntie Clara helped Lizzie open a business, and for all intensive purposes, Auntie Clara helped Lizzie find the man of her dreams. It had been a crazy ride, as they now referred to it, but Lizzie was here, and settled, and happy. And so was Auntie Clara.

Very happy.

After all Auntie Clara got what she wanted--her great niece to move here, and a cute husband for her niece to boot. And a business for her, and her pals to scrap book, and basically play store, though sometimes it was more like work.

A lot of work.

Auntie Clara's knarled hands tripped the lock, Auntie Bertie flipped the lights, but Auntie Blanchie lagged behind, thumbing through the morning mail.

"Girls ..." Blanchie started patting her elegant red up do. Of course they hadn't been girls in a very very long time but used the word loosely as a term of endearment. "Look at this ... The Grand Hotel on Mackinac Island is hosting a Murder Mystery week. The theme is the nineteen twenties."

And suddenly Auntie Blanchie longed for a trip. Back in time. Somewhere grand. Why the name alone implied it was. And it was ... Blanchie fanned herself with the flyer, wondering what it would take for them to manage a trip. Take a little time off from their 'job' and just be treated like the royalty they felt they were.

Well all but Auntie Bertie. Bertie was very down to earth. She wore brogues, heavy duty shoes, with Faire Isle sox from Scotland. and tweed trousers, practical, sturdy, like the shoes. Still she liked good treatment.

Thrived on it really.

As they did.

Auntie Clara sighed as she clutched her over sized tote to her over sized frame. A tote filled to the brim with whatever she needed to get through a day of work. Mostly snacks, a few pairs of spare shoes, and some new C Ds to keep them all tapping their toes. "Ah ... our time ..." She wore a deco day dress in olive and burgundy. A bird pattern. It looked old, preserved well but of a forgotten style and cut. And pattern. And of course the fabric, rayon, the miracle fabric of the war years. Whichever war that was hard to say ...

The dress was a look. A look any number of young people would covet as pure retro. Deco--a wonderful era. It was Auntie Clara. She had a closet full of other frocks very similar. It was her style, her look, and as the years had rolled by Auntie Clara felt no reason to give it up. She simply had bigger versions. To accommodate her slightly round, okay very round, figure.

"Are you sure?" Auntie Bertie asked as she turned the CD player to 'When We Going Home', Jim Hart's cut off his Atonic Tuning Fork CD. Age had crept up on Auntie Bertie; she wasn't sure when her era was, exactly. She wasn't even sure when age had crept up on her. Still Bertie knew it had. Mostly in the morning when she had to get moving, keep moving—warm it all up.

The music helped.

Woke up her slowed down system. Eased her in--into the day. The music helped--a lot.

"I do so love a good murder mystery," Auntie Blanchie drifted, her triple strand of pearls swaying along with her stately elegant long legs. Auntie Blanchie was elegant. She transcended time. And age for that matter. No one ever looked at Auntie Blanchie and thought her clothes looked retro. They just thought she looked smashing. And she did, of course. Look smashing. Whatever Auntie Blanchie wore she wore well. It was usually extremely expensive and extremely old, but still she wore it well.

Auntie Blanchie started in again about loving a good murder mystery.

Auntie Clara wasn't sure if she meant as in a book curled up with a cup of tea or … taking part in an actual murder mystery with the local police or … Maybe the one advertised by the Grand Hotel.

"And fashion. Vintage fashion. I do so love good fashion," Auntie Blanchie went on, "New or old. Well old. But I could like new if it wasn't, you know, so new …"

Auntie Blanchie was the fashion aficionado in their little group. Always had been and of course age wasn't going to change that. She simply had more years, and styles, to draw from. And Blanchie dressed the part every day regardless of her chores.

If she was sweeping, vacuuming up the shoppe, or just tending to customers she looked elegant. Perfect. True a little retro, but perfect none the less. Blanchie had always claimed good design transcended time and everything else. And it did. The good design part had a way of just always being the right note. Regardless the song. And of course a big pile of cash didn't hurt either—to acquire that good design.

Auntie Clara was opening a UPS box of pumpkin and scarecrow stickers, Auntie Bertie was tying a shoe lace on her very sensible oxfords. Auntie Blanchie was day dreaming. "I have a granddaughter fashion designer you know ... why she was even named after Coco--Chanel, that is."

Auntie Clara and Auntie Bertie knew.

They'd heard.

Many times.

They kept working. They also knew no one had heard from young Coco--ever.

"We could go ... to the Grand I mean," Auntie Blanchie said it with just a tad of a faraway look, like she was almost there. Maybe now, maybe way back when. She'd shelved her granddaughter and was back to the hotel. "You know girls we surely are due for a little break, from all this work. And it is right around the corner. Could be rather spontaneous of us. Just pack and go. And enjoy. Enjoy a little luxury ..."

Auntie Clara raised an eyebrow. Auntie Bertie tugged up her faire isle Scottish sox and clucked, "Can't leave the shoppe." It was unspoken. Their shoppe kept them on their toes ... and in town. They'd squabbled among themselves about their hours.

Auntie Blanchie felt as co-owners they could do as they wanted. And to her that meant come and go as she wanted, which she pretty much did anyway, leaving some of the longer hours to the others. Not to mention some of the more undesirable chores--chores that she didn't even know needing doing. Because they were usually done when she was off flitting around. Still Aunt Blanchie did her share.

More than her share.

They all did.

Auntie Bertie was old school. If you opened a business and said you were going to be there, well, someone better be there. Auntie

Clara's position was somewhere in between. She would argue that they were not a pharmacy, there was no life and death about being there all the time. No medicine to pick up. That someone would not die without their bunny stickers.

Even if Auntie Bertie disagreed.

Still Auntie Clara felt if you were a 'real' store you played by 'real' rules and that meant 'real' hours. Steady ones that people could count on. For their bunny stickers.

"Of course we can; Lizzie will be back from her honey moon and and ... Jinx's older friend Biscuit could help her." 'Older' was a loose term, as Blanchie, Bertie, and Clara were older than, well, everyone. Lizzie was Auntie Clara's great niece, the one who technically owned the scrap book shoppe. Or maybe she'd just been the excuse the Aunties used to open it.

Biscuit was a newer acquaintance of theirs, and good friend of Jinx, who owned the shoppe down the street a ways. Biscuit was older. Not as old as they were but well past her blush. Her blush was definitely gone. Still she worked, over at Dink's diner, a roadside restaurant. And the Aunties were pretty sure it was exhausting work.

But Biscuit also seemed to have a friend at the diner. A Mr. Jingles--silver haired, and also past his first blush. Well, as the aunties thought about it, maybe not ... They didn't know it for a fact, but they thought, well pretty sure, that Biscuit and the man called Jingles were an item. So Biscuit must have energy. For the item part. She could help out at the scrap book shoppe if they were gone. What with all that energy and all ...

"And we could have an adventure. A real adventure." Then Auntie Blanchie pulled her ace out of her pocket, "And then we'd come back rested, revived, and inspired. Ready to work ... even harder."

Everyone needed and deserved a little holiday. Everyone took one. They certainly fit into that category. They were 'everyone' ...

"Uh maybe ..." Auntie Bertie conceded. She hadn't been anywhere in a very long time. She wasn't even sure where her luggage was, or her old steamer trunk. The one she would never part with ... but couldn't find. Oh yeah, she was using it as a coffee table ... And even though she was a bit of a country woman, the Grand was just that, grand. A little luxury sometimes did wonders.

Auntie Blanchie started up again, "A trip! A vacation! Think of it! To Michigan. To the Upper Peninsula. To stay at the Grand Hotel! Or is the part called the Upper Peninsula up even farther? Doesn't matter though does it? I mean Michigan is a mitten isn't it? And the Grand, well it's on that mitten somewhere. Or is an island part of the mitten?"

Auntie Clara was pretty sure Blanchie was referring to the shape of the state. The mitten part. And no she had no idea. And really, did it matter? Of course not. Auntie Blanchie was still babbling but suddenly Auntie Clara was picturing herself sipping a Mimosa on the mile long Victorian porch, looking out over the crystal clear Straits of Mackinac. Well maybe six hundred foot long porch ... Still, Auntie Clara could see herself there. And maybe she was sipping on a lemonade with Pimms.

Didn't matter.

The length of the porch or the drink.

It was a day dream.

A good one.

The door clattered and Jinx, their shoppe neighbor from Fairchild's, wandered in, "Hi ladies, er Aunties," As they insisted on being called. She still clutched her brochure from the Grand Hotel. Jinx had left her husband Jefferson to wake up their shoppe, and was instead out shopping ... "I need a scrap book ... something nineteen twenties. Jefferson and I are taking a trip, and I want to get my plans organized." She waved the flyer about the Murder Mystery week.

The Murder Mystery at the Grand Hotel.

"And stickers. What do you have with a twenties theme? Flappers? Pearls? Hats?" Jinx was already digging through the racks, pulling out little packets, plopping glitter and glue on the counter. Her pile piling up.

Fate? Serendipity? It didn't matter. The three old friends looked at each other and answered as one. "Funny thing Jinx, we're going too!"

2

Coco pushed a strand of golden hair off her damp forehead, trying to smooth her bobbed page boy with one hand. She held her glue gun steady with the other, and attached another rivet to the robot costume she was working on. Well technically not a real rivet as it was being glued, and not 'riveted' in place. A faux rivet. And, well, technically she wasn't working on a costume.

She was working on an assembly line gluing little bolts in strips on futuristic robots pant legs. She kept going despite a glob of glue that escaped the gun and hit her mini skirted thigh. It was hot. Wasn't Southern California supposed to be balmy? Always seventy three degrees? She couldn't remember. She just knew in the bowels of the Los Angeles Designs Company it was sweaty, muggy, dingy. Not at all the commercial for sunny California. Not even close.

Los Angeles Designs! "Ha!" But Coco kept gluing, while her mind was drifting. True it was a design company but she was so far down the food chain the word 'design' was just that, a word on her pay check. Her meager pay check. She was a cog on an assembly line. She did one thing over, and over, and over. And then did it some more. She could almost be replaced by a machine.

Almost.

There just wasn't a machine that did such mundane work. Well there was. It was named Coco.

When had her dream of designing fashion--real fashion--gone sour? Her mind flitted back to her days at the Art Institute of Chicago and how not only had she excelled, her professors had recognized her boundless talents. Top of her class. Not everyone was top of her class. That's why it was the top. And she had been it--the top. Now it seemed she was at the bottom. Well pretty sure because she couldn't imagine anything lower. She picked up the next shiny bolt and squeezed the glue. Carefully this time, so as not to burn herself.

She'd come to Los Angeles with stars in her eyes, to design for the stars. But somehow her apprenticeship had gone bad. Very bad.

The biggest problem she had was she was in love.

In love with the black and white movies. The flowing gowns, the slinky satins, the swishy little pleats, the platform shoes. The suit jackets that nipped in at the waist with padded shoulders and peplums. A word she was sure no one, including her boss, knew what it meant. Yeah, she was in love all right, with black and white movies.

At a time when the world was in love with futuristic movies. Costumes that melded to the body in a rather neon way. Exposing everything in a tattooed kind of way. And raggedy grubby outfits. Well, of course not outfits. Just torn and dirty looking clothes. Clothes that sincerely did not look like anyone planned them, or coordinated them, or heaven help, designed them. Clothes that just looked like they had been in a heap until someone had thrown them on. Clothes, that to boot, didn't fit. Anyone. She tried, God knows she tired. But her heart was set on roushing and delicate pleats. Because she was in love...

ABOUT THE AUTHOR

 Jacqueline Gillam Fairchild writes cozy fiction stories that are escapes to countryside settings, and also on Nantucket Island. She writes of women who are ready to take the leap into starting their own business, or who just want to start over. At the heart of Jacqueline's writing is the belief we all want a life that is just a little bit prettier and maybe a little bit magical.

Jacqueline owns and operates Her Majesty's English Tea Room, and her British store Fairchild's, in the middle of the middle with her Scottish husband, and their Pekingese, Piewacket. A former Interior Designer who studied pastry at Le Cordon Bleu, her business was a finalist for *Gift and Decorating Accessories Magazine's* Retailer of the Year award. Her business is also the winner of the coveted Icon Award for branding from the Americasmart, Atlanta. Youtu.be/77XxtQ-WQ54. Jacqueline is also a script writer and is a cast member of the Grand Hotel Murder Mystery Troupe.

Enjoy her daily blog at jgfairchild.wix.com/tea-room-life, and on Facebook at Her Majesty's' English Tea Room.

Made in the USA
Lexington, KY
26 December 2017